SCHEMES, DISGUISES, & TRAPS

SCHEMES, DISGUISES, & TRAPS

A Novel

David Orsini

SCHEMES, DISGUISES, & TRAPS
Copyright © 2020 by David Orsini
First Edition Quaternity™ Books 2020
Quaternity™ Books
ISBN 978-1-943691-23-4
Cover Design by James Buchanan

This book is a work of fiction. Names, characters, businesses, organizations, places, events, and incidents are the product of the author's imagination or are used fictitiously. Any resemblance to actual persons, living or dead, or to actual events or locales is entirely coincidental.

Books by David Orsini

What's Left Afterward

Prisoners of Desire

The Price of Happiness

The Enchantments

The Reappearing

The Weaver of Plots

Schemes, Disguises, & Traps

Vanishing by Degrees

The Ghost Lovers

The Woman Who Loved Too Well

The Subtleties of Seduction

Bitterness / Seven Stories

CONTENTS

1 The Intruder — 11

2 Prisoner of Desire — 45

3 Mister Right — 85

4 Heir Apparent — 111

5 A Flickering Light — 135

6 Betrayals — 163

7 Schemes, Disguises, & Traps — 193

8 A Double Plot — 223

9 Death Trap — 261

10 Phantoms — 291

Alternate Ending — 315

There are no heroes here.
These are human beings, nevertheless, who make their fallible
journeys.

Chapter One
The Intruder

"We agreed that you were never going to come here," Lauren told him the moment he stepped foot inside the house. "If anyone sees you, you will ruin everything for us."

Her soft voice and petitioning manner could not conceal her angry resentment that he had come here so unexpectedly, complicating the scheme that they had been devising together, even though these days they were often apart.

He knew her too well to accept this petition as anything more than her fear of him. There had been other times when she had more persuasively disguised her fear or, with carefree words and a light caress of his arm, kept her fear at bay. But always her fear held her words in its chains. Always, the memory of how rough he could be with her subdued any impulse that might impel her to cross him. That she loved him despite this fear intrigued him. Such love, as far as he understood it, was a perversity of the will. It drove its energies against safe convention and against the expectation of quiet happiness.

For the moment, he met her softness with his own subdued response, a disguise that lent conviction to his husky voice and nearly affable manner.

"There's no need to worry," he said. "Most of the summer people have left the area. Besides, if any of the regulars here do recognize me, they will accept me as a friend of yours who happens to be passing through."

"But I do worry, Bryce," she said. "I do worry. One wrong move and everything we have worked for will be ruined."

The late September sun flowing through the panoramic window touched the whole lithe form of her: her long, curly black hair and dark brown eyes; her smooth olive skin; her exotic face with its turned-up nose and full lips; her firm, round breasts; and her sensual hips and legs. For a moment, standing before him in a green tweed jacket and tan jodhpurs and riding boots, she looked otherworldly and mysterious. Even in his brooding suspicion, he had to admit that her beauty still excited him. As if she were casting a spell, she stirred him in ways that surprised him. But on this Tuesday morning in 1977, as he observed her every move, he found her mystery to be very much of this world. No longer was she open with him. No longer did her words and gestures seem spontaneous. She was withholding herself from him. She was not being true. In these last months, something had happened to her. Someone had compelled her to hide her feelings. That someone, he was convinced, was Aaron Dowling.

Now he drew closer to her, his tall muscularity casting a shadow over her wary face. The thought that, by falling in love with their intended victim, she had betrayed the plan that could set them free goaded the fury he had carefully concealed. Yet he gave her no clear sign of his anger. Instead, he harnessed his words to playful intonations while he gently pressed his large, rugged hands upon her shoulders. She knew where he stood. She knew him well enough to recognize the undercurrent of menace.

"If anyone makes a wrong move, baby, it will be you."

She held herself still, accepting the ambivalent press of his hands as a show of affection. He could read her well. She was too smart to try to break free of him. That gesture might incite his anger. Not being able to break away, she would have to admit his press of hands was telling her that he could do with her as he willed. Instead, she met his gaze directly, her eyes gleaming with their matter-of-fact apprehension of who he was and of why he had come here so abruptly.

Now, he was aware, she chose words meant to placate his unease.

"I'll never make a wrong move," she said, after touching his mouth with a fleet kiss, "...not when we can win so much."

He pressed his hands more firmly upon her shoulders. Still he kept his voice low, yet insistent.

"I don't think you are leveling with me," he said.

She placed her head against his chest, trying to conceal the nearly imperceptible look of fear that was overtaking her face.

"What makes you say that?" she asked him, all the while maintaining her show of serenity.

His right hand clasped the back of her head now, her sunlit hair falling through and around his fingers. Once more he brought her face to face with him. He wanted to study her as she spoke to him. He wanted to watch her as she lied and schemed. The low timbres of his voice were making his words guttural and abrasive.

"You're playing your own private game with Dowling. You've fallen for him. You like going to bed with him."

She did not permit herself to move. No frown creased her brow. Nor did her voice rise in protest. Determined and resourceful, she chose to act nearly amused by his words.

"Dowling means nothing to me. He's a means to an end, that's all."

The hint of a smile touching her lips roused his anger. She was playing a game and leaving him at the edge of it. He was outside, peering into what he did not understand. For all he knew, she might be laughing at him. If she were playing him false, he had to put a stop to it.

He released her from his hold upon her and then, in the same instant, began slapping her while he spewed through his teeth a volley of questions and accusations.

"Why haven't I heard from you in more than a month? Why?" he asked her, his caustic voice dangerously low and threatening. "Tell me that, baby. Then explain why you left New York weeks ago in such a hurry. Make me believe that you are not trying to hide something from me."

She lifted her hands as if to deflect the next slap and to protect her face, which was already flushed and bruised from his assault of her.

"Don't do this," she gasped, as he lurched forward to slap her again. "Don't do this. You will ruin everything that's good between us."

In his anger, he heard her words as a threat.

He grabbed her now and began shaking her violently.

She twisted her body, trying to escape from his pinioning hold of her. For an instant, right after she kicked him in his left ankle, she nearly broke free of him.

"Stop it, Bryce!" she screamed. "Stop it!"

This time he slapped her so hard she fell across the long, richly upholstered sofa that dominated the south corner of the room. Only when he noticed the blood seeping from the corner of her mouth did he draw away from her. He held his body taut, as if with hair-trigger energies he was prepared to subdue any new adversary. Bitter now and unrepentant, he hurried to the bar to pour himself a scotch. Here, within the intimate north corner of this spacious reception room and amid her glamorous circle of friends, Lauren and he had in times past shared a few drinks as well as an intense need for each other. The memory of that intensity goaded his bitterness. His need for her still lived, urgent and distended, within the deepest secrecies that hid his real self, even from those who thought they knew him well. But, with almost imperceptible alterations and with nearly casual dissembling, Lauren had changed toward him. Her tightly controlled wariness, her undercurrent of fear, and her contrived exhilaration incited his doubt of her.

That he desired her so intensely, yet was willing to kill her if she crossed him gave him pause. He was not surprised by the savagery of his instincts or by the hardened will that pushed him to kill. What did surprise him was his fear of himself and of his willingness to kill this beautiful woman who roused his desire in a way few women had ever done. Whether that desire was a form of love, he could not say. Though he had slept with many women, he had made no lasting commitment with any of them. But Lauren was different. Working through her subtleties, she had gradually imposed herself upon his cold detachment. She had disarmed his inability to love anyone. The bond they had made involved not only their bodies, though their frequent copulation deepened and excited the urgency of the bond. Their pact also involved murder. Aaron Dowling was going to be their victim.

At first, their plan seemed a simple one. With her patrician background, Lauren could smoothly enter the world to which Dowling belonged. His world was also hers. Their meeting at a dinner party in a penthouse that overlooked Central Park or at a Manhattan supper club would be regarded as a natural thing. Observers with a romantic disposition might even call the pairing inevitable. Some of the wealthiest men who saw or conversed with Aaron Dowling and Lauren at these clubs and parties might favorably mention the two of them afterwards. They would refer to them during a game of billiards at their private club, maybe, or at the close of a business lunch at The Pierre, where they had spoken of many things including the current Wall Street merger and the success of a Broadway show in which they had made a substantial investment. He could imagine some prominent banker or a top-notch lawyer who had sighted Aaron and Lauren together later insisting that the collaboration of the Dowlings with the equally prominent Winters family from which Lauren derived was inevitable. He knew them well, these bankers, lawyers and other power brokers. For four years after his boxing days, he had worked for them. In different seasons, he had been their valet and their chauffeur. He had been their personal trainer and their bodyguard. Sometimes, he had lied for them when the business partners or the wives or the tax people whom they were stringing along suddenly closed in on them. They had paid him well for his skills. They had even looked the other way on those occasions when he calmed their troublesome mistresses by bringing them into his bed.

But he was not of their kind. He did not belong to their privileged class. Even when he was taking risks for them, these bankers and brokers and lawyers offered him curt directives and grim-faced reminders that he was strictly on his own if he failed in his assignments and drew to himself the attention of the police or of some sharp-eyed detective. Even then, when he was rescuing them from the backfiring effects of their crimes, they regarded him with the contempt that hides its loathing within cautious formality. He was the necessary intruder upon their secrets. He was the temporary interloper who could make things right for them.

Lauren belonged to their class, not his. She had been born into the wealth that anchors its powers to privilege and security and that makes life a freewheeling adventure. Though her family now placed heavy constraints upon her use of that privilege, she enjoyed nonetheless the prestige of her family's name and the easy acceptance of the well-to-do who, even had they been aware she was living off an annuity that suppressed her luxurious tastes, knew that by birth and blood and family connections she was one like themselves. Lauren's access to this world of wealth and privilege made possible the plan that, together with her, he had devised to murder Aaron Dowling and get away with it. She was going to make Dowling fall in love with her and then ask her to marry him. For a few months, she would will herself to be his dutiful wife. Then, like a thief hurrying into a night when Lauren was away and Dowling was alone, he would break into their Manhattan apartment and kill him with a Beretta pistol or a Colt semiautomatic handgun. For a while after that, she was going to play the role of a widow who was so grief-stricken she didn't seem to care she had inherited the bulk of Dowling's vast holdings. She would also inherit part of her parents' fortune, because she had married the right man and because she had stayed with him to the end. Later in the same year, while she was traveling away from the places that knew her well, she would meet him in Hawaii as they had planned. There, they would begin a new life, never looking back at the wreckage they left behind.

A year ago, they turned their plan into a living thing. Lauren and Dowling were now sleeping together and, more than a few times, he had spoken to her about marriage. But they had not yet married. Lauren had failed to meet the timeline of their plan to murder Dowling.

"I can't hurry Dowling into marriage," she whispered to him on more than one occasion when, appearing in public as strangers who by chance were standing near each other, they exchanged quick remarks. They sometimes stood behind the topiary of a heroic soldier carrying a rifle in a secluded corner of Central Park. Occasionally, they stood in front of a famous canvas in a private art gallery and once behind an array of roses in a florist shop. During each of these contrived encounters, Lauren would not look at him. As if she were an actress making wise choices for this intricate role she was required to play, she maintained her poise and offered him temperate words that were meant to calm him.

"Hurrying Dowling will rouse his suspicion," she would murmur. "Before our plan can work, I need to build his trust in me."

Always, he received her words with blunt, soft-spoken protests.

"You're stalling. You're making excuses. You're holding out on me."

Hearing his muted anger, she would keep her gaze upon the topiary or the canvas or the roses.

"Give me more time. That's the only way we'll get what we want."

Try though he had, he could not believe her. Lately, he had not heard from Lauren for weeks at a time. At first, he told himself she was using this time well. Desirable and seductive, she was making Dowling believe she was the most important person in his life. Without her, he could not live happily.

"Dowling is a romantic," she said, right after she met this wealthy man whom they were planning to make their victim. "He won't give me any trouble. He's going to play right into my hands."

"Don't be too sure," he warned her. "This Dowling knows the score. He's rich. He probably enjoys being a scoundrel. It's in his blood. It's the badge his class wears."

Confident and even lighthearted, she had parried his remark. He knew what she was thinking. By making their plan an active thing, she had entered an adventure to her liking.

"I'm not worried," she said. "You and I are going to be smarter scoundrels."

She had spoken those words seven months ago. Since then, a change had quietly overtaken her. No longer did she tell him every detail of her meetings with Dowling. No longer was she accelerating the plot that would bring her to a marriage with Dowling and bring Dowling to an early death. She had gone soft on Dowling. She had allowed him to take control of who they were together and of where they were headed.

When he first confronted her with these accusations two months later, declaring with his husky voice and the quiet undercurrent of threat that she was backing away from their plan to murder Dowling, Lauren had acted surprised. But she was careful not to display her anger or to take refuge in a fake protest of his accusations. Instead, she chose to be amused and to tease him with words that made her contrived response almost plausible.

"You're jealous," she said, caressing his shoulder and bringing into his grim awareness the gleam of her brown-eyed watchfulness. "I suppose I should be pleased. But, frankly, I'm disappointed. I thought you and I had gone past being the playthings of our feelings. You and I have made a plan to get everything we can from this world that loves nobody. I'm doing what I need to do to make that plan work. It is going to take time to get what we want, and both of us have to be patient."

On that spring afternoon, sequestered as they were within a solitary room of a Manhattan art gallery different from the one where they had met weeks earlier, she had brushed his cheek with her light kiss and clasped his right hand with the warm flesh of her own.

"Don't give in to feelings, Bryce," she whispered. "They'll mess up everything for us."

He did not believe in her lightheartedness. He resisted the rousing effect of her touch upon him. He saw her charming manner as yet another disguise meant to put him off his accurate understanding of her.

"It's *your* feelings I'm thinking about," he said while he held her in his steely gaze. "It's what you feel for Dowling that may ruin things for us."

She softly laughed.

"Nobody knows what I feel better than I do," she answered him. "I'm setting up Dowling just as we planned. He believes in me, and that is the important thing. I have him in the palm of my hands. Any day now, he'll ask me to marry him."

He grabbed her wrist and began twisting it until she winced with the pain he was inflicting upon her. But she did not cry out. Only the frown that creased her brow and the uncertainty in her rebellious eyes disclosed her fear of him. Tough-minded and jaded in her perception of who they were together, she played out the scene with a flippancy that stayed at the edge of cordiality. She knew she must not go too far. She must not incite his fury.

"Stop worrying," she whispered. Her voice was tremulous now because of the pain cutting into her wrist. "Dowling is going to marry me."

In this moment, he hated her for her self-assurance and for believing she could fool him if she had to. He was no Dowling. He wasn't the chump who was going to be murdered. Now, more than ever, he wanted to hurt her. He wanted to remind her of just how rough he could be with her

He pressed his big hand deeper into her wrist and, for one wild moment, thought of breaking not only her wrist, but also her arm—right there, in the secluded room where portraits by Rembrandt and Vermeer peered from the walls. But his own apprehension held him back. She might scream and draw from distant rooms the attention of the security guards and of the other visitors to the art gallery. Still, he would not let go of her wrist. When the pain of his grasp became unbearable, she began to whimper. More certain now that he was in control of what was happening between them, he released her from his hold.

Before she looked away from him, disguising her latest submission to his brutality by bringing her attention once again to the canvas in front of her, he saw that her face had turned pale and unhappy. His own face, he imagined, revealed a tight-lipped bitterness and a vague disdain of the remorse that made him feel like a stranger to himself. Quickly, he altered the look of his face, selecting as an appropriate identity a tough and unsentimental countenance. He was careful to keep the harsh undercurrent in his voice and to temper with grating insinuation the words he threw out to her as a warning.

"Maybe you're right," he told her while she continued to look away from him. "Maybe Dowling will ask you to marry him. But don't make me wait too long."

This meeting in the Manhattan gallery had taken place five months ago.

For several weeks afterwards, Lauren reported to him regularly about her dealings with Aaron Dowling. Her fear, he was certain, had compelled her to explain even the small details of her meetings with the man who was going to be their victim.

"Our plan is working like a charm," she assured him at their most recent meeting, which had taken place on a morning in June within the gardens of Central Park, shortly before she left the city for her summer retreat here at her aunt's home in Vermont. She was wearing a cobalt blue blouse, white slacks and slip-on loafers, a matching white turban that covered her hair, and dark glasses that concealed her eyes. He, too, wore dark glasses, as well as a white short-sleeve shirt that revealed his rugged arms, blue denims that closely fitted his long legs, and light brown penny loafers. He was carrying a Leica and put it to good use as he impersonated a tourist or, maybe, a newspaperman who had come to the park to capture on film the emerging summer day. He paused near the bench on which Lauren sat reading a book and now and then looked up as if she were admiring the vivid colors of the flowers and the imaginative shapes of the topiaries. Never did he look at her. Instead, he kept taking pictures and listened to everything she had to say about Dowling and her, while she pretended to read the book. Nobody strolled by. No passerby saw them. But never did they let their guard down.

"Aaron Dowling believes in me," Lauren whispered to him on that afternoon. "He keeps telling me that he and I were meant to be together. Fate had a hand in it."

On that afternoon, she put a special lilt in her voice as she worked to convince him that, with smooth precision, she was advancing the scenario which would bring them everything they wanted. Yet, even with the lilt, he detected the tension she was trying to conceal—the harnessed fear that made her words sound rehearsed and artificial. Hers was an ambivalent fear, bound as it was to her perverse need to be degraded and even beaten by him. The need had become sensual in its masochism. It roused and it disconcerted her. That he held such power over her roused him, as well. At times, it made even him uneasy. He wondered whether the ambiguous love they felt for one another would turn out to be a trap—the tripwire or snare that brought them to a bad end.

So, in those solitary hours when his brooding made the ghostly image of Lauren a nearly visible presence, he told himself.

The furtive meetings with her kept at bay his doubts of her. But then she suggested they not meet while she was away in Vermont. It would be hard for her to leave Stowe without drawing to herself her friends' questions and maybe even Dowling's curiosity.

He did not like the idea. But he went along with it when she promised she would phone him two or three times a week. At first, she had kept her promise, calling him when no one was around her and when she felt confident none of her friends could hear all that she had to tell him. But he still did not like this new setup. Hearing her voice wasn't enough. He needed to see her. He wanted to look at her when she explained to him the ways she was advancing their plan to get Dowling to marry her. He wanted to search her face for the half-truths and the subtle lies she might be telling him about the hours she and Dowling were spending together.

Then, the phone calls stopped. Lauren had denied him even the sound of her voice. During these four weeks when she had retreated to an unexpected silence, his doubts once more assailed him. Despite the fear that shadowed her relationship with him, Lauren was breaking their pact. She was leaving him behind. Not once in all these four weeks had he heard from her. That she had betrayed his pact with her became a troubled conviction, a disquieting certainty she was closing him out of her life. She was abandoning the plan that was supposed to make them rich together. Instead, she was teaming up with Aaron Dowling, the man whom they agreed they were going to murder.

He felt trapped, caught as he was inside his agony of doubting her. No longer anticipating her call and wary of drawing suspicion to her if, when he called, Dowling answered the phone, he waited until now to make his move. The summer season was over, and most of her friends had returned to their busy lives in New York. But she had not returned to her apartment there. The security guard who was assigned to protect her apartment building from trespassers and who believed he was her brother told him that Lauren had decided to remain in Stowe. She planned to return to the city in a few weeks.

The news angered and alarmed him. He knew Dowling had returned to New York. He also knew Lauren's aunt was traveling in Europe. That Lauren was still in Vermont convinced him she was avoiding him. He was more certain than he had ever been that she was double-crossing him. If that were the case, he was determined to kill her. Arming himself with a snub-nosed revolver, he made the six-hour drive from New York as if hastening through a nightmare. He arrived at the doorstep of this mountain style home at ten in the morning, just as Lauren was preparing to ride her favorite Tobiano or Arab bay across the early autumn landscape of Stowe.

So here they were now.

He had questioned her, and he had roughed her up a little. Maybe Lauren was staying on the level with him. Maybe, after all, they would win the jackpot.

Only after he poured himself a second scotch and quickly swallowed it, allowing its comforting sting to appease his wrath, did he direct his glance toward her. There, still on the sofa and with a gold cosmetic case she had brought from the pocket of her jacket, she was skillfully applying powder and lip gloss to conceal the bruises on her face and on her lips. She had shed no tears, nor did she reveal the fear of him that lived inside her. Instead, with a steady glance and confident voice, she hurried back into this dangerous game they were playing with each other.

"Pour me one, too," she said. "Straight up."

He knew she wanted him to see how tough she could be. She also wanted to calm him.

She joined him at the bar, while the light of the morning sun streaming through the panoramic window caught within its radiance the sinuous movements of her body. Her dark hair glistened, and her brown eyes gleamed. The sheen upon her olive skin and her delicate bones made her look otherworldly. When he handed her the scotch, she lifted the glass and saluted him. She was smiling now and drawing him into her lightheartedness.

"Here's to our partnership," she said. "Here's to making it work for us."

He was not ready to be lighthearted. Her words drew from him, instead, a blunt declaration that hovered about his anger and his despair.

"It *has* to work," he said. "I'm killing Dowling to get the big prize."

She set her glass on the counter and moved closer to him, so that she could touch his right hand.

"We are both going to get that prize," she said. "We are in all of this together."

He clenched his hand into a fist and lightly tapped her chin.

"Keep remembering that, baby," he said. "Then there won't be any trouble between us."

She brought his rough hand to her lips and kissed it.

"There will never be any trouble between you and me," she said. "That's a promise."

Her conciliatory manner pleased him, even though he did not really believe her soft words. But he allowed himself an ironic smile as he answered her.

"Maybe you'll keep your promise. Maybe you won't. I'll go a few more rounds with you in this thing. Let's see what happens."

She frowned, even as she kissed his hand once again. Then, wily and resourceful, she petitioned him.

"You have to trust me, Bryce," she said. "Our plan won't work unless you trust me."

He did not answer her. Instead, he withdrew his hand from her caress and silently drank his scotch.

Now Lauren lightened the mood once again and invited him to go horse riding.

A year and a half earlier, he had often gone riding with her and had hobnobbed with her friends. They did not really like him, despite his Ivy League veneer, because he was not of their class. But they never made a move against him, intimidated maybe by his streetwise muscularity. Or, possibly, they were waiting to see just how long Lauren would accept him as her latest adventure.

The rules changed for him once she met Dowling. It was important that he not be seen with Lauren. Dowling had to believe there was no other man in her life. He had made certain Dowling stayed unaware that Bryce Thompson existed. He had followed the rules strictly, and so had Lauren. His meetings with her were indirect and secretive. Even when they were in each other's presence, they were never together. That, on this September morning, the risk of his being seen with Lauren suddenly did not matter to her impressed him. She was trying.

She wanted to dispel his anger and his suspicion. She wanted to convince him they were still a team.

"I thought you didn't want me here," he said. "What if somebody sees me?"

"I'll take the risk," she said. "Besides, you and I need to spend a few hours together."

So, they spent that morning riding her aunt's Arab bays across the autumn flare of the land. For that brief time, he felt free. He was a man who had suddenly escaped from the prison he had made of his life. He was racing out of his own body. He was leaving everything behind him—all the grueling hours and days and years that had battered him and all the good ones that he had eventually betrayed. He was rushing away from even this hour, leaving in his wake the flickering imagery of Lauren sitting tall in the saddle and leaving also, as a spun velocity upon his seeing, the gleaming whiteness of the large main house on her aunt's property. Galloping now, he glimpsed as careening blurs quick verdant slopes and fieldstone retaining walls, ornately paved and planted surfaces, and many tiered, bluestone terraces. He saw as flashes of color and animation young men and women picking apples in a teeming orchard. Paddocks and stables and barns hurled themselves away from him. Houses and farm fields were another flare upon his senses, rising and instantly vanishing. Trees and hills and lake soared, wavered aloft, and disappeared. Even the mountains whirled past him, the pale sun tilted, and the cloud-laden sky darted, loped, and vaulted. He felt freed from all of it. He was someone new. He was claiming a totally different existence. The reality toward which he was hastening was another disguise that might hide who he was from all the people coming into his life and maybe from himself.

His Arab bay was galloping even faster now, at full stretch with body and neck lengthening and each leg fully extended as it powered along the winding trail. Behind his horse's neck, he tucked his upper torso precisely and fused the outline of their forms. He lifted himself out of his saddle, so that he could drop his weight down into his heels and push it further back, allowing his upper body to tuck in behind the horse's neck. Onward and more swiftly he went galloping, riding with shorter stirrups to make it easier to lift his weight out of the saddle. He kept his lower legs on the girth and kept his arms extended forward, as his horse stretched its neck within each stride.

Other teeming orchards, colorful brush, and wild flower fields went flashing by him. Women and men were harvesting a passing field, and a rugged man was driving a tractor over a northerly hill. Now five or six gray-haired couples canoeing on the distant lake leaped into his vision and just as quickly scattered away. A flight of black-backed gulls overtook fleecy clouds, entered their pockets, and then soared above the white cliff that rose out of the lake. He felt himself soaring, too—rushing out of the reach of the self that he was shedding even as he chased the self that was unknown to him.

Only when he saw in the looming distance two horses grazing in a paddock did he push his lower leg forward while still squeezing both legs against his horse's sides. He braced himself against the stirrup, shortened up his reins, and put the hand that held one of the reins tight into the horse's neck. He used his other hand to keep a strong hold on the second rein, as the horse started to listen and to slow down. The world that he had eluded for a quarter of an hour instantly reassembled its imagery for his seeing. His past hovered by him, ghostly and insistent. The brooding thoughts came back to taunt him. But he fought back. He stayed tough. His bitterness spurred his resolve. He wanted to hurry forward to the new, disguised self that he had only begun to devise.

"I'll do all right," he told himself. "So will Lauren. I've made a plan that can win her and me everything we want. I'll keep pushing her. I'll make her do everything she needs to do, so we can win the game."

Now he dismounted and led his horse into the paddock that was encircled by a cedar wood fence. After closing the fence, he waited for Lauren. That she would follow him here, he was certain. This secluded spot had always been their private meeting place on all the other afternoons when they had been out riding her aunt's Arab bays or Tobianos. When she joined him a quarter of an hour later, there was no need to call forth new words that might validate the bond between them. There were no words that could keep at bay his doubts of her or that could disguise the equivocal nature of their collaboration. Instead, they walked side-by-side along the trail that was flanked by lavender fields and scented meadows, accepting the silence between them as a reprieve from his dangerous anger and from her wily submissiveness. Only when this trail left the fields behind and led them to the top of a promontory did she break the stillness between them.

Standing there with him, upon one of the highest hills in the area, Lauren spoke words that revealed more than what his eyes perceived as her simulated elation.

"I love this place," she said, as she looked out upon a blue mist greenery of hills beyond hills, cloud laden implications of mountains, and the sun spotted expanse of corridors of space wheeling freely around and below and above them. "Whenever I come here, I believe in myself more than ever. Maybe, that's because the place gives me the illusion of concealment and a promise of safety. Being here gives me time to rally my forces. It convinces me that one day I will be rid of all my troubles. I will be absolutely free."

She was playing with him again. She was trying to fool him with her make-believe talk of escape hatches and happy endings. Swiftly now, with husky inflections that yoked themselves to a vague and quiet menace, he reminded her of the way things really stood.

"That won't happen without me, baby. You need me to get your freedom."

She turned to him with casual seeming attention. Her brown eyes gleamed, and her lips parted in a smile, showing her perfect, white teeth and enhancing her demure consent to his will.

"Of course I need you," she said. "That is why you are here."

Her gaze turned back to the colorful panorama that apparently solaced her. He, in turn, studying her every move, saw what, with clarified awareness, she was observing. Below them, a motorboat was speeding across the lake, leaving in its wake the spume and ripples of blue-green waters. In the faraway distance, at the edge of the sun tinted forest that stood across from the lake, Chilean willow trees, Scotch elms, and blueberry ash trees were bringing flares of excited color to the autumn morning. Higher than that, though still within the opaque blue furling of distance, a stray herring gull was curving the dark flash of its wings against the tumescence of ponderous clouds. After an instant's pause, it plummeted with wily skill to the consenting lips of lake waters, the better to pluck for its meal a raw, ample fish or a tiny, mackerel-tinted seabird.

Though the vision gave him back what he had not sought, a predatory image shown natural and insistent, he grasped comfortably its familiar message and found again his realistic measure for understanding things. Turning once more, still toward the east, he was not surprised to sight the zinc-white hang of a wind-bleached cliff glaring like the bones of a devoured world. The limestone solidity of the gargantuan form impressed him, as did the cliff's having endured a wilderness of centuries. The imagery put him in mind of his own resilience, as willful and time trapped as that was. In a world of uncertainty and violence, his capacity to withstand brute adversaries and wrenching betrayals was, he felt, his most essential weapon. The stark message he took from the cliff quickened his senses more acutely than any of the colors of the earth that surrounded him.

He noticed, too, across and above the disquieted lake and on the crest of sun glanced fertile hills—right there, at the wavering margins of the shadow-laden woods—a gray-blue immensity of swaying larches that apparently grew into the sky and, before his troubled eyes, joined all of heaven's restless and eerie motion. The sudden wind was billowing now, like a flare of wings lifted by lower winds and pushing upward against moist, lake-scented air. This feeling of space actively stirring, this sense that here on a sun-hued promontory the wind had come sweeping through the day's intricate layers and, spinning always its rapid coils, had come to claim him—it was this feeling that stopped his firm gait and held him in taut surprise back upon his heels while cliff and clouds and festive autumn colors went wheeling by him. The earth itself seemed to revolve with visible motion. He noticed once more the receding diagonals of the forest across the lake—a shadow flecked welling of foliage and trees, an instant's ambiguity of surface and space. He noticed, too, Lauren's scrutiny of that same sequestered place. He wondered whether in this moment she was maintaining her realistic sense of things. In so many ways, she was just as knowing as he about the world's equivocal promises, just as canny about its bruising, addictive textures.

She turned to him now, eyeing him steadily, as though she were coming back to him after a long absence. Her flowing black hair and olive-skinned radiance, partially concealed by the light that shimmered around her, gave her the spectral look of a mirage or an apparition. Then, because the whorls of slanted light began slowly to recede from her, he saw more clearly her enigmatic face and heard, with muted skepticism, her matter-of-fact appraisal of their surroundings.

"I've taken from this place what I need," she said. "It has served me well. Maybe it has done the same for you."

"Maybe."

She laughed lightly, giving herself completely to the pleasure of this moment.

"Oh, Bryce, it is wonderful to be happy here with you. Let's promise always to be happy together."

Her brown eyes were misty with tears as she touched his lips with a delicate kiss.

"That's an easy promise to make," he answered her, his words as direct as they were even-tempered. "I'm all for that. Just be certain you do your part to make us happy."

"You know I will," she said, her voice still touched with exhilaration. "I'll always do everything to make us happy."

He observed her quietly, but only for an instant. He was not ready to share her exhilaration. His ingrained cynicism required here-and-now proof of the happiness they were seeking. That happiness, spawned from a murder, would cost them their souls. Had she allowed herself to forget? Or, in the most secret recesses of her heart, was she more treacherous than he was? Was her contempt of people more furious than his? Was her despair more deeply rooted? He wondered, even as he persuaded himself to press his lips against her lips and, afterwards, found words to please her.

"Sure," he said. "You're my woman. You are going to make me very happy."

"Let's ride back together," she said, apparently satisfied that this hour had dispelled his brooding at least a little. "We'll change our clothes and then go on to Burlington for lunch. You can drive the Bentley you like so much."

"I do like the Bentley," he answered her. "And I am ready for lunch."

They walked back to the paddock and deftly mounted their horses. They cantered along the trail in unison. Though they spoke no words to each other, she imparted through her gleaming smile the lighter spirit she had permitted to attend her from the moment they reached the promontory. He, too, consented to a modulated variation of this lightheartedness.

During their brief stop at her aunt's home and all through the drive to Burlington and even during their lunch at a fashionable lakeside restaurant, he joined her in good-humored talk of the new happiness they would know after Aaron Dowling was out of the way. There would be an exciting life in Hawaii, occasional trips to the Bahamas, weekends of skiing in Vermont, and their frequent co-piloting of a Piper Cherokee. But there would be new happiness now, as well. Seductive and serene, she kept whispering romantic words, promising him in the hour or two they spent in Burlington that, when they returned to Stowe, she would bring him into her bed. They would see the colored lights again, as they had when they first made love together.

Their lightheartedness, a pre-moral complicity, temporized but could not dispel his distrust of her. With her, he would always be on his guard. That was the best way to handle her. That was how he was going to win this game they were devising every time they were with each other and all the times they were not.

To make their plan work, Lauren had to stay in it with him all the way. Her continued need of him was essential to his remaining in the game and to his gathering the rewards of the killing. That she might be distancing herself from their scheme pricked his anger once again. He had worked too hard to perfect the scheme to have her discard it because of a carnal whim or because she had convinced herself that her unanticipated love for Dowling was the real thing. He preferred Lauren's harder edge. He knew where he stood with her when she was being herself, the tough-minded realist who disdained conventional sentiment and fairy tale unions. Each of them had traveled far away from the safe paths of convention and fairy tales. Though she was reluctant to tell him all the disappointments and scandals of her past, he had drawn from Lauren enough of the story to understand she had made a mess of her life. But her being the daughter of a wealthy man protected her. The privileged circle that had spawned her continued to receive her as one of their own.

He had enjoyed no such protection. In October of 1938, he had entered this world as a foundling. Within the same hour of his birth, he had been left at the darkened rim of a slum's alley, the blanketed bundle containing him perched upon garbage cans. He had come into the world anonymously. He was illegitimate and abandoned. Without parents or known identity, he belonged to no one. Nor was he wanted by anybody. His very presence was an intrusion upon the acceptable order of things. From the start, the world treated him harshly and offered him a makeshift existence. Even the name the state orphanage assigned him was makeshift. A cold-hearted supervisor appropriated his first name from a war movie she had recently seen. The name Thompson, she took from an obituary. Later, when he was nine years old, he began telling himself that he was carrying the name of a dead man because in some mysterious way he, too, was dead. Only if he escaped from the orphanage would he have a real chance to live.

He escaped five times, hiding inside the back of trucks after their drivers delivered food, medical supplies, and furniture to a building on the grounds of the orphanage where by chance he had been placed on a work detail—scrubbing floors, maybe, or cleaning toilets. A few times, his getaway truck made a delivery to a farm that was located three or four miles from the orphanage.

On those mornings, he jumped from the truck before the driver had left his seat and scurried to a hiding place in the hayloft of a barn or inside a distant forest of elm trees. On three occasions, when he jumped from the truck right after it came to a stop, he found himself in the center of town, where he disappeared into a crowd of shoppers. At the end of the day, he concealed himself inside a large department store and, after it closed its doors in early evening, fed his hunger by breaking the lock of the glass case at the soda fountain that contained cupcakes, cookies, and candy.

Always, he was caught—usually by a night watchman or a store detective and sometimes by a cop—but not before he tried to punch and kick his way out of their rough handling of him. Though he was only nine and later eleven and thirteen, they punched him back, leaving him doubled up with pain shooting through his stomach or his chest. Because he was big-boned and tall, the men who came searching for him may have thought he was one of the older boys at the orphanage. The cop was the cruelest of his captors, with a crazed fury breaking his jaw and his left arm. This ugly cop, who was more rugged than the watchman and the detective, jeered at him, a gangly teenager slumped on the floor while he was bleeding and moaning in pain.

"Don't take it so hard, kid," he said. "The orphanage isn't such a bad place. They give you a bed and three meals a day. Besides, nobody in this town wants you."

Each time his pursuers returned him to the orphanage, the nightmare began again. No sooner did he recover from the injuries they had inflicted upon him than a sadistic barracks guard began beating him for no reason except the pleasure he found in causing him pain. One time, when the pain was too excruciating to bear, he fought harder than ever before and knocked out the guard. By then, he was fifteen and stood six foot, two inches. His body had filled out and, from his workouts in the gym, was rock-solid. Grown uneasy by the imposing sight of him, the head supervisor and the board of trustees wanted to expel him from the orphanage. They planned to press assault charges against him and recommend that he be confined to a detention hall for wayward youth.

But, after questioning him about his fight with the guard, Irwin Baxter, one of the gym teachers at the orphanage, defended him. He convinced the trustees and the senior supervisor that they would do wrong by pressing charges against a youth who had defended himself against the sadistic guard. In fact, they would draw the attention of the press, who were very likely going to create a scandal that would tarnish the staff and the trustees.

Baxter saved him from a prison sentence. Then he and his wife took him into their home as a foster son. By that time, Irwin and Clara Baxter were in their sixties. Their three sons were married and had their own children. Now living in Colorado, they had built successful careers as a team of architects. Though they missed their parents, they had settled in the faraway place where they could start their firm and then expand it.

When he became a part of their home in the spring of 1954, Mr. and Mrs. Baxter needed a foster son to replace the three sons who, born from their own flesh, had gone forward to independent lives. Baxter was a hard man, but fair. Mrs. Baxter was warmhearted and gentle.

"Always be true to your word," Baxter advised him. "Always follow the rules. Remember this: You identify the person you are through your actions. Strive to be good. Stay clean. Don't let the world corrupt you. Never let anger and bitterness destroy your goodness."

"I'll be all right," he had answered him. "I'll never make you ashamed of me."

In the same month that he began living with these temporary parents, Baxter persuaded him to train for the high school boxing team. He coached him and, for a time, turned his life around. In the fifteen years when he grew to believe he really was the fourth son of the Baxters, he became an honor student and won an athletic scholarship to New York University. He was on the boxing and fencing teams there, and he majored in American history. His years at NYU were his happiest, because the Baxters were his safety net and because he knew that he was moving up. His graduate studies at the University of Pennsylvania also kept him on his proper course, guiding him to a Ph.D. in British and American literature and to a tenured slot on the faculty of Columbia University.

Then, in the autumn of 1969, everything changed for him.

Meredith Templeton, one of the beautiful students with whom he had been sleeping, made the mistake to fall in love with him. She loved him with an intensity he neither wanted nor comprehended. When she discovered that he had been sleeping with two other beautiful students in the same semester, she swallowed twenty sleeping pills. Hours later, her university roommate discovered her sprawled on the bathroom floor. She called in the medics, but they could not save Meredith. Then she telephoned the girl's father and told him everything that she knew about the affair involving Meredith and her literature professor, Bryce Thompson. Meredith, her roommate explained and the autopsy report later verified, was four months pregnant with Thompson's child. It did not matter that he was in London on a sabbatical from his teaching assignments at Columbia. Nor did it matter that guilt and remorse racked his conscience and that his muted sorrow chained him to sleepless nights. The scandal that erupted brought him down.

Ian Templeton, who was a Wall Street broker and a major donor to Columbia's alumni fund, demanded his resignation. Nearly crazed with grief over the loss of his daughter, Templeton also gave newspaper and television interviews in which he spoke on behalf of his lost daughter. Bryce Thompson had used her. He had lied to her. He had driven her to an early death.

"Thompson doesn't belong at Columbia," Templeton said. "He belongs in the gutter that spawned him."

The newspapers and television had a field day. The young women at Columbia held a rally, demanding that Professor Thompson be fired.

The general public, choosing to forget its own sexual adventures, also protested against him.

The university fired him. In spite of his effective teaching and his highly praised biographies of F. Scott Fitzgerald and Ernest Hemingway, he had—the president of the university told him—failed his students, his community, and himself.

Eventually, Ian Templeton caught up with him. In a seamy bar in the West End of London, the angry father, maddened by his grief over his daughter's death, shot him.

"You killed my daughter," he shouted. "You drove her to a bad end. You were her death trap!"

He shot him again and again. But three physicians saved him for the makeshift life to which he had condemned himself.

After the scandal of Meredith's death and the news stories that sympathized with her grief-stricken father, he could not get a teaching post. Nor could he return to the Baxters, who had died within months of each other—Mrs. Baxter from cancer and Coach Baxter from a heart attack. During the scandal that brought him down, they had refused to see him. They could not forgive him for what he had done to the girl who had taken her life because of him. They could not forgive him for what he had done to himself. For a long time afterward, despite their turning away from him, he grieved because they had died. He grieved for them, even though they had left all their estate to their three sons. He understood. He knew the score. He had come into their lives as a displaced person—a young rebel and an outsider. They had rescued him. They had nurtured him. They had given him their guardian care. But, even though they had shown him genuine affection and had helped him in so many important ways, they had at the end not loved him. They could not forgive him his transgressions. They no longer regarded him as their son.

Once more his fate had tossed him asunder. The world he had been creating for himself was gone.

But he stayed strong. He stayed tough. He had a few good seasons as a boxer. Eventually, with muted regrets and some wily plans for duping others, he became a bodyguard and a chauffeur for the rich and, if need be, their convenient alibi.

Then, on a September evening in 1975 at an upscale bar in Manhattan, he met Lauren. On that same night, she took him into her bed. Their fates having cast them adrift, they saw in each other the promise of a rescue. Together, they could break free of all the conventions that were imprisoning them. Self-willed and rebellious, they could devise their own destinies. They could make their own rules. So, he told her in the summer of 1976, nearly a year after they had met, as she studied him with penetrating gaze and listened to his words with implicated willfulness. It wasn't long before he drew her into his murderous plan. They could win the jackpot if she collaborated with him. She had to choose a wealthy bachelor that fitted their scheme.

"Choose carefully," he told her. "Make the guy fall in love with you. Get him to marry you. Then leave the rest to me."

That she would choose the man who was going to be murdered intrigued her. Her bitter nature and her inbred perversity incited her consent to the plan.

"We'll play God, you and I," she said. "We'll treat this man that we have not yet met as harshly as God or Fate or Chance has treated us."

Not even a month later, she met Aaron Dowling, a thirty-year-old corporate executive, and began setting him up to be murdered. First, though, she had to marry him. Quickly enough, she had won Dowling's love. But he had not yet asked her to marry him. Whether it was Dowling or Lauren who was avoiding the subject of marriage, he was not certain. A day earlier, his distrust of Lauren had roused his anger to a fever pitch. He was certain that she was playing him for a fool. He had convinced himself that she had betrayed him. She had fallen in love with Dowling.

But these new hours that they had spent together dissuaded him from such thoughts.

He rose—naked and satisfied—from his place beside her in the oversized bed. A nightlight glowed from a table nearby, illuminating the soft flesh and sensual contours of her nakedness. During the night, she had tossed aside the scented sheets, and he wondered if in those moments hers had been an uneasy sleep. Now she lay deep in her sleep and apparently contented. He paused to look at her for only an instant. He did not want his sexual need of her to trap him. He could not afford to confuse that need with the vague stirrings of love that he sometimes felt for her. Turning from her sleeping figure, he hurried to shave and shower and to begin the ride back to New York. Today, he believed once again that he and Lauren were succeeding in their plan to use Aaron Dowling for their purposes. For today, at least, he could push away the fury that had impelled him to thoughts of murdering her. Her death, he knew, would mean the end of everything. If he killed Lauren, then right afterwards, with the wildness that made him his own enemy, he'd kill himself.

Chapter Two
Prisoner of Desire

Alone in her bed now, separated temporarily though never freed from Bryce's brooding presence and from his wily sensuality, Lauren leaned into the soft textures of her pillows as she bitterly reflected upon her life. The rum scented smoke from her Patagonian cigarette wafted, sinuous and furtive, around her, collaborating with the darkness that only partially accepted the sunglow of dawn and that intermittently concealed the ample nature and the sometimes-solacing influences of this room. The semidarkness that encased the autumn-cool atmosphere in a caul-like sheath disguised with ambiguous subtleties the glamorous textures and the seductive implications of her bedroom. On other mornings, when the tensions churning inside her had left her less wary and bitter, she would have accepted with amused cynicism the disguise wrought by the darkness. Disguise was, after all, her stock in trade. So, in 1966, when she was an already despairing girl of sixteen, her mother had told her, as she invoked once again the calculated disdain that overrode the warmer, maternal gestures she occasionally expressed.

"You are an amateur," her mother sneered. "You do not play the game well. Even country bumpkins see through you—if not immediately, then eventually. How could they not see through you? You do not believe in your disguises. You wear none of them with conviction."

On that occasion, a few hours after she had been compelled to withdraw from a private school in Connecticut, she had not merely disappointed her mother. She had angered her.

"You imagine yourself a rebel," her mother scoffed. "You steal away from your school and hurry to meet a sailor who is waiting for you at a pub near the base where he is stationed. He brings you to a room and goes to bed with you. Then, after he is finished with you and after you have reveled in the newness of the experience, you take fright at what you have allowed to happen to you. You make a scene. The police become involved. Your father and I are called to stand by you and to rescue you from the mess that you have made."

That afternoon, she openly challenged her mother.

"You did not stand by me. Nor did Father. You made the police believe that I was lying because I craved attention. You convinced the physician who examined me to assure the police that nothing had happened to me. So he lied and told them that I was still a virgin."

Her sudden rush of words made her mother pause. When she chose to speak again, her mother was calm and matter-of-fact.

"We were protecting you from yourself," her mother said, with the harnessed vehemence that banks its hatred in calibrated understatement and malice. "We were protecting our name. We were protecting the reputation of the school that, because of your father's influence, wisely allowed you to withdraw without the stigma of expulsion."

"You stood against me. It was you, more than Father."

"Of course, I stood against you. You are a foolish girl. For an hour or so, you acted out the role of a rebel, and then you panicked. Your rebellion was a sham. If you had gone to bed with that sailor and, afterwards in the privacy of a casual conversation, told me about it, I would have respected you. Your rebellion would have pleased me, because it was authentic and because it was not merely the scheme of a sullen schoolgirl who wanted to bring attention to herself."

How strange, Lauren mused on this morning eleven years later, when she felt trapped by the new disguise she had woven for herself, that her mother's caustic words should rise to taunt her. They were not the first rancorous words that passed between them. As a child and an early teen, she had sought ways to rouse the anger not only of her mother, but also of her father. She made herself look plain and sometimes slightly disheveled. Perverse and resentful, she presented her unhappy appearance as a testimony against the parents who often found reasons to be away from her and who refused to love her unconditionally. Not even the solicitude of her various governesses or the kindness of her classmates and teachers allayed her distrust of her mother and her father or dispelled the conviction that they had abandoned her.

Her mother knew a great deal about disguise. She had fled the poverty of her Patagonian background in 1935, when she was fifteen. Even then, she was a superb flamenco dancer and a dark-haired beauty. Using her feminine wiles and her razor-sharp wits, she eventually found celebrity through supper club performances and through lovers who included bankers, ambassadors, and gangsters. Shortly afterwards, after a Hollywood film producer had, by chance, seen her supper club act, she reinvented herself. No longer was she Estelita Figueroa. Now she was Maria Navarro, a glamorous film star. Critics praised her acting. Audiences admired her fiery personality and her sensual dances. Not only her male co-stars, but also a new roster of French and Spanish diplomats, British titled heirs, and Wall Street brokers—all of them with diverse and vigorous appetites—enjoyed her company in the pleasure haunts of Hollywood, New York, and the French Riviera, as well as in bed. They regarded her as a beautiful and famous courtesan, and they paid her well. With an ironic awareness of her current value and with the lighthearted worldliness that sparked her relations with men, she accepted their gifts of Cartier jewelry, Lamborghinis and Rolls Royces, and high-performing stocks and bonds.

"We get along well," she would tell her lovers, while teasing their fondness for the unconventional. "We know the ways of business. We are experienced negotiators. Ours is a smooth transaction that leaves each of us satisfied. There are no complicated feelings to punish our conscience or to rouse our nostalgia."

To her casual seeming honesty, her lovers responded in ways that revealed the subtle variations of their characters. Some smiled discreetly, pleased to find in their favorite bedmate the carefree and self-centered disposition that mirrored their own. Others studied her with hardened eyes as they attempted to fathom the authenticity of her indifference. Still others laughed exuberantly, caught up in the mutual recognition that their partnership was as spurious as it was temporary.

Only when she met Leonard Winters did her relations with a lover become complicated. She had gone to bed with many men who had been born into immense wealth and privilege. All of them were street-smart and duplicitous. All of them had expanded their fortunes into even more lucrative Wall Street ventures and into pioneering technologies that spanned the globe. In this respect, Leonard Winters was like them. But there was a wildness in Leonard Winters that the others lacked or that, despite their occasional forays into unconventional and rebellious behavior, made these sometime lovers appear vulgar or stupid. They lacked the genuine danger that was in Leonard. They could not summon the fiery spirit and the non-conforming responses that made him always exciting and, to her mother's mind, often original. She was favorably impressed when she learned from her lawyer that, even though he continued to achieve tremendous success in all his business investments, Leonard Winters' family regarded him as something of a scapegrace because he often flouted the rules society imposed upon men of his class. His parents, as well as his sister and his two brothers, kept urging him to change his habits. His association with shady politicians and scandalous film stars and his unorthodox trading on Wall Street were bringing him a notoriety that tarnished the family name. To their admonitions, he listened patiently. Then with a peremptory wave of his hand and with witty, devil-may-care inflections, he would choose words that never failed to startle or to displease these relatives.

"All that you tell me, dear parents and good brothers and sister, sounds prudent and cautious. But your words make sense for your own lives, not for mine. They suit your natures. They have no connection to the life that I have made for myself and that I shall continue to explore and to build. I know you have my interests at heart. Yet, despite our affection for each other, we think differently about these matters. What more is there to say?

When all is said and done, you have to go to your church. I need to go to mine."

His flippant dismissal of their counsel appalled his parents and his sister and angered his brothers. But, even though they distanced themselves from him and from his reckless pursuits, they continued to admonish him and to remind him of his obligations to his family and to his class. At times, when his rash deeds had drawn more unfavorable publicity, he offered his family temporizing words that suggested he was going to defer to their judgments. For a while, he would follow their Spartan rules that, to his mind, made his life unpleasant and ascetic. Then, with a shrewd awareness of having withstood the media's latest assaults upon his character and without heeding his family's counsel, he would hurry forward to new and even more turbulent episodes in his life.

His widely publicized affair with Maria Navarro roused his family's deepest censure. But, when they could not dissuade him from marrying her, his parents as well as his brothers and his sister willed themselves to attend his wedding in August 1944 and to welcome into the family the woman they regarded as plebeian and manipulative. That she brought into the marriage the millions of dollars that she had earned from her film and stage work, from commercial endorsements, from the lavish gifts of her lovers, and from judicious investments made her a different kind of fortune hunter. Not averse to Leonard's immense wealth, Maria was currently more interested in acquiring the rarefied name of Winters and of enjoying the prestige that it carried.

To this end, she began reinventing herself. No longer did she care to play so openly the role of the scandalous woman. With a new team of publicists, she created a more elegant version of the earthy Maria Navarro whom the public admired. Never denying that she had been born into poverty, she reminded her public that she had used her talent and her wits to escape the prison of her early deprivation. She assured them, through radio, television, and newspaper interviews, that most of her relations with men were platonic. These businessmen had guided her thriving career and her well-stocked portfolio. She assured this same public that she was providing substantial sums of money for her parents' comfortable retirement and for her brothers' horse farms and aircraft factory. She was careful not to mention her long alienation from her parents and brothers or the expedient nature and recent date of their reconciliation.

The Winters family took note of the more genteel persona that she was contriving for this current phase of her life. They looked with equally approving eyes upon the transformations she had wrought upon the character of Leonard Winters. No longer did his well-worn handsomeness or his sensual adventuring find a place in the tabloids and in television newscasts. Whenever his name and image appeared in the news, he was involved in some charity event or in a business leadership conference that brought him to Washington, D.C.; to Europe; and to South America. More often than not, Maria was there with him, skillfully playing her role of dutiful and demure wife. After she gave birth to a son in 1946 and, four years later, to a daughter, the Winters family and the global populace accepted as genuine the temperate personas by which Maria and Leonard were defining themselves.

But, Lauren mused, on this much later morning when memories of her family's history and of her own unhappy biography intensified her bitterness, her parents did not abandon their adventurous daring or their sensual inclinations.

"We played our games just as exuberantly," her mother told her years afterwards, while she was complaining against the blatancy of her perverse daughter's rebellions. "We go on playing them. But we play them away from disapproving eyes. We play them with style."

"I play the same games," she answered her that time, with the blunt insolence that makes allies of resentment and hate. "I play them just as well as you and father do."

She heard again, as though her mother were standing before her in this dawn shadowed bedroom eleven years later, the smoky voiced contempt of that worldly woman.

"You are an imposter. You play the games without loving life. You play without enjoying any of the pleasures. You play to spite your father and me and to shock the public whose attention you willfully draw to yourself."

By then, she had shed the drab appearance that, in her childhood and early adolescence, she had devised to undermine the fictive impressions her mother worked to create about herself and her children in the mind of the public. Two years earlier, when she was fourteen and wished to please the kindest of all the governesses who had guided her upbringing before she was enrolled into a series of private schools, she had consented to wear a beautiful azure blue dress, its delicate femininity replete with organdy and lace, to an after theater party where she would be seen by New York power brokers and their wives, as well as by their teenage sons and daughters. On that evening, she noticed that the beauty of her appearance roused her mother's vague discomfort and her nearly imperceptible envy. In those partying hours, her mother avoided being photographed with her. The epitome of glamour even at forty-four, her mother's beauty had, nevertheless, lost its freshness. Though the years had not visibly depreciated that beauty, they had subdued its splendor. Self-aware and unsentimental, Maria Navarro Winters knew that her time for competing successfully with blossoming teenaged girls and young, sophisticated women had passed her. For the most part, she orchestrated her public appearances so that her dark, rare beauty could work its powers as well as its illusion in the company of men and women who were her own age or who, while growing even older, were retaining at least some of their past splendor.

Perceiving her mother's discomfort, she adopted a glamorous manner. She—Lauren Winters, the unhappy daughter who, for so many years, had willfully appeared plain and disheveled—-suddenly became beautiful. Quite suddenly, while making a dazzling entrance at that New York party, she became someone who, if not actually different, was altogether new. Girls her own age instantly emulated her. Fashionable matrons approved her style and her decorum. Young men courted her favor, and seasoned men observed her carefully, imagining a more propitious time a few years later when they would seduce her.

Her mother acted swiftly against her. Within the next month, she enrolled her in a private school in Newport, Rhode Island. That the school was two hundred miles away from their New York penthouse pleased not only her mother, but also her father, whose disappointment in his daughter had become one more dark and palpable influence upon her acts of angry rebellion. In this bleak period, her parents distanced themselves from her even further by their travels to Europe, South Africa, and South America, as well as to Pennsylvania, Texas, and New Mexico. That her father's business holdings—his gold and copper mines, his oil wells and steel factories, and his vineyards—generated much of the travel did not allay her fears that her parents were shutting her out of their lives or appease her resentment that they were placing their hopes and their trust in her brother Calden. Unlike her, Calden followed all the rules. Conservative and judgmental, he concealed his disdain of his parents' extravagance and their secret misadventures. Instead, he worked hard, won honors at Phillips Andover and at Yale, and bonded with their plans for his advancement in the Winters Corporations. Toward her, his forlorn and willful sister, he concealed neither his disdain, nor his satisfaction at having eclipsed her status within the family.

Hardened by her parents' and her brother's betrayal, she initiated one scandalous episode after another as her acts of revenge against their abandonment and, perhaps, as her cries of despair that might call them back to her. In Newport, she began an affair with Winston Jackson, a man of her own class who had made a name for himself as a classical pianist and as a composer of film scores. He had married a New York debutante and, for a few weeks each year, summered in Newport with her and their two children. Athletic and rangy and, at thirty-two, driven by a fierce and reawakened sexuality, Winston was a man made new by his affair with her.

"You are my wonderful addiction," he told her one time after he had made vigorous love to her in the secret apartment he kept in nearby Middletown. "You are the best thing that has happened to me. These hours with you make my life seem real again."

"I feel the same way," she murmured, sated yet still excited in the aftermath of their lovemaking. "You and I are so right for each other."

Winston's wife disagreed. Gradually aware of her husband's subtle indifference to her, she hired a detective to discover the truth behind his frequent absences from their home. This detective succeeded admirably in his assignment. He and his equally callous associate managed to enter Winston's apartment in Middletown and to photograph him when he was in bed with her, the seventeen-year-old Winters girl who was acquiring a reputation for being reckless and promiscuous. The detectives also followed them into Boston. There, compelled by his obsessive need of her and unmindful of having to confront eventually the harsh consequences of his criminal behavior or of his having been photographed while he was making love to the melancholic girl whose beauty continued to draw him into its spell, Winston had brought her to an exclusive supper club, where they drank champagne and danced to the romantic melodies of Irving Berlin, Franz Lehar, and Cole Porter. The detectives also followed them into Little Compton, Rhode Island. Within the serenities of a beachfront summer home that his parents had given to him and his wife as a wedding present, Winston and she swam on a warm, sun glistening afternoon in May. Later that day, they sailed across the blue sheen of the bay and dined at an inn that was both picturesque and secluded. On an afternoon in June, from an airfield in Darien, Connecticut, they flew in Winston's Cessna 172 Skyhawk. Exhilarated beyond measure and attentive to his instruction, she learned the rudiments of copiloting. Even now, ten years later, she remembered those days with Winston as the happiest time of her life.

Then their affair was over.

"We had a great time together," Winston told her. An imported cigarette was dangling from the right corner of his mouth, and a grimace was spoiling his handsomeness. "But we are finished."

"I don't believe you," she protested. "I know you love me as much as I love you."

"Sure I do, honey," he said, keeping at bay his angry sorrow and choosing, instead to express himself with matter-of-fact briskness. "But I do not plan on spending any time in prison, not even for you. Come back in a few years. Maybe we can strike the spark again, when you are old enough to make it legal."

The detectives had already paid a visit to her parents and informed them that Winston's wife planned to go to the police and to the newspapers, unless their daughter was sent out of the country. Wary of unfavorable publicity, for fear that the scandal would damage the prestige of their corporations and jeopardize their portfolio of blue-chip stocks, her parents quickly collaborated with Winston's wife. They were glad to defuse the perversities of their daughter's carnal relations with a married man and to relocate her far away from their immediate jurisdiction to an exclusive school near Lausanne, Switzerland.

Her losing Winston ignited within the deepest part of her rage, her earliest suicidal thoughts. That she might fling herself from a snowy Alpine precipice when she had joined her classmates for a weekend of skiing would make her death appear accidental. Neither her parents, nor Winston would perceive that their betrayals had driven her to suicide. So, she rejected that scenario, which might invoke their nostalgia for the happier episodes they had shared with her and their regret for the episodes they could never share with her, but which would absolve them of any complicity in her death. Swallowing arsenic or some other poison might prolong the agony of dying and might twist her face into an ugliness that was horror-stricken and repellent. She rejected that plan, too. Firing a single bullet from a snub-nosed revolver straight into her heart would bring instant death. Both Winston and her parents would know for certain that they had driven her to suicide.

She told herself, though without much conviction, that her mother might experience not only a wrenching grief, but also a punishing guilt. The Smith and Wesson snub-nosed revolver belonged to her mother. The once-fearless and now sometimes-apprehensive Maria Navarro had carried it inside a glamorous purse whenever a bad dream of a gangster boyfriend from her lurid past disturbed her self-possession or after she had glimpsed in a crowded New York airport the volatile business executive she had played for a fool in England or the sadistic polo player she had left behind in Buenos Aires. That she, Lauren Winters, the troubled daughter whom her parents regarded as immature and troublesome, had been clever enough to take the revolver from the drawer of her mother's night table and, just before embarking on the journey to Switzerland, conceal it effectively within the lining of a ski jacket lifted her spirits at least momentarily. Her theft of the revolver goaded her desire to kill herself. The thought that her mother might never recover from her death pleased her. To imagine that her death would deprive her mother, as well as her father and Winston, of the happiness they so often took for granted satisfied her need to avenge herself against them.

But her grudging awareness that they would not grieve for long gave her pause. She knew them well. Her parents and Winston would permit themselves to forget her. They would go on without her, reveling in the contrived pleasures and the unabated joys of being alive. Now she resolved to avenge herself against them in a more lasting way. She would not kill herself. She would live as scandalously as they were living. But she would live more openly, defying the rules that made them wary and secretive. She would fill her life with careless and self-centered adventures and with relationships both ruthless and promiscuous.

In Switzerland, she began sleeping with Tristan Garnier, a rugged seventeen-year-old athlete who was attending a private school only a mile away from her own. The son of a Swiss banker, Tristan was the most handsome young man she had ever met. His tall, blond virility and his keen-eyed perceptions; his mastery of swimming, boxing, skiing, and horseback riding; his crafty piloting of a Piper Super Cub; and his inventive riffing on a jazz trumpet—all these emblems of identity influenced and enhanced his confident negotiations with the world. Though he did not regard himself as a narcissist, he enjoyed, nevertheless, her adulation and her deferring to his every whim. At first, the intensity of her love intrigued him. Incapable of so profound a commitment, he quietly studied her responses during the first months of their being together. He wondered (he once told her) whether her capacity for idealizing a lover made her passion more pleasurable, if not more profound. If that were the case, her love was a false passion that embellished a reality she found insufficient. She loved him not as he was, but as she imagined him to be.

"Love me for myself," he said. "That should be enough for you. Do not make me a plaything of your fantasies. Do not confer upon me virtues that I neither possess, nor care to represent."

On that October night, hours after they had shared an exhilarating day of skiing across intricate Alpine slopes and right after they had made love within the comfortable privacies of a Swiss chalet, she answered him with lighthearted words.

"I shall love you exactly as you want me to love you. I shall teach my eyes to see the real Tristan Garnier. But that will be a difficult lesson, I think, because even in a single day you are never the same Tristan. You are so many Tristan Garniers, and every one of them fascinates me."

Tristan laughed.

"You see magic where there is none. You tell yourself you have found a god, though I am only a man."

"That is how I love," she said. "I cannot love otherwise."

Tristan laughed again. Even now, nearly ten years later, the memory of his laughter saddened her. Hearing his words then, for the first time, she understood in a flash of recognition how far from the mark she was in determining who he was when he was with her and when he was away. But not only the memory of his laughter saddened her. Now, long after that night with him, an even more disturbing memory revived for her bitter awareness the casual manner in which he separated himself from her view of their relationship.

"I have never met a girl like you before," he said, as his hands gently caressed her face. "You are a bona fide romantic."

"So are you."

"Not even a little bit," he said, understated, yet insistent before pressing his lips just for a moment upon her lips.

Once again he studied her, trying to fathom the wishful thinking that convinced her he was a romantic.

"Then I promise to make you a romantic," she said, feigning the lightheartedness that had just left her. "That is a rule that all lovers learn to obey."

"Forget those old-fashioned rules," Tristan said. "The only rule we need is to tell each other the truth."

"That rule is easy to follow."

"Of course, it is. We'll always level with each other. We'll always tell one another how it is with us."

For all that school year and for much of their first year in Paris, while Tristan was enrolled at the University of Paris and she studied at École des Beaux-Arts, she enjoyed the fierce passion and the natural ecstasy of their love. With Tristan, she discovered new levels of sensuality. His prowess as a lover and his confident exploration of her body gave to their relationship a joy that was both mutual and authentic. The café afternoons and nightclub evenings in Montparnasse, in St-Germain-des-Prés, and on the French Riviera; the lively conversations with poets, novelists, and philosophers in Montmartre and in the Sorbonne; the midnight jazz sessions in the Latin Quarter, where she (at the piano) and Tristan (with his trumpet) accompanied the moody blue notes of top musical pros; the kayaking excursions to Finland; and the copiloting of a Piper Super Cub in England—all these more-than-ordinary occasions intensified her belief in Tristan. His earthbound realism smoothly complemented even as it deflected the idealized subtexts and the obsessive implications of her love for him. Yet his was no fair-weather love. He was always honest. He was always true. He was always there to advise and to rescue her whenever she called out to him.

Only in their final weeks together did he close himself off from her. Only then, when he was no longer her advocate, did he look upon her with a hardened and pitiless gaze. Then his brooding tension and blunt arguing displaced the harmony they had so casually shared. At first, she thought the pressure of his studies and the wily, competitive spirit of his classmates had darkened his spirit. Never had he met with caustic remarks her sorrowing recollection of her parents' animosity. Never, in the two years that they freely loved each other, had he dismissed with contemptuous sneer and cold-hearted detachment her petitions for his sympathy.

"You are a mess of neuroses," he said, on that final afternoon when he had quickly expressed his impatience with her. She had returned from a university lecture to find him packing his trunk and several suitcases in the bedroom where he kept most of his belongings, but where he slept only on those nights after studying long hours for his examinations. He was emptying his wardrobe closets of his trousers, suits, and coats and removing from a chest of drawers his shirts, socks, and underwear.

"What are you doing?' she asked him, imagining that some unhappy news from his parents or from his brothers was calling him to them. "Where are you going?"

"I'm moving out," he said, without pausing in his haste to fill his suitcases with his belongings. "I want a different scene."

He kept moving past her or around her, as he gathered his possessions. She, in turn, followed him while tracking his every step.

"Then I'll go with you," she said. "Living in a new place will be good for us."

"Not if we are together."

"Of course we'll be good together," she said, her voice suddenly tremulous with apprehension. "We always have been."

"Not now," he quickly answered her, sullen and insistent. "We're not good together now."

"Tell me what I've done. Tell me what's wrong. I'll do whatever you ask me. I'll be whoever you want me to be."

He was moving into her bedroom now. She followed him, always hovering near him as he continued to take hold of all the belongings that signified his having lived here. Now he flung open the drawers of the night tables that flanked the bed in which he had so often made love to her. From the drawers of the table on the left side of the bed, he took one of his textbooks, a stack of letters that friends from South America and from the United States had written to him, a gold watch that he had casually left there, and a carton of cigarettes imported from Patagonia. He placed the watch around his wrist. But all the other things he placed in a large traveling bag, even as he went on explaining to her who she was and why he was leaving her.

"It's not any good being with you," he said. "You are a leaner. You depend too much upon my sharing your problems and even solving them. You mess around with me. You try to draw me into your neuroses. You want me to fall into the same traps that are holding you back."

"No, I have never wanted that. I have never wanted you to feel trapped. I depended on your remaining strong. I believed that you would show me the way out of the traps. And you have. Your being there with me has so often helped me to free myself from my nights of terrible memories and from all the days that have punished me with the latest news of my parents' and my brother's hatred."

"You will be on your own now. You will have to fight your battles alone."

"I can't," she cried out. "I can't. I need you here with me."

"You need to grow up. That is what you need. You need to let go of your parents. Stop blaming them or your brother or me or anyone else for your unhappiness. Learn how to stand up to the world alone, without expecting that everyone is going to treat you fairly."

"I don't care about everyone," she softly answered him, while choosing temperate words to allay his anger. "But I care about those to whom I have given all my love. I expect them to love me in return. I expect them to comfort me when I go to them with my sorrows. I want them to stand with me. I want them to show me that I am not alone."

Still the sneer remained at the right corner of his mouth. Still the cold-hearted dismissal of her feelings pushed his words forward.

"Everyone is alone," he said, as he started to hurry away from her and from the plush amenities of their apartment. "That is the way things are."

"Wait," she called out to him.

With her hand gently touching the back of his shoulder as he turned from her, she made him pause in his tracks.

"What has happened?" she asked him. "Why has everything changed between us?"

"Don't you know? Haven't you guessed?"

"I don't know anything until you tell me."

"I have met someone else. We hit it off right away. She is better suited to me. She's what I need right now."

"You said you loved me."

"I did love you. For the past two years I loved you. But things change. I've changed. I need to go forward without you."

"You can't mean that. Everything has been so real between us. What we have felt for each other can't be over. Genuine love isn't like that."

"I told you that I am not a romantic. Love comes. Love goes. When it goes, it is better to face up to the truth. It is better to walk away as quickly as possible."

"Is it because I dissuaded you from the hunting trip to South Africa? Or is it because I talked you out of that trek to the Australian outback? Is that what has turned you against me?"

"You were right about South Africa and about Australia. You did not belong in either place with me."

"But this new girl does."

"Yes."

"She will never love you as I do. You could never be for each other what we have been."

"I don't want your kind of love anymore. I don't want a woman who depends upon my love. I want a woman who treats love as a plaything and who can toss it away after using it awhile."

Just then, before she could find other reasons why he should stay with her or petition him to come to his senses, the doorbell rang. Tristan opened the door to one of the porters assigned to their apartment building. The porter, a tall, muscular man in his middle years, gave no sign that he noticed the tension that hovered between her and Tristan. Instead, while carrying out an assignment that, she guessed, Tristan had given him hours earlier, the porter grabbed the trunk and one of the suitcases and hurried away.

Alone with him once more, she implored Tristan to stay.

"Don't do this," she said. "We can work something out. We can make all of it good again."

"It's too late for that," he answered her. His voice was pitiless and unyielding. "We have had our time together, and now we are finished."

He was turning away from her and, while carrying two of his suitcases with confident ease, was hurrying toward the door. He opened the door and was about to step into the hallway.

In that instant, she felt herself going outside herself. She felt that she was plummeting through space, without a parachute or safety hatch or ballasting apparatus to save her. The sight of Tristan's walking away from her left her disoriented and breathless. Fear and rage were confusing her senses. As though she were caught inside a bleak dream, she was only vaguely aware of hurrying to the secret drawer inside her dresser and taking hold of the snub-nosed revolver. Nor did she accurately remember until months afterward her piercing shriek and her taut voice calling out to this man who was leaving her.

"Tristan! Tristan!"

So wretched was her cry, so broken and lost did she sound, that he stopped in his tracks and turned back to her.

Without uttering a word, she shot him in the chest. The impact of the bullet threw him backwards, as the suitcases fell away from him. He struggled in vain to remain standing. Then, he dropped to his knees and leaned forward, as if he were moving in slow motion and resisting the fall upon the carpet. Blood was trickling from his chest and rushing out of his back. He grimaced with pain, just before he noticed new blood welling from his chest and covering his right hand. She watched his astonished face trying to comprehend what was happening. She saw him looking with horrified awareness upon her. She waited while he slowly lifted himself to his full height and groped toward her. His hand was reaching out to balance his wavering movements, perhaps, or to take the gun from her, or simply to make an appeal.

"No! No!" he yelled with a voice gone raspy, as he saw her aiming her revolver again. "Don't do it! Don't do it!"

Still he groped toward her. Still his right hand reached out, as if in appeal. Still his blue eyes flashed, horror-struck and unbelieving.

She shot him again, the bullet glancing off his right temple. Now he fell backward, his long and athletic body landing with a soft thud upon the thick carpet.

Tristan's body lay very still. His eyes were closed, and his mouth was slightly open. Though she hurried to the place where he lay and stood over him with her hand tightly clasping her revolver, she could not tell whether he was dead or merely unconscious. Her eyes could not see his body with any clarity, so blinded by tears was her vision. Now, as though she were being overtaken by a wild impulse, she lifted her hand that held the revolver and pointed it toward her right temple. She studied the pistol's barrel length of three inches and the compact nature of its carbon steel. She placed her index finger around the trigger, convinced that the press of that finger would swiftly kill her. But, in that instant, her fear held her back. She could not fire the bullet that would throw her out of existence. She could not, at the last, bond with the dark and wild impulse that her bitterness had often called to her. With a quick, jagged movement, she tossed the revolver away from herself, vaguely aware that it came to rest at the right foot of Tristan's body. She heard herself sobbing, and the wretched sounds filled her with pity for herself. There flashed in her memory quick scenes of all the earlier days that had misused her and of all those other persons, including her parents, who had betrayed her. But only for a moment did her mind hold these images. Only in the instant after she shot Tristan was she alone in the room with his body.

Right after that, a security guard and a gendarme rushed into the room, their revolvers pointed at her until the gendarme grabbed hold of the pistol that lay at Tristan's feet. The security guard examined Tristan's body. She heard him whispering to the gendarme, but all of his words were lost to her hearing. Nor did she comprehend the words he spoke so hastily into the telephone. The room was folding into itself, and she—even as she stood, weary and motionless, over Tristan's body—was floating apart from herself and from the two men, as well. Now the security guard gently took her arm and led her to the sofa. Then he and the gendarme began prying her with questions. She answered none of them. She could not comprehend what they were asking. Their voices seemed so far away, as their words rose up in fragments to baffle her.

Nor could she understand why Tristan's best friend, Guillaume Dussolier, came rushing into the room, his ruddy, handsome face looking apprehensive and grief-stricken. His girlfriend Cécile was with him. On that afternoon, her beautiful oval face looked pale; her long, slim figure seemed vulnerable and awkward; and her brown eyes were filling with tears as she, finding a place next to her on the sofa, took hold of her hands. Her voice tremulous and sorrow-laden, Cécile began speaking to her. But (Lauren remembered on this morning so many years later) she could not make sense of any of the words, so far away and indecipherable did they sound to her. She was more aware of Guillaume, though he never approached her. She saw him with grieving face place two pillows beneath Tristan's bleeding head. She watched him hurrying into Tristan's bedroom and quickly hurrying back with a blanket that he placed around Tristan's body. Only once, after he became aware of her gaze upon him, did Guillaume look up at her. But he said nothing.

Now a tall, wiry man with curly black hair and a studious calm made his way into the room. The black leather physician's bag that his large hand clasped and the equally young, auburn-haired nurse accompanying him told her why he was here. His penetrating brown eyes, quickly scanning the richly upholstered room, caught sight of Tristan's inert body and Guillaume's first-aid care of it; and Cécile and her sitting together, forlorn and silent, on the sofa. Just then, the room and all the people in it floated away from her again. Once more she felt herself going outside herself. This time she plummeted even more swiftly through space, her free fall hurling her toward a darkness that she tried, without avail, to resist. Before her clouded seeing, the room sparked and flashed as if exploding, and the people and the objects before her scattered away from her vision into the darkness that, with waves like bruising tentacles, overtook her. When the darkness threw her back, the nurse was taking her pulse, and—right after that—Cécile, flanking the other side of her, was urging her with a quiet, ingratiating voice to sip water from a small paper cup. At the same time, the brawny security guard was recording with his Leica what she vaguely perceived as the disarranged and lopsided imagery of the snub-nosed revolver that the gendarme held in the palm of his hand for the camera's inspection; Tristan's supine body; and two agile medics who were in that very instant, under the watchful eyes of Guillaume and the physician, lifting Tristan onto a gurney, as though it were an open casket, and hurrying out of the room with it. Guillaume and the physician with his nurse, without looking at her, but nodding respectfully to Cécile as well as to the gendarme and the security guard, quickly followed. Their faces became a blur to her in the instant after she glimpsed them. Yet Tristan's ashen and blood-smeared face stayed with her. His eyes were still closed, and a rigid stillness had overtaken his body. She believed that he was dead, so lifeless and discarded did he appear to her eyes as he was carried away on the gurney.

But Tristan did not die. The first bullet had missed his heart by an inch or two. The second bullet merely grazed his right temple. On that bleak afternoon, however, *she* died. It was one of her many deaths. She had believed that her love for Tristan would show her the way out of her wilderness. She had convinced herself that the fervor and authenticity of that love would transform Tristan's casual sensuality into a genuine and unconditional love that mirrored her own. Her love for him did not save her, though. Nor could he be her rescuer. He had not really loved her. Betrayed by his spurious affection, she had become his would-be destroyer. So quickly did her love for him turn to hate that, for months after she shot him, she wondered whether her feelings for Tristan were spawned, after all, not from authentic love but from a perverse obsession that derived its power from wild impulse and from an inordinate desire to possess completely the object on which her obsession fed. This idea that, never having been truly loved by anyone, she might be incapable of genuine love maddened her. It condemned her once again to the wilderness that she sought to escape. It stole her hope. It left her bereft, a wayward creature cast adrift by her self-willed fate and by self-defeating impulse.

"You are the prisoner of your desires," her mother complained to her, after the shooting of Tristan and after the news media had thrown the family into another scandal. "You never learn your lesson. You will come to a bad end."

On that day in the spring of 1969, her mother and her father signed the papers that placed her inside a sanitarium.

"Some of your luck has stayed with you," her father said, without concealing his contempt for her. "Your sometime lover,

Tristan What's-his-name, has decided to do the gallant thing. He will not press charges. I imagine that he is weary of being vilified in the press and on television. His being a cad has made him the latest public sensation. Though the police have frowned upon his gesture of forgiveness, my money has paid them well for their pangs of conscience. Your lawyer has placated them further. He has agreed with them that you need to spend some time in a Swiss clinic."

Her father was standing at the foot of her hospital bed. His commanding height and well-groomed, athletic body drove with quickened energies the self-possession that was an inherent part of his nature. His silver hair and brown-eyed steely gaze lent him further distinction. His sleek tan revealed to her eyes that, before the police called him back to Paris, he had been vacationing in Tahiti.

Her mother was also tanned, yet almost imperceptibly. The tan had merely deepened her already dark complexion. Though Givenchy had designed her white chiffon dress, the darkened skin gave her the look of a Spanish peasant or gypsy. She was standing at the iron-grated window, where the light of the sun suffused with eerie radiance her vivid appearance. More formidable than a wily peasant or a dangerous gypsy in this instant, she might have been a malevolent spirit who had come there, in this secluded room within the hospital, to invoke a life-long spell upon her or to seal, as an eternal fate, the curse that would disguise the unhappiness that was in store for her.

"Maybe Dr. Triesault will help you unravel the mess that you have made of your life," her mother said. "Maybe he will make you see why you are your own worst enemy."

Before the room could float away from her again, she struggled to find the words that would keep her parents at bay.

"You are my worst enemies," she said, her voice at first pitched low and tremulous. "The two of you have always made things difficult for me, even while pretending that you know what is best for me. You are glad that I am here, strapped to this bed. You are pleased to see me held prisoner in this clinic. You are waiting for me to tell you that I am sorry for the way that I have been living my life. You want me to beg your forgiveness. You want me to say that you were right about everything. But I will not say it. I will never give you the pleasure of hearing me say it."

By now, her voice was strident and filled with rage. A gray-haired nurse rushed into the room and jabbed her arm with a needle. Standing at the entrance to the room, her grim-faced parents, who started to take leave of her, were speaking carefully measured words that she could not hear. For an instant, their faraway voices seemed like her own—a confusion of resentment, bitterness, and anguish. Then, with disarranged abruptness, the room disappeared, leaving in its wake her fleeting glimpse of the tight-lipped nurse who was hovering by the bed and, just before a murky darkness overtook everything, her vague awareness of the ambiguous faces of her parents. They stared at her, just before leaving this new, angry scene that she had wrought. A moment later, caught within a spell that she imagined she had cast upon them, both her father and her mother vanished.

That was not to be the last rancorous scene between her parents and herself. After the extended absences that followed each of their confrontations, they always managed to devise some temporary accord or to find their way to a reluctant compromise that permitted them to continue their relationship. But in 1971, two years after her angry meeting with them in the sanitarium, her parents were killed in a plane crash over the Southern Andes. With swift and pitiless finality, the Fates denied her the tattered remorse she might otherwise have felt. Her parents had died before she could resolve her acrimonious relations with them and before she could negotiate the sort of peace treaty in which many unhappy families take weary refuge. When her parents died, she felt no remorse. What she felt was a surge of panic, yoked as it was to her awareness that, even in death, they had expressed their disapproval of her. From the grave, they continued to betray her. The irrevocable will that, with her parents' meticulous instructions, four lawyers had drawn up a year earlier dashed all her hopes. It threw her down again, into the abyss of despair from which her "rest cure" in the Zürich clinic had tenuously saved her. Neither her entrapment in the clinic, nor the seven months when she was surrounded by precision-drilled nurses and by calculating psychiatrists, nor the electro-shock therapies that overtook her disarranged senses had left her feeling so helpless, so abandoned, and so ruthlessly punished.

As far as she was concerned, her parents virtually disinherited her. They left most of their fortune to her adversarial brother. The trust fund they established for her provided a comfortable security that was to be doled out to her quarterly, the sum of each increment sufficient to the needs of a Winters heiress, without complicating her life with prodigal amenities or scandalous excess. So, her parents' lawyers explained. Yet her parents did not fail to leave her one of their Manhattan penthouses and one of their Bentleys. They also left her a house in the Hamptons and a villa on the French Riviera, with the proviso that she could not sell the Manhattan penthouse, the house in East Hampton, or the French villa without the permission of her brother or the approval of the four eminent lawyers who were the executors of her parents' estate. In those hours when she was alone and able to reflect calmly upon her situation, she admitted that her parents had not completely disinherited her. They were too clever to publicize their antipathy. Had they done so, they would have brought shame upon themselves. Nevertheless, their will made clear, to her at least, that they had no intention of financing their daughter's wayward escapades. They had endowed her with the security that befitted a young woman from a privileged class. But they had not left her the forty million dollars that, as a free-flowing liquid asset, would allow her to experience the adventurous life that she craved.

A codicil to the will expressed her parents' conflicted regard of her even more clearly. This amendment to their will called out to her to change her life. If her future conduct gave evidence of a new maturity as well as of a genuine transformation, a substantial bequest would be added to her inheritance. To earn the forty million dollars, she not only needed to reform her ways. She also needed to marry a man of substance. He must belong to the same privileged class. He must have the mental agility and the solid character to make his life worthwhile and to increase his fortune. He could, if he so desired, become a leader in state or national government.

The codicil infuriated her. It condemned her to a too-cautious existence that suppressed her individuality and imprisoned her within its rules and its conventions.

"To hell with the codicil," she told her lawyers. *"I'll* choose the way I live my life. You can bury the codicil with those two strangers who called themselves my parents."

As though she had been cast adrift and left to discover new capacities for manipulating her fate, she reveled even more flagrantly in the party scenes that brought her away from the New York and Los Angeles cabarets that viewed her apprehensively because of her reputation for flinging champagne glasses and dinner plates at the latest gigolo who was duping her and because, on more than one occasion, she had fired her snub-nosed revolver at the young men of her class who drank even more than she did and who slapped and punched her whenever she taunted them with the details of her latest infidelity or, with brazen perversity, refused to bring them to her bed. For nearly two years, she lived with extravagant wildness in Paris, Rome, London, Buenos Aires, Madrid, and Barcelona. She was cynically aware that, in her rebellious flouting of both civil and moral codes and with a sensuality that disguised its promiscuity through glamorous decorum, she was replicating the early life of her mother. Loveless though not unloved, she became the temporary mistress of an Italian banker and two British stockbrokers, of a French film producer and a Spanish duke. As her mother had done before her, she regarded her associations with these men as business transactions.

"We play this game well," she would tell her lovers, knowing all the while that she was appropriating the role her mother had often inhabited during those years when she was known as the famous film star Maria Navarro. "We satisfy each other's need of an exciting partner. We raise the stakes as high as we like, and we always win the game. Afterwards, we take away what satisfies us most of all. You take the memory of our nights together. I take the gifts you freely offer. The game always plays the way we choose. We make it a smooth transaction. There are no pangs of conscience. There are no false promises. There are no regrets or confused feelings. There are only the hours that we enjoy together."

Whenever she expressed her carefree point of view, most of her partners responded with a worldly detachment that matched her own. They grinned in wily accord. In these moments, they offered no romantic words that might elevate the pragmatic nature of their relationship. Their affairs with her succeeded because she, as well as they, disdained the sentimental remarks and conventional gestures that violated the unspoken rules of their free-spirited associations. But her more introspective partners, wondering whether their feelings for her had become too profound, grew very still when they heard her casual appraisal of their partnership. They observed her with even more careful attention than was their habit, searching now as they did for the tremulous lilt in her voice and the misty glow of her eyes that might betray the heartfelt emotions she was hiding from them. But her voice carried no tremulous lilt, nor did her eyes fill with the mist of melancholic yearning. Never did she violate the pact that she had made with them. Never did she reveal to these more contemplative partners any disposition other than her inveterate narcissism.

But then she went too far, plunging herself recklessly into the lowest depths of her rebellious nightclub life. Upon her return to the United States, she began traveling with a drug-addicted crowd of pleasure-seekers in New York and Los Angeles. The three young men that she too carelessly befriended in this ill-fated cycle belonged to her class. Like her, they were in conflict with the wealthy families that pampered their needs and paid for their follies. Although they were very young, they were already on their way down. They were arrogant and hollow men who had been rendered effete by the soft gentility that produced them. Already, only a year or two later, she had forgotten their names. But the memory of the wild nights she had shared with each of them remained with her. The wildness seldom involved their sexual prowess. Too far gone in their cocaine or heroin addiction, they could no longer make copulation a vigorous and satisfying experience. Nor could their cocaine and heroin fixes bring them to the safe harbor they were seeking. Without hope of rescue, these lost men fell deeper into their addiction. Bitterness fired within them the savage inclinations that had always been dormant. They took perverse pleasure now in declaring themselves the enemies of any man or woman who looked too self-assured or quietly vulnerable or genuinely happy. There were frequent nightclub brawls. There was the careless sharing of drugs. There were police raids. There were arrests that were well publicized in the tabloids. There was the shooting of a well-known saxophonist while he was performing a medley of love ballads. The bullets fired into his chest nearly killed him. His brown skin and his success as a lover of white women had roused the envy and the hatred of the most savage of the three men whose appeal for her derived from the degradation into which they had fallen. Willfully, she fell with them, though never so far as to join them in their heroin fantasies. Cocaine fed her gestures toward self-destruction, without imposing upon those gestures the bleak finality from which there was no rescue.

In these months, she outraged her brother once again and even those friends of her parents who had always remained loyal to her when her scandalous escapades drew the attention of the police as well as of the press. But this time the scandal made her look tawdry. It tarnished, even by their oblique association, the members of her family who shared the name of Winters. Worse than that, she had become involved with three men whose bad conduct had betrayed the established honor of *their* families. An accessory to the drug-addicted sprees of these three worthless fellows and, with its racist implications, to the shooting rampage of the most savage of the three, she had violated the terms of her parents' will. This time, because she had given false testimony in defense of the man who had shot the saxophonist, she had mired herself in scandal that clearly identified her as a criminal. Her brother, as well as the lawyers who served as executors of her parents' estate, acted swiftly. Once again, they discreetly used the Winters' money and political influence to absolve her of any criminal charges. At the same time, they reduced the sum of money that the Winters' trust deposited into her bank account every quarter. They also invoked more stringent rules that required her to conduct her life with well-reasoned and temperate choices. If she failed to do so, she would forfeit even more of the privileges that her parents' will was providing for her.

She felt worse than lost. She felt trapped—not only by the events that had closed in upon her, but also by herself. There seemed to be no way out of her dilemma. For a few months, because of the scandal, New York and Los Angeles were finished for her. She could go nowhere without drawing to herself tabloid reporters and hostile detectives who hated wealthy people and who thought that she should be serving time in prison. So, for all of that summer, she withdrew to her aunt's home in Vermont. When she returned to New York, she took care not to become involved with the troublesome crowd that made a mockery of the rules for civil behavior. She wanted to live differently. She wanted to reinvent herself. But she lacked the inspiration and the training that would guide her into a meaningful career. Nor could she persuade herself to resume the university program that would turn her into the fashion designer that she had once planned to be. Try as she might, she could not summon the discipline that would change her life for the better. Even with its stinted rewards, the annuity that her parents had left her provided a measure of security that made ambition seem gratuitous, an awkward appendage to a life that appeased itself with inherited gifts and unearned privileges.

Whether her ingrained perversity or her tightly coiled despair kept her from rescuing herself, she could not say. Perhaps, it was the rage festering within her that subverted her desire to become somebody new and altogether different. Possibly, her cynical expectation that her uninhibited sensuality would win her passionate lovers and, eventually, a loyal husband kept her from becoming self-dependent and new. Only recently, and all too belatedly, she had grown aware that the prominent men of her class might use her to sate their various lusts, but they would never marry her. As if her fate had canceled all her chances for happiness, she could draw to herself only temporary men who, intrigued by her scandalous past or weary of their demure wives or roused by her glamorous facade, willingly shared with her those pleasures that were illicit and self-serving.

In the winter of 1975, at an upscale bar in Manhattan, she met Bryce Thompson. He was thirty-seven and already on his way down. She was twenty-five and burning fast the fuse that ignited her vitality. Though he did not belong to her class, she saw in his brooding virility, in his contempt for the rules that had sometimes thwarted him, and in his wily negotiations with whatever scenario was unfolding around him a rebel who matched her own dangerous willfulness. He never told her much about himself. Yet she understood the sort of man that he was. They shared the same narcissistic self-enclosure—the same, adamant refusal, after years of failed relationships, to connect deeply to any other person. He had arrived at a sinuous turn in the road on which his fate had placed him. She met him on that same road, as conflicted as he was and nearly as desperate. Now, looking back on their first year together two years later, she was startled by the ease with which they had agreed to murder a man that they did not even know.

"Find a wealthy guy from your own class," Bryce told her. "Make him fall in love with you. Get him to marry you. Then leave the rest to me."

Their plan fascinated her. They were going to choose the man who would die. Equally devious and implicated, they would—this one time, at least—overturn the prevailing rules that had so often constrained their wayward desires and subverted their wily powers. She would also make a mockery of the codicil in her parents' will that required her to reform her character and to marry a substantial man who belonged to her class. She was going to marry such a man. Then, she would inherit, from her parents' estate, the forty million dollars that she would be allowed to keep as long as she did her part to make her marriage successful. After Bryce killed her husband, she would inherit that man's fortune, as well, and, with Bryce as her wayward partner, resume the free-spirited living that quickened her days and nights.

"For once, we'll deal with loaded dice and get away with it," she said. "We'll play God and win the game."

Her need to avenge herself against her parents and against the world that had treated her with rough indifference drove her into the plan. Only a few weeks later, in September 1976, she met Aaron Dowling, the man whom she selected to be the victim in the murderous plot that she and Bryce had devised. Meeting him for the first time at a glamorous party hosted by long-time friends of her parents, she decided that Dowling fit all the requirements of the victim that she and Bryce had imagined. He was wealthy. He was single. He wore his privileged status with an arrogance that, in her first regard of him, displeased her. But then she came to know him well. The arrogance that she had carelessly sighted in Aaron Dowling was, she perceived later, an inherent self-assurance that gave him a convincing authenticity. He was a strong-minded man who was not afraid to express a hard-won truth or to defend a controversial principle. He was an extraordinary man who had mastered four languages, who had flown bombing missions over South Vietnam, and who was an executive on his way up in the Dowling Corporation. He was also a romantic man, sandy-haired and handsome. By this time, because she had allowed herself to see him as he really was, she had fallen in love with him. That he had fallen in love with her, as well, quickened her spirit. His love persuaded her to believe that she could, once again, be that Lauren Winters of her childhood who loved life and who wanted to bring into the world life-affirming discoveries and worthwhile deeds.

In July of 1977, when they were vacationing in Newport, she married him in a quiet ceremony that took place in the town clerk's private chambers. Paul and Leah Cohen, who were Aaron's trusted friends, witnessed the marriage and promised to keep it a secret. In time, Aaron told her, they would have a church ceremony and a New York festival kind of celebration, to which they would invite hundreds of guests. For now, though, he preferred to establish himself even more solidly within the Dowling Corporation, before they revealed their secret marriage to her brother and to any of the other essential persons in their lives. His rising success as an architect would, Aaron explained, increase both the rightness and the value of their marriage not only to her brother and the lawyers who stood watch over her inheritance, but also to the executors of his uncle's fortune. If he did all the right things, he would reap a third of the Dowling fortune.

"We hold the right cards," Aaron told her. "We have to play them well, if we want to win the game."

His realistic sense of things appealed to her. Its materialist subtexts gave to his romantic fervor an earth-bound gravity that she respected. The secrecy of their marriage also pleased her. It gave her time to release herself from Bryce's hold upon her.

No longer did she want to make Aaron the victim of Bryce's and her murderous plot. But Bryce wanted to kill him. Now, when he suspected that she had fallen in love with Aaron, he wanted to kill him very soon. Thus far, he was unaware that she had married Aaron. She wondered whether she would still be able to keep Bryce at bay. She had grown uneasy and even frightened when she was in his company. If she had come to know Aaron well, she had, in these complicated months, come to know Bryce with even more incisive certainty. She had been drawn to him at first by his vigorous sensuality and by the flashes of sensitivity that were as intermittent as they were awkward. Lately, though, she realized in new and bitter ways that he had made her his prisoner. Conscious from the start of how much their relationship was costing her, she had, nevertheless, reveled in the late nights and early mornings of sex with him. The immense pleasure that he gave her solaced her for hours afterward. For those hours, the pleasure dispelled the bruising intensities of the real world.

No sooner had she met Aaron Dowling, however, than she began detaching herself from her dependence upon Bryce. She admitted, at last, that Bryce manipulated her feelings for him—both the fear and the love—so that he could control her behavior. She had readily submitted to that control. It was a fair payment for the pleasure that he brought her. Now, with a clarity that resisted her self-deluded view of things, she saw him as her enemy. To break free of Bryce, she would have to activate her capacity for devising clever ruses and even wilier schemes. She would have to anticipate all the moves that he planned to make against Aaron and even against her. As if this thought were compelling her to initiate the rescuing plan that she had only, during the last hours, constructed, she rose from her bed and hurried to meet the day's conflicted powers. She would leave Vermont and return to New York, where being with Aaron would revive her hope and allow her, with charming naturalness, to introduce her plan. Without mentioning Bryce and without confessing her perverse attachment to him or their murderous plot, she must persuade Aaron to accompany her to Europe. Taking flight from Bryce was the only strategy that could save their lives.

Chapter Three
Mister Right

Lighthearted and confident as always, Aaron Dowling laughed a husky laugh, coiled as it was within his steel-true masculinity. Then, he casually brushed Lauren's cheek with a kiss.

"Your plan for Europe is a good one," he said, right after the kiss and after with natural ease he pulled away from her, so that he could study her response to him. "You are a clever girl, and your business instincts are right on the mark. But your imagination is moving too fast. This is not the right time for Europe."

He noticed the vague lines of a frown touching her brow and the graceful gesture of her clasped hands as, with beseeching subtexts, she spoke new words that might draw him to her will. He noticed as well the genteel timbre of her voice, with its modulated artifice. The soft and mellow rhythms had displaced the smoky and seductive inflections that more naturally represented who she was. She was a confused girl, and the fault line in his cultivated hard-heartedness permitted him to pity her a little. She was, after all and in spite of her wary efforts to suppress her emotional destitution, so needy. But the pity did not diminish the subtle contempt he sometimes felt for her. Nor did it persuade him to defer to her need or, by compromising his own purposes and by subduing his own will, to allay her apprehension. Instead, he let her talk, while he listened with calculated patience to whatever new problem was festering inside her spoiled life. Today, though, he detected a difference in the neurotic appeal that she was making to him. He heard genuine fear in her voice, and he saw that same fear in her eyes.

"You can make Europe work for you, Aaron," she murmured, infusing her petition with a decorous intimacy that meant to disarm him. "The Dowling Corporation will be pleased to have you there. An assignment in Europe will give you a splendid push forward. It is the best thing that can happen, and I will be with you.

He found the intimacy charming, but his hardened nature, with unobtrusive willfulness, resisted her appeal nonetheless.

"New York has treated me very well," he said, while allowing his big hands to cover the delicate skin of her own. "I am moving forward very smoothly right here. Besides, this is the place where everybody that counts knows me. This is the place where architectural commissions and real estate development really matter. This is the big city that gives you and me a good time."

"Of course it does," she quickly agreed, while he gently pressed the cool flesh of her hands. "But there is so much building going on in Europe right now, and Dowling is at the center of it. You can do really creative work there. You can make an even bigger success for yourself."

He did not answer her at once. Instead, while placing his left arm around her waist and, with his right hand, clasping her hand, he led her to the terrace of his penthouse. The romantic implications of this courtly gesture would please her. The two of them were, as she saw them in this moment, young lovers at their ease, reflecting upon the day that was unfolding its reality around them. So, he told himself, while he calmed her anxiety with a precisely calibrated self-control and with his own strong-minded purpose guiding him. Whether her terrace-view of the city pleased her, he could not say with any certainty. But what *he* saw pleased him very much. Here, within the Upper West Side of Manhattan on this bright September afternoon, the sun glowed upon the busy city eighteen floors below them, enhancing with glittering emphasis the skyscrapers and historic landmarks, as well as the long streets teeming with upscale shops and wealthy patrons, and with Broadway theaters and art galleries. That same sun also touched with radiance the neo-Gothic dome of a cathedral, the presence of an Ivy League university and other prestigious schools, the greenery of well-tended parks, and the meandering currents of the Hudson River. In the far distance, at the southern tip of Manhattan, the freewheeling business district and the austere banking center were muted, though still colorful, impressions upon his scanning glance.

Only now, after his view of the splendid city confirmed the rightness of his opinion, did he respond to Lauren's remark that, if he were to accept an assignment in Europe, he could become more successful.

"I have all the success that I want, right here in New York," he said. "I do not need to chase success in Europe."

To these words, which he spoke with gentle under-statement because he was negotiating with her trust of him, she did not at first reply. Instead, she leaned toward him, inviting him once again to the intimacy that was a private bond between them. Her full-bodied sensuality and her lavender fragrance were exciting influences upon him. Her brown eyes were alive with love for him, as she planted a soft kiss upon his lips. He returned the kiss, just as softly, and waited for her to say the new words that would urge him to her will. Before she chose the words, though, her nearly imperceptible fear hurried back to displace the love that had brightened her eyes, and the tension that she could no longer suppress enfolded her inflections.

"If you stay here, you will miss a rare opportunity. You may never again get such an opportunity."

Still he held her carefully in his embrace, his big frame offering her the protectiveness that might subdue the fear that she was struggling to keep at bay. To dispel that fear without compromising his decision to remain in New York and without yielding to her remark about rare opportunities, he answered her this time with self-assured playfulness.

"You seem to forget that I am a Dowling. That is the best opportunity of all."

His remark brought a smile to her lips, imbued though it was with melancholy. Harbored momentarily within her stillness, she looked up at him with a searching gaze that could not conceal her apprehension.

"I envy you your freedom," she said. "You can go anywhere you like—New York, Paris, or London—and success will quickly follow you. But I do not have your knack for making things work in my favor. Some places are traps for me. New York is one of them."

"What makes you think so?" he asked, while with a simulated casualness he probed for the cause of her apprehension. "Has something happened?"

She hesitated before she answered him. She was, he imagined, calculating the risk of telling him too much and the folly of altering too radically the self-willed and sophisticated persona that she had, until this afternoon, brought to their relationship. So he coaxed her further.

"Tell me what is wrong. I want to help you. I'm good at fixing dashed hopes and broken aspirations."

"You make it sound so easy. But it isn't. Not here. Not in New York"

"Try me," he said, confident as always and solicitous. "I'll do everything that I can to make things better for you."

She hesitated for a moment longer, still uncertain of the path on which her words would bring her. Then, with a flash of the self-possession that had, months earlier, first roused his notice of her, she hurried to say the words that he needed to hear.

"I have too many friends in New York who draw me into frivolous pursuits," she said. "They are all so likable, that it is hard to resist their influence. But, really, they are not good for me. They are wild and capricious and superficial. I have become like them. Whenever I am with them, there are so many dazzling parties and so many extraordinary adventures. Whether we are skydiving or mountain-climbing, skiing or piloting Piper Super Cubs, we live on the cusp of danger that quickens our senses and makes existence seem a tremendous experiment. They are brave and foolish friends who enjoy mocking the fate that binds all of us. They find pleasure in goading the specter of death that is usually hovering near us. I love each of them. But, if I do not get away from them, I shall become as lost as they are. I need a new place. In Europe, I have friends who are creative and who are doing wonderfully artistic things. I want their kind of life. I need to return to school in Paris. I'd like to resume my study of fashion photography at the École des Beaux Arts."

All these things, she told him in a rapid delivery of words that left her slightly breathless and that imparted, with skillfully modulated nuances, a poignant conviction. Though, for his ears, her words could not elude the disingenuous purposes that impelled her, he admired nonetheless her smooth immersion into the soul-searching complexities of her party-girl persona. That an inherent sensitivity drew her inward glance made her, even from his jaded perspective, rather intriguing. But the intricate layers of her identity, yoked as they were to her subtle deceptions and to the concealed truth of her nature, did not dissuade him from reminding her how much her own country could do for her.

"You can study fashion photography right here in New York. The New School for Social Research has an excellent program."

Once again, she became very still. Then, after touching his lips with a fleet kiss, as though her kiss might stir his empathy or because the delicate gesture might charm him, she made her words sound even more urgent.

"I need to be in Paris. I want to work with the teachers who first inspired me. I would also like to see my classmates from Beaux-Arts. We have remained friends ever since we studied together seven years ago, though now we see one another only occasionally. All of them have begun successful careers. They will have much to tell me about the world of fashion photography. They will be my teachers, too."

That she was running away from something or from someone was, to his keen-eyed perceiving, very clear. Fear had not left her eyes, nor had it left her vaguely tremulous voice. Whether that fear was spawned from some imagined adversary or from her self-centered whims or from the bleak memory of her unhappy past, he could not tell. Her estrangement from her parents and from her brother had disoriented her. She had lost her bearings. She was no longer certain of where her life was taking her or of why she kept betraying her better inclinations. So he had learned from one of her discarded boyfriends on an evening, months earlier, in an upscale bar in Manhattan. During those after-midnight hours, while plying the weak-willed and wealthy fellow with drinks and, at the same time, arranging a secret assignation with the beautiful film starlet that this same fellow had too carelessly escorted there, he had also learned about the other scandals that had marred Lauren's reputation and that, like vengeful spirits, continued to haunt her life.

Seven months earlier, he learned even more from Elsa Marling, a lovely Norwegian blonde who sometimes shared his bed. She was a secretary in the prestigious New York law firm that had drawn up the will of Leonard and Maria Winters. Although she was the mistress of the aged CEO of the law firm that employed her, Elsa always found time for her secret meetings with him.

"I like you because you are athletic and because you are as young as I am," she casually remarked on a Sunday morning when they were spending one of their weekends together, skiing and partying in Maine. "I like you especially because you are handsome and because you excite me. You are a different breed from my high-and-mighty keeper."

He had risen from their bed and had drawn open the curtains to the panoramic window to allow the February sunlight to float its radiance into this well-appointed room within the second story of the country house that his cousin allowed him to use whenever he wished. He could feel the warm glow of the sun touching his naked muscularity and bringing to its strength an artful emphasis. In the far distance, the snowcapped mountains rose, massive and proprietary, toward a cold, pale-blue sky and toward wind-blown wispy clouds. Men and women were skiing down curving slopes of the mountain, their spiraling forms so many flashes of color within the wintry scene. Hearing Elsa's words, he turned to gaze upon her once more. Their morning sex had left him contented and even newly energized, the festering wounds of his bitter life eased by the prolonged thrill of their consummation.

Elsa was lolling against a galaxy of pillows, while the scented satin sheets that she tossed aside only partially concealed the seductive curves of her naked body. She might have been a well-paid model posing for calendar art or for a museum canvas or an even better paid call girl whose morning copulation had left her satisfied. On that specific morning, she was even more carefree, because her formidable CEO (her "high-and-mighty keeper") was out of the country. He was traveling in Europe with his wife and their three children. That she considered her keeper a different breed from him, the Aaron Dowling whose sexual vitality equaled her own, amused him, even as her remark prodded his cynical view of things.

"Don't be too sure that your keeper and I are different," he said. "When you see him, you may be looking at the man I could be thirty-five years from now."

Elsa laughed, her blue eyes brighter with exhilaration, and her moist lips and gleaming teeth enhancing her smile.

"Not a chance," she said. "My keeper was never as young or as daring as you are. Oh, you may become a CEO. But you'll never become the tight-ass that he is. Being repressed or conventional is not in your blood. You are made for more exciting responses."

"Sex and money—they are what I am made for."

His words pleased her.

"You and I think alike," she said. "We are not afraid of telling the truth. We call a spade a spade."

He walked back to the bed, his tall and husky manhood a preening emphasis upon her steady gaze. After climbing in next to her, he fondled her ample breasts and then, with his big, powerful hands, gently caressed her face. Only after that did he touch her lips with a kiss.

"Tell me about Lauren Winters again," he said. "You haven't told me all of it yet. Tell me how she figures in the codicil to her parents' will."

She pulled away from him now. Her face expressed neither displeasure nor approval. Her level glance and her even-tempered inflections suggested matter-of-fact detachment. Her incisive awareness of the world's ironies and deceptions was her stay against confusion and against any emotion that could dispel the afterglow of the hour they had just shared. Their conversing here in this bedroom, about another woman whom he was plotting to use for his self-centered purposes, did not unsettle her. At any other time, the irony of the situation might have drawn her derisive laughter. But to laugh at his hardheartedness or at her jaded receptivity to all that he represented might have disarranged her composure. Instead, she grew very still. The stillness that came upon her did not disturb him. He knew her well. Her silence was a strategy for taking control of the moment. After reaching for one of her imported cigarettes from the gold cigarette case on a bed table nearby and after bringing it to the flame of a gold lighter, she leaned once more into the galaxy of pillows that, in a minor way, extended the comforts of the morning. She took a few drags on her cigarette and watched the smoke wafting around them. Once or twice, she looked at him, the intensity of his blue eyes and the warmth of his solid flesh a vivid presence beside her. All this while she lingered within a silence as natural as it was reflective. He joined her in the silence, unwilling to hurry her into the words that he was waiting to hear. When, at last, she did speak, she did not refrain from mentioning where they stood with each other.

"You are using me," she said. "But I don't mind. We use one another, and the games we play always leave us happy. This weekend, though, isn't really about us—at least, not all of it. We are here together because you need information about Lauren Winters. She is the big prize that you are going after."

He was not surprised by her tough-minded appraisal or by her refusal to sentimentalize their association. With him, Elsa was a straight shooter. Had he been less than honest with her, she would have seen through his dissembling. She was willing to tell him as much as she knew about the distribution of the Winters' estate because he had leveled with her about his relationship with Lauren and because she enjoyed his company in and out of bed.

"But how big a prize is she? You haven't told me that yet."

Before she answered him, she took another drag on her cigarette and once again studied the wisps of smoke billowing around them. Then, while turning to him because, he imagined, she wanted to study his reaction, she spoke the words that he was eager to hear.

"Lauren Winters will be forty million dollars richer, if she stays out of trouble and if she marries Mister Right."

His pulse quickened. His wind-burned skin flushed. It took him a moment to harness his feelings, so that he could choose street-wise words to deflect the excitement that was rushing through him. Before he found the right words, he leaned toward Elsa and kissed her. He took hold of her cigarette and enjoyed a few drags upon it, its coiling smoke rising and hovering around him, as though it had come there to conceal his face. Only then did he speak the words that kept him anchored to the hard-edged version of himself with whom he felt comfortable.

"Well, what do you know? I've struck the mother lode."

Elsa laughed. It was not the first time that she found his sly wit to her liking.

"You are a cool hustler," she said. "You know an opportunity when you see one. Lauren Winters doesn't have a chance of escaping you. Not that she'd want to. You will be Mister Right because she thinks that you are."

"I haven't staked my claim yet. I'll have a better chance of winning if I don't move too fast. Otherwise, Lauren and her brother will see the way things are with me. Sure, I like her—most of the time. But I like her money even more. I have to move cautiously if I am going to win the prize."

He handed Elsa her cigarette and, after she took another drag on it, she spoke matter-of-fact words. As she spoke, he watched her keen-eyed gaze upon him and her knowing smile, and he heard the words that teased his uneasy introspection.

"That, my sometime lover, you have already done. You have won the prize. But be ready to pay for it. Nothing comes free."

Seven months had passed since that weekend with Elsa. In that time, he had married Lauren. He had staked his claim to her and her fortune, though he had not yet made his claim public.

Now, here in this New York penthouse that his Uncle Liam had given him and his cousin Gavin to share equally, he found himself using temporizing words to placate Lauren's neurotic apprehension and her sudden desire to be in Europe. He did not want to lose the prospect of merging with her forty million dollars.

"I do see Europe in our future," he said. "Whether that happens for us tomorrow or next year, I cannot say. Maybe one day I will convince my bosses that I'll make more money for them in Paris, Berlin, or Rome."

His words gave her hope. They subdued the fear that was stalking her. They stirred her anticipation.

"You know how to deal with your bosses," she said. "You will win them over. But you must win them over as soon as you can. Then we can be free of New York. We will have an even more exciting life in Europe."

"Sure we will," he said, casually easing her tension. "But, until that happens, let's enjoy everything here."

"Not here," she said. "Please. Not in the city. We can enjoy ourselves in so many other places."

"Of course, we can," he agreed, still noting her unease. "I have a few days free until I begin my next assignment. We'll have a good time."

He brushed her forehead with a kiss and hurried out of the bed. He intended to meet the day with quickened vitality. He wanted Lauren to do the same. He chose to be lighthearted and agile, as he drew her into the busy day awaiting them.

"I'll shave and shower and get dressed," he said, as he headed into his bathroom. "Get into your powder room and make with the magic. Last one dressed is last."

He did not turn back to observe her wistful smile, though he imagined that he had brought a smile to her lips. Except for a few excursions that would bring them away from the city, he had no intention of abandoning New York. He was not averse to accepting Dowling assignments that sent him temporarily to Florida and to San Francisco. He had fulfilled similar assignments on previous occasions. But Europe did not fit into his plan to use New York as his strategic headquarters. He wanted Lauren to stay here with him. What he decided to do now was to wean her away from her fears of New York, even as he discovered the cause of them.

For ten days, he drew her into a spate of activities that wakened her exhilaration and appeased her desire to leave the city. In East Hampton, about a hundred twenty miles away from New York City, they cruised brisk autumn waters in a pristine yacht that the Dowling Corporation made accessible to its young, vacationing executives. There, in the Hamptons, they stayed in the luxurious beach house that Lauren had inherited from her parents. While he and Lauren were staying in the house, a middle-aged couple, dutiful and meticulous, who usually drove in twice a week from their home in a village nearby to maintain the place, now served their needs every day as housekeeper, cook, and groundskeeper. For the most part, though, he and Lauren were elsewhere. That they were seldom alone helped him to dispel her anxiety. Whenever they were navigating the rush and spume and rising wake of Montauk, Long Island waters in the Dowling yacht or kayaking in a Catalina sloop, they intensified their freewheeling experience of each new day because they were in the company of young, married friends or equally attractive twosomes who had shared other convivial days with Lauren and with him. These were not the troubled friends who had led her astray. This circle of ten friends who brought fun-loving and life-inspiriting capacities to their current visit to the Hamptons made all the right moves. He did not mistake their *joie-de-vivre* for careless abandon. All of them were as ambitious and as wily as he was. They were on their way up. They could not afford to break the rules set by corporate power brokers or violate the codes defined by conservative dowagers. Yet, even while harnessing their sensual inclinations, these friends knew how to have a good time.

In their company, Lauren thrived. Before his studious eyes and their affable witness, she came to life again and proved herself a reliable partner who could help him negotiate his way forward. A gala party hosted by his boss within a splendid yacht club in Sag Harbor showed her aptitude for impressing the power brokers. On this occasion, Lauren helped him to spark the evening. While—politic and adept—he waltzed with his boss's wife, Lauren inspired his boss, usually an awkward dancer, to break free of his inhibitions and give himself over to the three-quarter tempo of the rhythms, accompanied as they were by the flair of violins and by the excited riffs of trumpets, flutes, and clarinets. At the same time, the boss's wife, an elegant woman in her early forties, enjoyed dancing with him, a man on his way up in the corporation and twenty years younger than her husband. She was even more elated when, as the orchestra extended the waltz rhythms with the melodies of other ballads, Lauren induced his boss to change partners, so that he could dance with his wife and Aaron could dance with her. Never before had Lauren appeared so happy. Nor had her face ever imparted so lovely a glow or suggested so unconditionally an authentic serenity.

"You two belong together," she said, after—arm in arm with his boss—she had made her way around the edge of the dance floor so that he could join his wife. "You make a perfect couple."

"We've had years of practice," his boss said, in this moment as casual as he was jovial. "As you can see, we are still practicing."

Having said so, he led his wife into the waltz with a smooth poise that he had rarely expressed on a dance floor in all the years of their marriage. He absolutely delighted his wife.

Aaron was to learn later that evening, after he and Lauren returned to his apartment, that his boss's wife had expressed a warm regard for her when they shared friendly words during a visit to the powder room.

"You are a clever girl," she told Lauren. "You will be well-liked in our circle if you trust the instincts that you followed tonight."

A day later, still in the Hamptons, when they and two of their friends were fishing from a chartered boat, Lauren caught four striped bass. Once again, she was elated with a spontaneity that she had never revealed to him before this week. In that moment, for his eyes at least, she retrieved her lost innocence. Always before, when a night of vigorous lovemaking or a festive occasion stirred her exhilaration, he detected a guarded edge to her excitement. Even then, she remained keenly aware that her happiness was merely temporary, a fleeting instance that kept her ingrained melancholy at bay for an hour or two after he made love to her or during lavish afternoons of parties and friends. But here, in East Hampton, her happiness knew neither qualification nor inhibition. Here, on this September afternoon when they were fishing in Montauk waters, she revealed a hidden layer of her existence. Once again, her spirit rose high, as it must have soared when she was a young girl who believed that her father and her mother loved her and that the multifaceted world apart from them was a friend that she could trust.

That she trusted Paul and Leah Cohen, the newly married couple in their fishing party, intensified her belief in the solacing influences of the day. Paul, all rugged good-heartedness while he was away from the competitive Dowling arena, summoned a gentle deference whenever he conversed with her about the latest books and films and about their mutual interest in horse riding. His wife Leah, a petite, raven-haired beauty who wrote and illustrated children's books, bonded with her in a sisterly manner. She was well trained in art, music, and literature. She spoke three foreign languages that, a few years earlier, helped to make her a proficient student in Paris, Buenos Aires, and Rome. She also proved herself a first-rate partner in tennis, and she was an accomplished swimmer. But Leah had never gone fishing. Uneasy that she might embarrass herself and, even worse, disappoint her husband, she approached their day of fishing with shy reticence. Too busy applying his mastery as a fisherman to his pursuit of Atlantic striped bass, Paul did not notice the vague traceries of her unease.

But *he* noticed—he, Aaron Dowling, who, Leah affectionately reminded him every once in awhile, was at the top of the list of the four Aarons that she knew. Before he could offer his own assistance, though, Lauren—with extemporaneous helpfulness that deflects attention from itself—quietly showed Leah how to execute a proper side cast, desirable or even necessary when the fisher is constrained by windy conditions. In that hour, Leah learned how to begin her cast with the rod low and pointed slightly outward. Using her wrist and forearm to flex the top section of the rod back and forward, she released the line just before aiming the rod tip at its target. Concise and agile, she followed through with the forward motion to bring the line in front of itself. As a result, she caught two streamlined, silver bass, each weighing approximately twelve pounds.

Overjoyed, she began to heap praise upon Lauren, her generous teacher.

"You are a miracle worker," she exclaimed. "You showed me how to turn my fishing rod into a magnet for catching fish."

Pleased at the success of her pupil, Lauren beamed, even as she gave full credit to her.

"You have a gift for fishing," she told Leah. "Today, you have only begun to tap it."

Hearing her words, which gave full credit to her initiative and skill, Leah fell silent. Her brown eyes were misty, even as her lips formed a grateful smile. Paul smiled, too, while he found lighthearted words to celebrate his wife's achievement.

"Lauren's right," he told his wife. "You have a gift. You are going to be a first-rate partner whenever we fish for cod or bass or tuna."

Late that afternoon, when they had returned to Lauren's beachfront home and while they were dressing for an evening that they would spend with the Cohens at a glamorous nightclub in the Hamptons, Lauren remarked upon Leah's innocence. Just for an instant, an abrasive edge touched her matter-of-fact words.

"The world has never played rough with Leah," she said. "I hope it never does. Anyway, Paul will show her the ropes. He knows the score. Nobody who works in New York stays innocent."

But here and now, while their chartered boat hurried across the rising waves of dark green ocean waters, what to his eyes made Lauren even more remarkable was her serene disposition. Sensitive and reflective, she observed with uncommon appreciation the vivid reality unfolding around her. He watched her discreetly as, with studious gaze, she peered at the solid forms that identified nature's ambivalent presence. He wondered whether that ambivalence might jostle her serenity. He wondered, too, whether her ingrained tough-mindedness would prevail over her tenuous inclination to see the world as a bright, affirming possibility. Was she sighting the same world that he perceived? Right then, with his usual trenchant awareness, what he saw within the azure-blue furling of distance, what directed his gaze to the floating pastel sky, was the dark ripple of a black-backed gull curving the flare of its wings against vaporous, sunlit clouds. After a second's pause, it plummeted with cunning precision to the consenting waves of ocean water, the better to pluck for its meal a wriggling, striped bass or a tiny mackerel. Because the vision gave him back what he had anticipated, the image of danger shown natural and implacable, he recognized its familiar message and confirmed his realistic measure for understanding things. Turning once more, still toward the west, he was not surprised to sight the limestone-hang of giant cliffs glaring like the sea-whipped bones of some lost, ancient world swallowed by an angry sea. He noticed, too, across and above the wide span of quick Atlantic waters and on the crest of autumn-bronzed hills—right there, at the wavering margins of the nebulous woods—a gray-blue immensity of swaying larches that, before his searching eyes, joined all of nature's restless and proprietary motion.

What Lauren saw, he could merely guess. On any of the other days that they had shared before this vacation in the Hamptons, her view of things would have remained wary and unsentimental. Only when she turned to him was he certain that her serenity was influencing what she saw.

"I'd love to paint this scene," she said.

Her smoky voice was melded to the muted excitement that hovers at the rim of contentment.

Excitement and contentment stayed with them for a while. They skied on brisk Long Island waters; they went clay shooting in the scenic Hudson Valley town of New Paltz, seventy-five miles from New York; and they alternately piloted a Bell Ranger helicopter into Camden, Maine, where they met some of his friends, two CBS television executives and their girlfriends, for an Indian summer weekend of more swimming, sailing, and partying. On each of these occasions, Lauren knew, as if for the first time, the quick velocity of happiness. So secure did she feel during these days, so completely at ease with herself and with him and with the new friends she was making, that there was no talk between them of hurrying away to Europe. The words that she shared with him when they were alone were as buoyant and lighthearted as the carefree repartee that she exchanged with their friends. Sometimes, when they were dancing at a fashionable nightclub in the Hamptons or dining by themselves at an equally fashionable oceanfront restaurant during a two-day visit to Newport, her words became softly intimate. Her eyes glowed with love for him, and the gentle touch of her hands upon his skin connected him once again to the warm-blooded vitality that was coursing through her veins. During one of these evenings, while they were dancing, she looked up at him with a gaze that was not only affectionate and seductive, but also vulnerable.

"You are my lucky charm," she said. "Whenever I am with you, I believe that the world isn't such a bad place, after all."

Though he did not believe in "lucky charms," he gratified her need to believe that they existed.

"I'll always want to charm you," he said, "in any place and at any time."

She smiled prettily, while he held her closer and while a band of musicians played a romantic ballad and a tall, dark-haired man sang about the love that lasts forever.

If he did not believe in "lucky charms," he believed even less in this new person that Lauren had willed herself to become. Her voyage into the sentimental and the demure was a backward step. To his razor-sharp awareness, she seemed unreal. She seemed false. Her strongest suit had always been the veiled cynicism and the tough-minded acuity that hovered at the rim of who she was. Her willing herself to become someone else, someone who appeared conventionally romantic and innocent, suggested—to his mind, at least—the desperation and the despair that were compelling her to impersonate a stranger, a ghostly image from her childhood with whom she had made a brief acquaintance and who no longer existed.

He knew something about desperation and despair. His battle with those adversaries was spawned from self-sacrifice and enforced asceticism. His father, Ryan Dowling, was a Protestant missionary who, as a young man, brought his religious fervor, as well as his skills as an architect and builder, to Northern Rhodesia. With an equally dedicated wife and a pliable son, he led (and continued to lead) a Spartan existence in a politically volatile and often dangerous environment. He taught the Rhodesian natives how to build solid homes and churches and how to connect them properly to their cultural environment. Within the first months of his assignment in South Africa, his father created cadres of excellent planners and builders. With his father working beside them, they built whole communities of functional homes and attractive landscapes.

The Reverend Ryan Dowling was, from the years of his young manhood, an intensely religious man who believed that he had to perfect the here-and-now environment he inhabited if he were to gain a place in the Afterlife Heaven he anticipated. His skills as an architect could have made him a wealthy man. Those same skills made his brother Liam wealthy. Liam was a multi-millionaire, having garnered a fortune not only from his architectural firm, but also from his partnerships in oil and steel corporations. But his father chose to explore a different path.

Whatever profits he made from his building commissions, he gave to his church and to the care of the needy. With his wife, who shared his beliefs and his altruistic spirit, he devoted his life to helping the poor, the maimed, and the aged.

He was a tall, gaunt man. His brown mane of neatly combed hair, his blue eyes that looked with direct and honest gaze upon every person that he met, his deep voice, his strong handshake, and his masterly self-restraint—all these emblems of identity made his father a formidable man.

"We are called to help other people, Aaron," his father often told him during those sessions at home when he would read aloud to him those passages from the Saint James Bible that he regarded as especially helpful to a schoolboy. "All human beings are our brothers and sisters. All of them deserve our respect and our assistance."

One time, when he was fourteen years old, he found the courage to question his father's beliefs. Earlier that day, he had defended himself against a bully at school and had broken the boy's nose. Afterwards, he resisted the bully's efforts to make peace with him. Even then, despite his father's careful mentoring, there was in the dark recesses of his character a bitter and cynical streak. But his father, patient and compassionate, urged him toward a better way.

"Make peace with the boy. Forgive him. Always forgive. Always try to help others when they want to be better. Always do the right thing."

That time, because he loved and trusted his father, he obeyed his counsel. But, try as he did, he could not bring himself to like the bully. At his best, he merely tolerated the reformed person that the bully was becoming. On rainy Sundays, when, reflective and alone in his room, he searched his heavy heart, he could not find the compassion that defined his father's every action. Even then, at fourteen, he understood the predatory nature of most human beings. He was acutely aware of the violence that left its bloodstains upon the land. With his own eyes, during chance encounters (after which, with his classmates and a schoolteacher or a building foreman or fellow athletes, he hurried to conceal himself within a safe building or a field of tall grasses or an obscure, used-book shop) he witnessed the political murders and the racist killings by British henchmen in so many parts of Rhodesia, including Lusaka, the capital city.

Each time, he told his father what he had seen. Each time, he sought from his father some clue that could help him make his way through a world that sometimes turned savage and threatening. Each time, his father answered him with the same firm clarity.

"There is evil in the world. There is violence. But you must never allow evil and violence to tarnish your goodness. Nor must you league yourself with a killer."

"But what if someone wants to do me harm?" he asked his father on an afternoon when he had grown skeptical and impatient after listening to him. "What if someone wants to kill me? Do I have the right to kill him before he kills me?"

Rather than answering him quickly, his father paused. A stern gravity made his calm demeanor even more austere.

"You have the right to kill him," he said, "because your intention is to save your life. You have a moral obligation to save the life of an innocent person. In this case, *you* are the innocent person."

Having said so, his father paused once again. Vague wrinkles touched his brow as he pondered the matter even more deeply. When he resumed speaking, an iron-willed certainty drove his words.

"If you can subdue your opponent without killing him," he said, "then you do not have the right to take his life. If you use more than necessary violence against him and end by killing him, you are his murderer. You have taken a life that only God has the right to take."

His father's answer pleased him. It echoed the answer that he had discovered within the secret workings of his own mind. Although, even then, he had begun to resent his father's Spartan rules, he respected him. Ryan Dowling was an authentic man. He was a dedicated minister who translated his beliefs through honorable behavior.

Since boyhood, he—Aaron, his father's only son—had been an earnest apprentice collaborating with his own intuitive gifts and with his father's careful mentoring. During free summer days and sometimes during a spring or late autumn recess from school, he visited the sites where his father and other architects were building new landscapes and constructing pristine homes. With a keen appraisal of things, he perceived, because of his father's tutelage, how the implicated reality of the environment— particularly its geology and vegetation and climate and the construction techniques and local materials transforming it—can inspire an architect as well as the builders and landscape architects with whom he creates.

He learned to observe carefully, as immense variations of the earth, the spatial mosaic of fields and hills and plains defining the circumference of an ample farm. When he found himself on property that overlooked the Zambezi River, he noticed the contours of the land hurrying toward the rapid waters. He also noticed on that same property, elevated and proprietary as it peered upon the long and sinuous river, the amplitude of a three-story home with decorous gables and wrap-around porches. So perceiving, he remembered that his father had advised the builder to install with a crane twenty steel I-beams and countless special connectors—the better to brace and protect the house from high winds or uplift. When he was back in the main section of Northern Rhodesia and was surveying the latest community of houses that his father's team had recently built, he understood why his father, in structuring these larger homes, had designed many curved rooms and spacious archways and detailed millwork. They were control points that established centerlines, curves, and intersections for each house—from basement to rooflines. Two years later, as a young man of sixteen, he began to work with his father and a savvy team of fellow architects to implement the designs that he, the son whom his father's partners called a gifted newcomer, had drawn up for a group of office buildings on the streets of emerging business districts that joined their modernist breeding to the handsome formalities of tradition.

But the money that he was paid for his innovative designs and for his labors as a builder was a mere stipend. The future that he was paving for himself while under the tutelage of his father merely replicated his father's missionary zeal and the self-abnegation of that rigorous man. Weary of being eclipsed by his father and by religious creeds that he regarded as outworn, he broke free of his father's influence and of turbulent Rhodesia, a country from which he had always felt alienated. For five years, as a well-trained American pilot, he flew B-52s in the war against North Vietnam. Wounded twice, but each time rescuing himself as well as his plane, he returned to the war after grueling convalescent leaves, even more determined to rain bombs and death upon his adversaries. The bitterness that he had harbored within the hidden recesses of his feelings had fed his need to inflict pain upon others. His Air Force buddies nicknamed him "the killing machine" because of the number of Vietnamese jets that he had shot down and the number of cities that he had bombed.

"You are a really fine killer," one of the pilots in his squadron told him, his voice a thick Georgian drawl, after they returned from a successful bombing mission. "I'm glad that you are not my enemy."

Chapter Four

Heir Apparent

Aaron might have stayed in the Air Force even after the war. He enjoyed the excitement of firing bombs upon his foes or, in peacetime, of policing the sky. But, unexpectedly, Liam Dowling, his wealthy uncle, entered his life and in that April of 1968, when he turned twenty-two, began to change it for the better. During a visit to his quarters within Andersen Air Force Base in Guam, where his bomb wing was deployed, his uncle outlined a plan that, if he played his cards right, would make him a wealthy man.

"After this thing is over," he said, "after you get all this killing out of your system, I want to put you on a track that will bring you into my corporation. I've seen the buildings that you designed for your father's charity organization. You have something special. But you need more training. I want you to study architecture at Yale. At the same time, you can work with my team on various assignments in the New England area. If you do well, I'll treat you as my second son. But you will have to prove yourself. You will have to make all the right moves."

His uncle was a tall, lean man in his fifties, though his white hair and cragged features made him look ten years older. His imperious manner, yoked as it was to a cold, blue-eyed gaze and to brusque, deep-voiced inflections, was off-putting, at first. Not even his generous offer could dispel the hint of disdain in his voice or convince him, Aaron Dowling, the nephew from a penniless background whose father had chosen to be a religious zealot, that kindness and sentimentality had inspired his uncle's sudden interest in his advancement. Liam Dowling was a hardhearted businessman. He expected an extraordinary return on any investment that he made.

So he did all the right things. He made all the right moves. With the promise of a bright future before him in 1969, he immersed himself in his studies at Yale, even while he found time to join the rowing team, to sleep with the prettiest girls from Radcliffe, Barnard, and Vassar, and to hobnob with the famous architects, corporate heads, and investment brokers that he met at the parties that Liam and his second wife hosted in their Manhattan penthouse and in their Connecticut mansion. Liam's new wife, Sara—lovely, blonde, and elegant—was only five years older than his son. She was twenty-six years younger than Liam. He kept a respectful yet cordial distance from Sara. He did not want to rouse Liam's notice of him as a potential rival for Sara's affection. He also managed to bond occasionally with Liam's son, Gavin, who—at twenty-three—was his age. Most of the time, though, Gavin lived away from the United States, studying architecture in London, Paris, and Copenhagen after his undergraduate studies at Cambridge University and eventually working for the Dowling Corporation in Berlin. Whenever he was in New York, they shared the palatial Manhattan apartment that Liam had given them after they completed their university studies. Reserved yet good-natured, Gavin looked uncannily like him—Aaron Dowling, the ambitious son of an impoverished minister. Their strong resemblance made it easier to accept each other as a brother.

After he was graduated from Yale in 1973, his uncle came

through with some of the rewards that he had promised him. Not only did he give him the sixteen-room Upper West Side penthouse, a gift that he shared with Gavin. Liam also gave him a top spot in the New York offices of the Dowling Corporation. Whether he was involved in the renovation of a renowned museum in lower Manhattan, the design and construction of a concert hall in Lincoln Center, or the remodeling of a luxurious apartment in Sutton Place, he was making his gifts known to the people who mattered, not only in New York, but also across the globe. He was on his way. He was going to be a rich man, through his own efforts and through the immense fortune that his uncle was going to leave him. That he was planning to leave him a fortune, his uncle made very clear on a gray November morning when he was visiting him in a hospital shortly after he had sustained a heart attack. In 1975, no remedy existed for congestive heart failure, not even for a rich man. Liam knew the score. His time was running out. But the imminence of death did not alter his tough-mindedness or induce an eleventh-hour reformation.

"I've had a hell of a life," he said. "I had the good sense to hurry away from my father and my brother. They may be good ministers, but religion has kept them poor. I'd never trade my life for theirs. I've helped to build a modern world. I've lived the adventure. I've worked with and for the change-makers and the power brokers. I began with nothing, and I have become a very rich man. I have made a fortune."

In that telling moment, his face looked pale and worn-down. Propped against a galaxy of pillows, he gazed with rheumy eyes upon him, the rugged nephew that he had chosen to be his second son. He was, nevertheless, in full command of himself. Alone with him in this hospital setting, a suite of rooms filled with flowers and with cordial messages from close friends and politic enemies, his uncle spoke the words that promised to bring him the wealth that he craved.

"You will have a third of my fortune," his uncle said. "You will share it equally with Gavin and with my wife. But not right away. Even after I am gone, you will have to keep on doing the right things for several years before you can get your share. My lawyers will keep their eyes on you. The same rules may apply to Gavin. He has a long road to travel before I decide when he gets my money. He also has to earn the approval of the lawyers who are the executors of my will."

He was not surprised that Liam was making rigid demands of Gavin. His uncle wanted his son to understand that nothing in this world comes free. He wanted him to *earn* the rewards that the Dowling legacy promised him, by proving himself to be tough-hearted and enterprising. So, he—the nephew who stood to reap a fortune if he, too, remained steadfast and aggressive—imagined. He read Liam well. He recognized the ruthless streak that defined his character. He understood the predatory instincts that had served his uncle well in the corporate world. That his uncle kept his son at a distance, even while he monitored his every move, was to his mind a calculated strategy for testing Gavin's cleverness and his resilience. His uncle appeared to leave Gavin to his own devices, though he was tethered always to the Dowling maneuvers that would bring him back to his proper station, should he try to break free of it. Liam was not a sentimental man. Whatever love he felt for his son was conditional. His son was not a son if he failed to perform well in the cutthroat arena that called itself "big business."

On the few occasions when he was in his company, his cousin Gavin rarely spoke of his father or, for that matter, of his stepmother.

"They want the best for me," he pushed himself to say, one time when he, Cousin Aaron—no longer a stranger from Rhodesia, but now a brotherly friend—asked him about them. "They want me to make a success of my life."

That time, when Gavin spoke, he felt that he was looking not at Gavin, but into a mirror that showed him his own reflection. In that year of 1975, when they were twenty-nine, they were on their way up. To strengthen their friendship, they did not need to see one another very often. Their uncanny physical resemblance became a strong bond between them.

During this period, he decided that he would not wait for the windfall that Liam had promised him. To make his potential security even more secure, he must marry into a prestigious family. Thus far, his portfolio consisted of an immense potential and a proficient launching of his career as an architect. But he wanted to anchor his emerging success to established wealth that he could share as soon as he took as his bride a well-bred heiress. At first, he met a few young women who met his requirements. But their families rejected him after they discovered that he was the son of a penniless minister and that his inheritance from a rich and powerful uncle belonged to a far-flung and nebulous future.

Then, one evening in September 1976, at a grand party in Manhattan, he met Lauren Winters. He was immediately attracted to her dark beauty and to the sensuality that, in spite of her understated appearance, played upon her makeshift self-assurance and upon her contrived decorum. With her, he imagined, the sex would be exciting and even experimental. Their life together might be driven by a bit of adventure and by their capacities for entering intriguing episodes that concealed their wild and rebellious dispositions. Yet, when he learned about the troubled relationship that she had wrought with her parents and heard the rumor that they had practically disinherited her, he stopped seeing her for a while. He reignited their romance a month later, after Elsa Marling, his sometime bed partner, searched the files of the law firm where she worked and uncovered what was, for his mercenary purposes, good news. Lauren Winters was going to be a rich woman if she married a successful man who won the approval of her brother, Calden, and of her late father's lawyers.

He courted their approval. Because of his Dowling connections, it was not difficult to enter their circle. He played tennis with two of the lawyers, and he golfed with her brother. With him, he copiloted a new Cessna 206, and he served on a committee that raised funds for children who had been afflicted by polio. He devised what appeared to be an unexpected meeting at the Metropolitan Opera, when Calden was there with his wife and when he, a Dowling who was making his way up, was escorting Lauren, the sister whom Calden saw only at tense conferences with their parents' lawyers. On that evening at the Opera, Lauren embodied with subtle nuances and demure conviction the gestures of a well-born young woman. Influenced by his friendly regard for her brother and by the glamour of the colorful evening, Lauren greeted Calden and his wife with a winsome smile and a warmhearted manner. She spoke all the right words, and she mingled with the conservative men and women whom her brother respected.

"You are good for my sister," Calden told him two days later, after they joined forces effectively against formidable, yet amiable opponents for a game of squash at their private club in Manhattan. They were leaving the locker room, having shared a round of bourbon there with their opponents after they had showered and dressed and were about to return to their busy offices. "You are bringing her to life again. You are inspiring her to follow her better instincts."

"That well may be," he answered him, as cautious as he was sly. "I shall always want to inspire her. I think that she is very special. I am glad to have her on my team."

Calden was pleased. He perceived him as a Dowling who was making his mark. He was a man who counted. He was the man who might reform the sister who had tarnished the Winters' family with her bad conduct and tabloid scandals.

That he would have access to the forty million dollars that Leonard Winters left his daughter thrilled him. He did not really love Lauren, except perhaps for the sex. She *was* good in bed. He felt no compunction about marrying her without loving her and about sharing the fortune that was coming to her. He was earning his right to the money. He was helping Lauren to reinvent herself. He was going to be the husband who rescued her from her bleak and tawdry life. Without him, she would not inherit the money. But to get what he wanted, he had to move fast. In July of 1977, he married Lauren. Aware of her whimsical inclinations and her perverse impulsiveness, he was not going to give any of her former lovers the chance to re-team with her and win her forty million dollars. At the same time, he preferred to keep the marriage a secret. Eventually, Lauren and he would make a proper announcement. They would have a big wedding, to which they would invite her brother Calden and all the lawyers who evaluated Lauren's and his claims to their inheritances. By then, he would have secured his success as an architect. He would be more than the sum of his current prospects. He would be making his own fortune. To Calden and the lawyers, he would appear to be a worthy inheritor of Dowling and Winters money. He had money of his own. He was moving to the top of the ladder. He belonged to their class. In this favorable way, he told himself, Calden and the lawyers would perceive him. He would not rouse their suspicion that he was an opportunist and a fortune hunter.

Their having been in Newport for their marriage was an auspicious sign. They had missed the electricity blackout that had darkened New York City for two days and that had set rioters and looters on a rampage.

So, here he was now, vacationing with Lauren in the Hamptons and in Newport two months after their secret marriage and, all the while, easing her neurotic apprehension and promising her the storybook happiness for which, in spite of her street-wise realism, she secretly yearned. Because he had, for the most part, dispelled her fears without yet fathoming the cause, he was able to persuade her to return to New York City for the closing days of their vacation. In the first weeks after their return to the city, they saw a popular musical with a cotton-candy disposition in a Broadway theater. They dined with more Dowling executives and their wives in five-star restaurants and in private clubs. They made the rounds of supper clubs in West Village, in Harlem, in Chelsea, and in Manhattan. Tamping down their capacities for high spirits, they reveled nonetheless in the spontaneity and the momentum of their partying. During all of these occasions, Lauren appeared genuinely elated. The ghosts from her past that were trailing her had, for these days and nights at least, vanished.

But, quite suddenly and without warning, her fears returned. One evening, in the grand ballroom of The Waldorf Astoria, while he was dancing with the wife of a senior executive from the Dowling Corporation, he saw in the distance, beyond the edge of the dance floor and inside the entrance to the skyline terrace, a tall, dark-haired man caught in what appeared to be a furtive exchange with Lauren. His initial impulse was to abandon his partner in the midst of their dance and hurry to Lauren's side, as a strategy for displacing the prominence in the scene that the stranger had appropriated. But his well-calibrated instincts held him to the dance. Only when the music stopped and after he delivered his partner, a glamorous woman in her fifties, to her husband, who was conversing with other couples at their festive table—only then did he walk briskly out to the terrace. Lauren was still there, and so was the dark-haired man. No one else was on the terrace, though the crisp autumn air, the elegant furnishings and table settings, and the starlit sky had drawn several romantic couples there earlier that evening. Lauren and the sullen man were still caught within the muted tension of their meeting. Her softer voice told him, at once, that she was negotiating with this man, who appeared to be in his mid-thirties and—even in a tuxedo—looked rough at the edges. His broken nose and battered face had altered the good looks that he may have once possessed. So intent was Lauren in appeasing this man's suppressed anger, that she did not notice him, the Aaron

Dowling who meant so much to her, approaching the terrace. By that time, he could hear her soft intonations without comprehending the words that were overtaken by the exhilarated voices floating from the ballroom into the terrace. He heard, as well, the clipped inflections of the man who was standing with familiar intimacy close to her, his deep voice with hushed power carefully harnessing his displeasure. But, once again, the words were lost to his hearing.

Now, as he stood suddenly by them, they noticed him, their hushed words consumed by a taut stillness. Lauren's eyes stared at him in fearful surprise. But, as quickly as this flare of unease had taken hold of her senses, she recovered her poise. Though to his eyes her self-possession was an artifice, a ruse to cloud his perception, he listened with ironic awareness to the lighthearted words with which she greeted him.

"I'm glad that you are here, Aaron. I was coming to look for you. I want to dance with you."

If she intended to introduce him to the stranger who was standing so close to her, the sullen man gave her no chance. Instead, after studying him with piercing gaze, he hurried away from the terrace without saying a word and, with ingrained wiliness, disappeared among the meticulously appointed tables and the glamorous guests that were bringing to the ballroom a festival atmosphere.

Aaron probed further.

"Who is he?"

For an instant, Lauren did not answer him. Only after she summoned a smile and a carefree manner did she speak.

"He's nobody you need to know about. He is just a

former boyfriend that I'd forgotten until he showed up this evening."

"What is his name?"

"You don't need to know."

He remained cool-headed, yet insistent.

"I want to know. You owe me that."

Once again, she hesitated and then hurried forward.

"His name is Bryce Thompson. But he doesn't mean anything to me. Not anymore. I told you that, until tonight, I'd forgotten him. "

"He hasn't forgotten you. Maybe, you haven't forgotten him as much as you thought you had. I caught the vibration between the two of you."

"There is nothing between us. Whatever we had together was finished a long time ago."

"He was standing too close to you, as if he were claiming you for his own uses. You share an intimacy with him. But the intimacy is mixed up with your fear."

"You are wrong, I tell you. He means nothing to me."

"You are afraid of him. I could tell by the tone of your voice and by the way you looked at him. He's the reason that you want to run away to Europe."

She took a gold cigarette case from her purse and offered him one of her Patagonians. He shook his head slightly, in polite refusal. With a graceful movement of her right hand, she lifted a cigarette from the case and brought it to her lips, which were moist with a sensual gloss. Right after that, but with merely a hint of his usual *savoir-faire*, he brought from his jacket a gold lighter. In the next instant, she was inhaling the fragrant aroma of her cigarette and, while standing near a tall, exotic plant, began peering out at the star-filled night and the silver clouds that were concealing part of the moon. She was stalling. She was struggling to find a way around his remark that connected Bryce Thompson to her need to take flight from her life in New York. When she found the words that might allay his suspicion, she answered him with remarks that melded the matter-of-fact with half-truths.

"Maybe. Maybe Bryce is the reason that I want to get away. He's certainly one of the reasons. He has a bad temper. When he is angry, a wildness comes over him that makes me afraid."

"You dumped him, and he doesn't like it."

"Yes."

"That is no reason to be afraid. It's no reason for running away to Europe."

"He is not the only reason. I've already explained this to you. I need a new place. I need different people who can help me make something out of my life."

"I'll help you. You can stay in New York. I've met many talented people since I have been here. I'll put you in touch with them. As for this thug who makes you afraid, I can handle him. I can set him straight. He won't bother you again."

Her eyes flashed with apprehension.

"No, Aaron. No. You must stay out of it. Bryce is not a man to cross."

"You *are* afraid of him."

"I don't want to bring trouble into my life. I don't want to find myself at the center of a scandal or on the front page of a tabloid."

"There won't be any scandal. I'll see to that. I'll deal with your Bryce Thompson. He won't bother you again."

Tense though she was, she smiled as if she were pleased that he wanted to be her protector. She brushed his lips with a kiss. Then, with petitioning words that nearly concealed her unease, she tried to dispel his concern for her.

"Stay out of it, Aaron. Bryce will not be a problem. Tonight, he was drinking too much. He knows that whatever was between us is over. So, ease up. Let's go back to the party. Ask me to dance."

There was, he felt, no point in challenging her contrived remarks about Bryce Thompson. He planned to keep an eye on Thompson. He'd make certain that he stayed a step ahead of him.

They went back to the ballroom, and they danced as though the brief moment on the terrace was unimportant, a mere ripple on the otherwise smooth surface of their evening. But, for the rest of that evening and for days afterwards, the face of Bryce Thompson would not leave him. It was a rugged face (some women, craving a dangerous partner, might think it sensual) that was marred by his anger and by his arrogance. The anger and the arrogance made him look brutish and even sinister.

Days after their return to the city, when they were about to leave his apartment for an evening on the town, Lauren spoke once again of her need to run off to Europe. But this time he joined his casual manner to a curt reply.

"I doubt that I can transfer to Europe, at least not right away. Maybe the Dowling people will reassign me next year."

She frowned with dismay.

"You can always leave ahead of me," he said. "I could join you later."

"No," she answered him. "We have to leave together. It

won't be good any other way."

"Don't let it worry you," he said. "I'll work something out with my boss. Maybe we can get to Europe by the beginning of next year."

"We must leave sooner than that," she said. "Our lives there will be so much better."

In spite of the bright smile that she offered him, her smoky voice was tremulous, and her brown eyes were misty with her love for him and with the fear that she was struggling to conceal.

For that moment, he pitied her. He found words to calm her, even though he had no intention of leaving New York.

"I told you that I'll work something out," he said. "Stop worrying. Forget Europe for tonight. Let's have a good time."

His words allowed her to keep her smile.

"Yes," she agreed. "Let's enjoy this evening."

They hurried away from his apartment now, drawing out of their hardened natures the proper enthusiasm that their socializing with friends at a Manhattan supper club required of them. But, even while he was dancing with her or drinking a few rounds of scotch or eating the delicious food or conversing with his friends, he kept recalling the face of Bryce Thompson. It was a rough face. It was an angry man. It was the face of an adversary who, when taking his leave from the Waldorf terrace, had glanced at him with the cold eyes of a killer.

The swift days that followed gave him little time to ponder the dangerous implications of Bryce Thompson's glance. Instead, a surge of good luck overtook him. An important client had asked him to design and build a palatial home in Palm Beach.

The Dowling Corporation was sending him there with two assistants to study the site on which he was going to oversee the building of the home and oversee, as well, the landscape architecture. In this preliminary phase of the assignment, he planned to stay in Florida for a week, during the middle of October. He would be working from the state-of-the-art Dowling offices there. A month later, when the construction phase of the commission began, he and a much larger team of assistants would return to Florida and spend the winter in Palm Beach. Lauren agreed to join him, even though she would have to defer her plans for Europe. That she would be away from New York eased her apprehension. Whatever fears New York roused in her, the news of his assignment in Florida instantly dispelled.

Before he and Lauren left for their preliminary week in Florida, his cousin Gavin returned, having completed a year's assignment in Berlin. He would be staying in the north wing of the penthouse that Liam had left to each of them. There, within eight of the sixteen rooms that dominated the eighteenth floor of their Upper West Side building, Gavin would enjoy the same privacy that he and sometimes Lauren shared within the south wing.

"I plan to spend a few months here in New York," Gavin told Lauren and him, "before I begin a new assignment in London."

Meeting him for the first time, Lauren found Gavin good company. She was drawn to his quiet self-possession and his air of masculine reserve that, in her eyes, yoked itself to mystery and to charisma. Her enthusiasm for the qualities that his cousin represented might have displeased him, if she had not included him in her praise.

"You could pass for Aaron's twin," she told Gavin, as she looked upon him with warm regard. "You have his rugged appearance and his confidence. Your voice, though, is even more husky, and your walk is brisker."

Gavin found her remark amusing.

"Aaron and I are actually quite different," he said. "You'll find out."

"I should hope so," Lauren lightly answered him. "Otherwise, I'll become a very confused woman."

He joined them in their breezy exchange. He was pleased that Lauren had favorably impressed Gavin. Having Liam Dowling's son on their side strengthened the probability that Lauren's brother and his lawyers would strongly approve of their marriage. With this thought in mind, he offered his own spark to Lauren's remark about Gavin's and his close resemblance to one another.

"We promise never to confuse you deliberately," he said, a casual irony infusing his words. "Only accidentally."

The three of them laughed, carefree and compatible.

For the next few weeks, Gavin busied himself with meetings at the Dowling offices that acquainted him with his new assignment in London. He also attended the dinner parties that Dowling executives and some of his long-standing friends gave in his honor. Gavin's itinerary often mirrored the freewheeling activities that he, himself, had recently experienced with Lauren. Gavin attended theater and opera in Lincoln Center, and a much-praised artist's exhibit in a gallery in Soho. He rode his favorite Belgian warm-blooded jumper over a turf-laden trail within a friend's horse farm in Bridgehampton, he piloted a Bell Ranger helicopter over Manhattan, and he kayaked in Newport. That Lauren and he sometimes joined Gavin for these holiday occasions strengthened their bond with him. Always, Gavin was partnered with a different young woman, with whom he flirted and laughed and shared lighthearted kisses. Always, he brought to each gregarious moment a life-loving spirit and a genuine cordiality. If, in those private moments when they were alone together, Gavin appeared guarded or enigmatic, he attributed his cousin's untypical moodiness to an ancillary part of his character. His cousin was not given to gratuitous explanations of his emotional state or to self-pitying analyses of his disappointments and follies. He was an enterprising individual who knew how to seize each day and, most of the time, make it work for him. In this respect, as well as in their physical resemblance, Gavin was his exact counterpart. Beneath the manly poise and the shrewdly modulated assertiveness lurked mysteries that they had not yet sufficiently explored and that even their closest friends had never fathomed.

Once, though, by chance, in the summer of 1976, he glimpsed part of the mystery that shrouded Gavin's character. Late one Sunday evening, having returned from a weekend in Vermont earlier than he had expected, he was surprised to see the dimmest light streaming from that part of the wrap-around terrace that connected to Gavin's apartment. As far as he knew, Gavin would not be returning from a long weekend in Newport until the following Tuesday. Imagining that the same thief who had been breaking into Manhattan penthouses had found his way into Gavin's apartment, he quickly took hold of the snub-nosed revolver that he kept in a drawer of his bed table. Looking cautiously about him for the murderous thief, he hurried through room after expansive room in his own apartment. Convinced, then, that the thief was not in his own apartment, he left it behind him and hurried into the corridor that led to Gavin's apartment. With a passkey that he and Gavin agreed they would use only in an emergency, he opened the door to the apartment. He made no sound, invoking with wily acumen the agility of a panther. Quickly, he made his way through the dimly lighted reception room, drawn as he was toward the hallway that brought him beyond the open door into the bedroom. There, propped against a galaxy of pillows, lay Gavin and his stepmother, Sara. Completely naked and apparently sated after an exciting hour of sex, they were lolling in the afterglow of their consummation. Gavin was smoking an imported cigarette and studying with vague satisfaction the rings of smoke that kept rising vaporously about him. Sara, her blonde beauty more radiant than he had previously observed it, was nestling beside him. They had tossed the rumpled sheets away from them, their bodies still heated by the intensity of their copulation.

They looked lost in their dreams. He wondered whether they had snorted cocaine or had smoked a joint of marijuana, so removed were they from the reality around them. He would have hurried away, because he did not care to embarrass them. But Gavin noticed him. He did not rise from his place in the bed with aggressive threats or hurry to grasp his own revolver from the drawer of the bed table. Instead, he covered Sara's nakedness with the scented sheets. Then, with no alarm and a cynical acceptance of the moment, he called out to him.

"Aaron, buddy. What the hell are you doing here?"

"I thought you were a thief."

Gavin laughed. A cigarette dangling from the right corner of his mouth, he hurried out of the bed now and reached for the robe that, an hour earlier, he must have tossed upon the richly upholstered chair not far from the bed.

"We are all thieves," he said. "Surely, you know that. All of us steal from each other, in one way or another."

"I've heard stories about it."

Gavin was face to face with him now. His blue eyes looked with penetrating gaze upon him. He was taking his measure. He was seeing an adversary, streetwise and devious, who was suddenly capable of ruining things for Sara and for him.

"Maybe, you are ready to make a new story of it," he told him, his voice even-tempered yet blunt. "Maybe, you want to tell my father about Sara and me. Maybe, you want to win more of his favor. Maybe, you intend to steal our inheritance."

He, Aaron Dowling, was much smarter than that. He knew where Liam Dowling had placed his allegiance. Gavin was his lifeline. In him ran the same blood and the same predisposition for immense success when he entered the Wall Street jungle and bestrode all the other battlefields of the business world. In contrast, he—a poor man's son—was not a lifeline, at least not to Liam. He was a prop—a makeshift rival to rouse Gavin's anger and jealousy. Liam could be a loose cannon. He might turn against him for the slightest reason—*him*, Aaron Dowling, the nephew who was too ambitious for his station. To tell Liam of Gavin's treachery would seal his own bad fate. The truth would turn Liam against him, the poor minister's son who was always reaching for the gold cup. It would also make Gavin his enemy. He preferred to keep Gavin in his debt. Gavin could be an important ally. A good word from Gavin would consolidate

Liam's trust of him.

With no show of emotion and with matter-of-fact words, he told him so.

"I'll have my share of the Dowling fortune," he said. "I don't need to steal what belongs to both of you. Besides, if I told your father about you and Sara, he'd end by hating me more than he might hate you. He'd hate any man who made it impossible for him to regard you as his son."

Gavin permitted himself a diplomatic smile. If he resented being in his debt, the ease with which he received the favorable terms that were being offered to him overrode any negative feelings that he might be harboring.

"Well, then," he answered him, "maybe we are going to be real friends, after all."

Sara, who had been watching them carefully, echoed Gavin's good will. While he and Gavin were busy with their negotiations, she had taken a cigarette from a gold case and, with a gold lighter, had ignited her imported cigarette. She took a drag on it as she lay against the galaxy of pillows that were adorned with needlepoint designs. Her blonde hair and fair skin, as well as her curvaceous body that the satin sheets concealed, were enhancing the tension between her genteel appeal and her carefully modulated seductiveness. Yet, to his eyes, her assurance was inauthentic. She had dared herself to be adventurous. She had made her stepson's bed the setting for breaking the rules that, he guessed, had—before she met Gavin—always confined her. As she called out to him, he heard the tremulousness in her voice that was competing with her lighthearted manner. Her beauty had already roused him. But this hint of vulnerability won him over completely.

"You are in the big league now," she said. "You are learning to play the game very smoothly."

"You two are all right," he said, addressing himself to both Sara and Gavin. "We are going to enjoy being friends. We think alike."

That unexpected meeting had taken place more than a year earlier. After that, he did not need to push or even coax their acceptance of him. They stayed on his side. They knew the score.

These new weeks during the early autumn of 1977 that he and Lauren spent with Gavin and his many friends and with the various girlfriends who were the unwitting covers for Gavin's love affair with Sara helped to dispel the tension that had hovered about Lauren. The news of his Florida assignment cheered Lauren most of all. During this period, her apprehension overtook her only once. At a Manhattan supper club, while they were partying with Paul and Leah Cohen a few evenings before he and Lauren were to leave for Palm Beach, Bryce Thompson suddenly appeared. As though they were replaying a scene that had occurred weeks earlier, they saw Thompson in the distance when they were on the dance floor. Once again, he was sitting at the bar, apparently alone, because his back was turned away from the men and women who were there together, drinking and conversing. Bryce was nursing his scotch, while he glared at Lauren and him as they moved with rhythmical assurance across the dance floor.

When Lauren saw him, she stopped dancing. Fear overtook her.

"Let's leave," she said, petitioning him with the tremulous urgency that, only in rare instances, subverted her tough-minded disposition. "We'll make our excuses to Paul and Leah. I'll tell them that I have a headache. They will understand."

He coaxed her back into the dance. Not far from them, the Cohens were enjoying their dance. If he and Lauren left the dance floor abruptly, Paul and Leah would know that something was wrong. They would ask questions. They might even guess that someone, right there in the supper club, had disturbed the happiness that they had genuinely represented at the start of the evening.

"We'll do nothing of the sort," he said, with gentle inflections that yoked themselves to confidence and protectiveness. "We are staying. We are not running away from Bryce Thompson. His being there, at the bar, will not spoil this evening for us."

Fear was in Lauren's eyes now and even more noticeably in her voice.

"I don't want Bryce to make trouble for us."

"His looking our way doesn't mean a thing. He's probably looking for the new girl that he intends to go home with."

At that very moment, a red-haired woman, who appeared to be in her mid-thirties and whose tight-fitting black dress enhanced her sensuality, happened to approach Bryce. Possibly, he had brought her to this upscale supper club. Just as likely, she was returning from a visit to the powder room. Whatever the case, she now took her place beside him and joined him in a drink.

The sight of Bryce and the red-haired woman drew from him new, encouraging words.

"What did I tell you? He wasn't looking at us. He was looking for his new woman."

"Maybe," Lauren said, reluctant to let go of her apprehension. "Maybe not."

"He has found a new woman. You have nothing to worry about. Besides, I am here. I'm not allowing him to get anywhere near you."

The music stopped. The orchestra had finished their set and would take a break now.

He and Lauren returned to their table and were instantly engaged in high-spirited conversation not only with the Cohens, but also with three other young couples who belonged to their circle. The waiter brought champagne for the ladies and scotch and bourbon for the men. Lightness of heart sparked the atmosphere, and a genuine pleasure in being there intensified the ongoing exhilaration. Even Lauren was caught up by the merriment. She had, at least for the moment, put Bryce out of her thoughts. With clever remarks and frequent laughter, he, too, managed to sound both witty and elated. Yet never did he lose sight of Bryce Thompson, whether he and his redheaded partner were sitting at the bar, enclosed within the intimacy of their being there together, or whether he was dancing with her across the wide span of the burnished floor, once the orchestra had returned to play a new set of ballads about bittersweet love and broken promises. From time to time, when Thompson was drinking scotch at the bar or dancing with his new partner only fifty feet away from the table where he and Lauren and the others were sitting, he noticed that the tall, dark-haired man was glaring at him. From this closer perspective, he studied Thompson's features. What he saw confirmed his initial impression. Bryce

Thompson had the rough face of an angry man. It was the face of an enemy. It was the battered face of a man who had the cold eyes of a killer.

Chapter Five
A Flickering Light

Gavin Dowling awoke trembling. Caught as he had been inside his uneasy dream, he saw as an after-image, ghostly and surreal, the flare of the midnight sun upon the steep, jagged cliffs of Bergen, Norway. He saw, as clearly, the face of his father, his chiseled features relaxed now as he drew him to the place beside him, there on the top of the cliff that they and their rugged guide had been trekking for two hours. The three of them were wearing navy blue winter caps that covered their ears and matched the blue of their insulated jackets and their thick leggings. The guide, who was a husky man of medium height and in his thirties, stood several feet behind them and could not hear what they were saying. But he, the son who was learning to be reliable, heard. He heard the wind howling from somewhere deep inside the blaze of light, and he heard, as well, insistent and proprietary on the edge of that wind-sound, the deep voice of his father.

"To own a part of the world, you have to be like that light," he said. "You have to be the force that influences whatever terrain you inhabit. You have to be the man that counts. You have to be the one who negotiates with each moment, so that you can sustain your power and even increase it."

In that faraway midnight, his father's words had thrilled him. He was nearly twelve years old then, tall for his age and lanky and already honing a razor-sharp awareness of things. To his father's words, he at first said nothing, so enthralled was he by their implications. His father, in turn, observed the blaze of light for another instant before he turned to study him carefully and to wait for the young, reflective words that hinted at the strong-minded individual that he was becoming. He felt his father's hardened gaze upon him, while he—the privileged son who regarded him as his alter ego—peered at the giant cliffs that rose, eerie and mysterious, out of the sun-welling light as though they were the bones of a discarded world. On that night in February of 1958, which had lived in his memory all these years afterward, he believed that his father was drawing him into a secret understanding of the new world that was unfolding around them and that only power brokers claimed for themselves and, sometimes, for their sons. His need to be like his father, to replicate his confidence and his experience, pushed him out of his momentary stillness to ask the question that pleased his father.

"How does a man keep his power? How does he hold on to it and increase it?"

His father answered him with matter-of-fact assertiveness.

"He makes a plan and runs with it. He stays flexible. He keeps his options open. He changes course, if he has to. He maneuvers the best of his troops into strategic situations. He leaves behind the faint-of-heart and the conventional. He forgives no man his mistakes. Nor does he forgive himself for his missteps. But, if he has guts, he keeps moving forward in an unexpected direction. He goes on fighting for more victories and more power."

Once more, his father's words thrilled him.

"I want to be that kind of man," he told him. "I want to be powerful."

With brown, piercing eyes, his father continued to study

him. He was calculating his potential. He was guessing how long it would take before experience drained him of his boyhood insecurities and his occasional sentimentality.

"You will be powerful, if you do the right things. You will be powerful not only because you are smart, but also because you are becoming street-wise. You are getting to know the world. You are learning how to maneuver your way through it."

"I want to be like you."

"That is good. It is important to choose as your mentor a man who has power. But, remember, as you grow into your success, you cannot be me. You have to be yourself. You have to be the Gavin Dowling that other men will want to emulate."

He hurried to say the words that he knew his father wanted to hear, though he, himself, did not completely fathom their complexities.

"I'll work hard. I'll work for your corporation. But I'll become successful in my own way and on my own terms."

His father allowed the suggestion of a smile to cross his lips. Then, proceeding briskly, he resumed this extemporaneous lesson that he was imparting to his son, there at the top of a jagged cliff that rose, adamant and prevailing, above the port of Bergen.

"At first, success may come easy to you," his father warned him. "You are already a Dowling. But don't let success make a fool of you. Don't believe that success will stay with you if you become soft or lazy. Strive to be new. Always make your life an adventure."

"I don't want to think of my life in any other way. I'll always want adventure."

"Those words are good to hear. Do not forget them. Do

not become one of those men who are trapped by their easy lives. Whatever light shone through them when they were in the adventure grows dim and weak. Their light becomes a mere flicker that influences nothing."

All through this exchange with his father, the wind never ceased howling. Nor did the radiance of the midnight sun diminish even slightly. Soft white clouds, tattered by the wind, floated in the azure sky. Far below the cliff on which he and his father stood and below the vast surround of hills, the glistening waters of the ship-laden port swirled. On a promontory that overlooked the waters, the grand hotel where they were staying shone like an elaborate beacon. Huge evergreens, foreshortened by the distance, wavered within his fleet glance, and a cluster of village houses appeared as miniature objects. Now, having spoken the words that he needed to say, his father turned to observe once more the flare of the midnight sun and the heft of the tattered clouds, the arrival of an American cruise ship within the windswept port, and the pastel colors of the village houses that were scattered across his quick glance. Then, as abruptly as he had brought his attention to the scene, his father signaled their guide. They would begin the trek down to Kirkenes, the tiny Arctic Circle town from which they had made their journey up the rugged path that brought them to the top of the cliff. After signaling the guide, his father directed new words to him, the son who, even in his boyhood, was already emulating him.

"It is time to move on," he said. " There is much that we have to accomplish. There are many new adventures that we have to enter."

A year or so after that time in Norway, his mother died. The heart ailment that killed her had prevented her from accompanying his father and him to Bergen. Nor had she been present during all the other excursions that strengthened the bond that he shared with his father. His mother was an elegant woman, still beautiful at forty despite the illness that made her so fragile. She was a sensible woman whose patrician background had taught her to disdain self-pity and to find pleasure in the bond that her husband was fostering with their son. Her illness did not prevent her from managing the large staffs that worked to maintain the splendid Dowling homes in Manhattan, the Hamptons, London, and Paris. Her cosmopolitan manner made her a luminous presence at the sumptuous parties and balls that she and his father hosted for a foreign ambassador, perhaps, or for a five-star general or at the glamorous dinners that honored a Wall Street mogul, a pioneering scientist, a famous artist, or an eminent playwright. She chaired important committees that raised funds for college-bound students, for needy refugees, and for the post-graduate studies of physicians and nurses. In all these ways, she enhanced the name of Dowling, and she intensified the love and respect that made her marriage to Liam Dowling an extraordinary union.

When his mother died, the light within his father did not blaze quite so powerfully. But never did he allow his suppressed grief to steal the light that empowered the intricacies of his journeys. It was in this period that he directed more of his attention to him, the essential thirteen-year-old son whom he had always been mentoring.

In the years that followed, there were many adventures that he and his father entered together. Always, his father was observing him. Always, he was setting new tests for him. Always, he was measuring his agility and stamina, his resilience and quick-wittedness, and his character. Again and again, he—the privileged son and heir to a vast fortune—had to prove himself worthy of the Dowling name. With his father, he trekked the High Atlas Mountains in Morocco. He hunted red stag in Patagonia and lions in South Africa. He paraglided over the Chamonix Valley within the Rhône-Alpes region, and he skied on the rugged slopes of Gstaad, Switzerland. For every one of these experiences, the light of the sun shone upon and around them. There were other sources of light, as well. He and his father were their own light, flares of excitement that made life fast-paced and vivid.

Never in this period did he resent his father's iron-willed mentoring. A superb athlete even at forty-four, his father competed aggressively against his son's vigorous physicality, his well-honed discipline, and his newly acquired daring. He, the obedient son who adulated him because of his stoical manner and because of his extraordinary influence upon other corporate leaders, consented to every test that his father devised for him. Though he still competed against his rugged peers at school and worked effectively to equal or to exceed their proficiency on athletic fields and in academic classes, he regarded the bond that he was forging with his father as essential to his wellbeing and to his self-definition.

Only later, after Sara came into their lives, did he resist his father's influence. By then, he was eighteen and, impelled by a rebellious spirit that, for eight years, he concealed from him, he made passionate love with the woman that his father had taken as his second wife two years earlier.

Sara banked her fires. Her cool exterior concealed her lonely destitution and her refined suppression of desire. Never did he regard her as his mother. How could he? She was only five years older than he. Nor did his father ever refer to her as a surrogate for the mother that died so early. Sara was herself, distinctive and talented. She was the daughter of Malcolm Lancaster, the eminent British scientist who had helped the British in Birmingham, England, and the Americans in Oak Ridge, Tennessee, during the Second World War to build the atom bomb that won the allies their victory in the Pacific. Because she made a favorable impression at her debutante's ball and because she was the daughter of Malcolm Lancaster, Queen Elizabeth had invited Sara to tea at Buckingham Palace. Even then, as a seventeen-year-old girl, she had already made a success as a gifted writer of historical fiction. When she was eighteen, Sara married Craig Halston, an American aeronautical engineer and an Air Force pilot who died two years later during a bombing mission over the North Vietnam sectors in Laos.

A year after she became a widow (Gavin sometimes reflected), Sara married his father, the internationally renowned Liam Dowling, who was trying to recover a portion, at least, of his lost happiness.

In those first years of his father's second marriage, he—the only offspring of the first marriage—was often away at school in Switzerland or on holiday in Europe and South Africa with his school friends and with well-travelled professors as scholarly guides and, shortly after he had completed his university days in Cambridge, Paris, and Copenhagen, on architectural commissions for his father's corporation in South America, in Australia, and in China. Whenever his busy life permitted him to spend time at his father's homes in New York City, in the Hamptons and in Newport, as well as in Palm Springs and in Paris, he and Sara made it a point never to see each other alone. Their polite detachment from one another concealed the illicit nature of their relationship. Although, at times, Sara appeared guilt-ridden because of their betrayal of Liam, he (Liam's devious son) was too enthralled by their need of each other to feel any guilt. He reveled in his sexual powers and in the exciting pleasure that he brought to her and that she gave him. In this same period, his busy life kept expanding the range of his experience, anchored as that experience was to adventurous pursuits that tested his proficiency and his courage and that forged new bonds which he created with athletic fellows like himself and with genteel girls who belonged to his privileged class and with whom he occasionally slept, without loving them.

On the occasions that he regarded as most challenging of all, during his teens and in the self-determining years of his early manhood, his adventuring partnered him with his father in hunting, mountain climbing, and flying excursions that brought them into wild and dangerous locations and into episodes requiring the use of razor-sharp instincts and well-honed aptitudes. To test his mettle and to plumb the depths of his emerging character, his father drew him into territories of danger that he, the son who adulated him and who sought his approval, had never before dared to enter. If he pushed his son into perilous occasions, his father shared the danger every time. From Liam Dowling's perspective, the *raison d'être* of their adventures was the strengthening of his son's character. He wanted his son to make a friend of pain. He wanted him to develop the bold resources within his nature that would enable him to confront the world with confidence and with authority. He wanted him to bring a keen-eyed realism to his comprehension of that devious world. The tests, which were always grueling, yielded rewards that nurtured his spirit and deepened his sense of the man that he was becoming. But his satisfying or even exceeding his father's expectations meant more to him than any other reward. In those days, he never doubted his father's love of him. Only later, when he was twenty-six, did he detect the streak of cruelty that sometimes prodded his father's actions toward him and toward all the other persons in his life.

Sara came into his life obliquely. Only by indirection did their paths cross. Only through chance did their fates converge. She never took part in the adventures that he shared with his father. Perhaps, his father dissuaded her from joining them because of the rigorous challenges and the dangerous tests that defined the journeys. Possibly, he invited her to accompany them, on the condition that she remained at the sidelines, outside their peril. If that were so, Sara would have rejected the scenario that confined her to the role of a passive spectator. More likely, Sara expressed no interest in joining them, so caught up was she in the research and writing of her latest historical novel. Usually, when he and Sara were in the same room together, they were surrounded by his father's partying friends or by his father's business associates and their wives or by foreign ambassadors, renowned scientists and philosophers, and film producers who were courting his father for investment capital, research grants, or other favors. As Liam's only offspring, he was expected even in his teens to mingle with the guests while he shared their enthusiasm for sports, politics, and art and while he made himself known, as well, to their sons and daughters who were his age or a bit older.

But one evening in 1963, at the end of the first year of his father's second marriage, while a grand party in the ballroom of the Waldorf Astoria in New York was offering sumptuous music, delicious food, and prestigious guests, everything changed for Sara and for him.

Weary on that evening of having to fulfill the role of his father's goodwill ambassador, he had stolen away from the party, colored though it was with glittering surfaces, buoyant personalities, and extravagant appurtenances. He intended to absent himself only long enough to calm his vague dissatisfaction by lighting up and inhaling one of the Patagonian cigarettes favored by his father and, in secret, by himself. The autumn breeze wafting across the wide expanse of the nighttime terrace quickened his senses and mitigated, in part, the melancholy that was overtaking him in spite of the festive occasion. That he had temporarily abandoned not only the party, but also the pallid daughter of a British emissary intensified the rush of satisfaction that stirred his awareness of the vivid moon and the star-filled sky in the vaulted space above him and of the efflorescent panorama of New York City that sparkled below him. As far as he was concerned, the only thing that he had in common with the British girl was his age. They were both seventeen. When he hurried away from her, he did not elude the party completely.

With the polished assurance that gave him a courtly manner, he had left the reticent British girl to dance with his father inside the wide circle of other couples. He had made his way with equal assurance and with brisk gait away from the dance floor and on to the rim of the crowded dining room, filled as it was with couples in tuxedos and gowns and made painterly by the yellow-gold of dahlias, the lavender of camellias, the red of hibiscus, and the peach hues of roses that flared their beauty in precise arrangements at the center of each table. But, even when he entered the skyline terrace that had been temporarily abandoned by the partygoers who had given themselves over to the exhilarated camaraderie of the dance, the sounds of the party followed him. Behind him, as a faraway impression, the melodious rhythms of a Cole Porter love ballad were navigating the blue-jazz sounds of piano, trumpet, and violin. The smoky voice of the woman who was singing it rose with aptitudes both seductive and poignant. The voices of the guests, intermittently hushed or cacophonous, were another riff upon his senses.

Yet the merriment of the party could not displace the tremulous sounds of a woman who was weeping within the shadows of a marble column not more than ten feet from where he stood, just beyond the entrance to the terrace. For a moment, he debated whether he should stay or go, so disinclined was he to become involved in the problems of this distraught woman. When she moved forward, out of the shadows that, even now, partly covered her tall, slim frame, he noticed—without yet apprehending her face—her blonde hair and young, fair-skinned arms. Still weeping, she took a handkerchief from her purse and, while she was drying her tear-stained face, she struggled to regain her composure. He might have turned from her and hurried back to the party. But, right after she placed her handkerchief inside her purse once more and moved forward again to peer ruefully upon the glittering city below her, the light of the moon caught her in profile. Now, with quickened heartbeat, he saw who she was. This weeping figure was none other than Sara, the beautiful woman whom his father had taken as his second wife.

With no hesitation, he hurried to her.

"I see that I am not the only one who values privacy," he began. "Being caught in a crowd has never appealed to me, either."

She turned quickly to peer upon his face. His husky, matter-of-fact voice had startled her. She was not anticipating him or, for that matter, any other person. With the cool detachment that he recognized as the armature of her self-possession, she met his remark with clipped inflections.

"We have something in common, then, you and I. But I never imagined that you enjoyed looking up at the stars and an autumn moon while you were alone. I know very little about you. But what I do know tells me that you prefer this here-and-now, earthbound world. The moon and the stars might be a convenient backdrop when you are with one of your girlfriends. They are a means to an end. You are not a dreamer. In that respect, you are like your father."

"Ah, but I did come here alone, and I was looking up at the moon and the stars."

"So you were."

"But I was not crying."

These words made her pause. When, after a moment, she answered him, her voice anchored its sorrow to a harder edge.

"No, you were not crying. You have no reason to cry."

"But you have."

Once again, she shrouded herself in silence. Beneath the artifice of her composure, he discerned her struggle. She was uncertain of him. She did not know whether she should explain the cause of her sorrow. Now, as if to clarify the person that his rugged demeanor represented, she looked upon him with a more studious gaze. Only then, while choosing carefully measured words that kept in check the anguish that she was experiencing, did she declare herself to him.

"I was thinking of Craig. Perhaps, your father has mentioned Craig Halston to you. He was my first husband. On this day, twenty-four years ago, he was born in Philadelphia. On this same day, two years ago, he was killed during a combat mission in Vietnam."

"You still love him."

His words were precise, yet blunt. They sounded accusatory, as he meant them to be. Tonight, he was still on his father's side. Where she was concerned, his loyalty to his father had not yet been tested. His probing words made her defensive. Her quick reply, weary and angry at the same time, yoked itself to the grim reality that her first husband's death had left her to live through.

"Of course I love him. But what does it matter? He is not here. He will never be here with me."

"You have gone forward with your life. You have married again. That is a good thing."

Once more she looked pensively upon him. Only then did she accept the truth of his remark.

"Yes, it is a good thing. Your father rescued me. I like to believe that I have also rescued him."

He pressed further.

"Do you love my father?"

Her words came more quickly now, extemporaneous and matter-of-fact. She wanted, in this moment, to tell him how it was with her. She wanted him to understand who she was.

"I do. But I do not love him in the same way that I loved Craig. Craig was my first love. He became my lifeline and my passion. At times, I think that he was my obsession. I could never love any other man in that way."

"Yet you married my father."

"Your father and I understand each other. We have no illusions about our relationship. When I first met him, your father was struggling through the grief that he felt after your mother died. I had heard many stories about your father. But never had I heard that he was a man capable of grief or despair. I was impressed and moved that a man with his strong-minded temperament and his formidable capacities could grieve so profoundly and for so long a time. I told myself that he and I shared the same spirit. Ironical, isn't it? Our grieving for our lost loves became a bond between us."

"I think that you and my father go on grieving, though you grieve mostly in secret—even from each other."

"Our being together makes grief bearable. Your father becomes even more important on an evening like this, when memories bring Craig back to me. Because your father is here, I can turn away from my ghost. I can go to your father and, without speaking a word, he will take my hands and comfort me."

"Then, you must allow me to bring you to him. Parties are not meant for ghosts."

His words were softer. They suggested his empathy. Sara allowed herself the hint of a smile. But melancholy did not leave her voice, and her blue eyes remained clouded with her grieving. Nevertheless, and without any reluctance, she took hold of the arm that he extended to her so that they could return to the party together.

"Yes," she said. "It is time to leave my ghost—at least, for tonight."

He brought her back to his father, who was sitting at the bar, conversing with two business partners about the stock market. As he and Sara approached, his father scanned their faces. He noticed at once the rapport between them. He noticed, too, that Sara had been weeping. His son's courtly manner toward her did not displease his father. As her stepson, he was granting Sara the respect that was her due. He was doing what needed to be done. He was a true Dowling. He was offering consolation to a melancholic woman.

After that evening, for the many months when he held himself to rigorous discipline that appeared to him, at least in retrospect, as perverse masochism or self-defeating asceticism, he was rarely alone with her. He did not need to be alone to share with her the furtive glances and to savor the pleasures of dancing, as if casually, with her at the grand parties that she and his father hosted in Manhattan, in Dallas, in Santa Barbara, and in London. The guests, as young as he was and older, accepted his courtliness toward her as a natural reflection of his strong bond with his father and of his careful breeding, yoked as his conduct was to a reserved demeanor and to well-modulated propriety. He was not alone with her when, in late August, they played tennis with a newly married couple at his father's home in the Hamptons or when, in November, he skied beside her while, not far from the private school that he attended, he was spending a weekend in Gstaad, Switzerland, at the family's chalet with her and his father and with several of his father's business friends and their wives. Nor was he alone with her when, during the Christmas holidays, they swam in the heated pool of his father's home in Paris or when, in April, they rode their Tobianos on a horse farm in Camden, Maine. Yet, on every occasion, whether he was seated next to her at a dinner table or guiding her through a waltz or conversing with her at the bar of a supper club or standing beside her in front of an Impressionist canvas in an art gallery, he conveyed through the press of his hand upon her shoulder or through the sensual implications of his husky voice or through his seductive glances the passion that was stirring within him. Because of the canny instincts that he had cultivated by means of his realistic negotiations with the world, he kept his passion a secret to everyone except Sara.

In the first months after the surprise of their meeting on the terrace of the Waldorf Astoria, Sara regarded his attraction to her as a schoolboy's infatuation. So she told him later. She found his attention charming. She recognized the poignancy in his ardor. She noticed, too, the care he took to conceal his feelings from everybody except her. His secrecy was a device for protecting her reputation and for avoiding public declarations of his love that could throw the two of them, as well as his father, into turmoil. Yet he was no callow youth. Her closest girlfriends had, a year or so earlier, told her about his less than discreet liaisons, from the time he was sixteen, with a film starlet, with a nightclub chanteuse, and with the equally promiscuous girls who were his age and who belonged to his social class. She could forgive him his follies. She could tell herself that he was testing his prowess with all these women in sexual encounters that were, to him, satisfying biological acts that involved no profound emotions and no commitment beyond an hour's sensation in an upscale hotel or in a private ski lodge or in a well-appointed cabin on a pristine yacht.

In these same months, she began to fall in love with him.

Though she struggled against the willfulness of the passion that must have lain dormant from the moment she saw him in a different way on the Waldorf terrace, her need to be with him became both urgent and troubled. As if to escape from the guilt that her passion inflicted upon her, she immersed herself in the writing of her new novel. She hosted dinner parties for Liam's corporate friends and their wives. She volunteered as a nurse's assistant at a New York children's hospital. She accompanied Liam on business trips to California, Texas, and New Mexico. Yet, no matter how many hours she devoted to her writing and to her obligations as Liam's wife, her passion for *him*—Gavin Dowling and Liam's son—haunted her, as though it were an implacable Spirit pursuing her or grimacing Truth pointing an accusatory finger at her.

Then, within the late autumn of 1964, in the first year of his university studies in England when his absence seemed a careless abandonment of her, the Fates conspired with her suppressed desire and with the wily sensuality that yoked itself to his need of her. Liam's business travel was drawing him away to South America and to Australia. He planned to be gone for weeks at a time. Sara, in turn, would be journeying through England, France, Switzerland, and South Africa to complete the research for her current book. Against her prudent judgment and her cautious fidelity to Liam, she telephoned Gavin an hour after she arrived in London. She was staying in the Dowling suite on the seventh floor of the Dorchester, the elegant hotel that overlooked Hyde Park and that was renowned for its restrained opulence and for its meticulous amenities. He was fifty miles away, at Cambridge University, where he was studying architecture. When he heard her voice, modulated as it was to self-control and cordiality, and heard as well the quiet suggestion that he join her for dinner on that Saturday, he was thrilled in a way that he had not anticipated. Though there was in her voice no promise of intimacy, there was, palpable and vivid, the prospect of being with her for an hour or two.

Even at this meeting, they were not alone together. Sara was determined that the public should view her as a dutiful stepmother who was sharing an enjoyable visit with her husband's son. For that reason, she had invited Tim and Nancy Flanagan to join them. Tim was a neurosurgeon, and Nancy was a pediatrician. With his tall, lean frame and brown-haired crew cut, Tim appeared much younger than his thirty-five years. His wife, a petite redhead whose fair-skinned appeal was enhanced by blue eyes, turned-up nose, and a gleaming smile, was thirty-two. But she could have passed for twenty-five. The Flanagans were "safe" guests. They had been happily married for ten years, and they were the parents of two sons and a daughter. Their varied interests made them ideal companions at a dinner table, on a trans-Atlantic flight or on a cruise ship, and at a sumptuous ball. They were avid skiers, proficient swimmers, and excellent horse riders. They loved opera, as well as jazz and country western ballads. They spoke French, German, and Gaelic, and they gave to their English speech precise inflections and brisk rhythms. Sara had always found them to be witty, empathetic, and loyal. They were altogether likable.

So Gavin remembered on this uneasy morning thirteen years later, here in the sixteen-room Manhattan penthouse that his father had given him and Aaron to share.

The two hours that Sara and he spent with the Flanagans at that long-ago dinner went reasonably well and nearly dispelled their unease, his and Sara's, at being observed together by this good-natured couple. Tim and he established a natural rapport because of their interests in soccer, horseback riding, skiing, and travel. Sara and Nancy appeared to his eyes as mutually supportive sisters who brought a spark to the afternoon with their talk of theater, books, and the global political scene. Feeling comfortable in their presence and made convivial by a few glasses of wine, he and Sara fully consented to the joy of being there with each other. He recalled placing his hand with casual-seeming intimacy upon Sara's shoulder. He whispered a witty remark in her ear. He brushed her lips with a kiss when he and the Flanagans were toasting her. Only when Nancy, while gazing at Sara and him, seated as they were across from Tim and her, burst into affectionate praise of Sara, did they pause before the tranquil surfaces of their deception.

"You have recovered yourself," she exclaimed. "You have gone past your grief. Your marrying Liam has been good for you. He has helped you to take a new path. And you have acquired a son, as well."

"Yes. Liam has been good for me," Sara said, while accompanying her words with a demure smile and genteel inflections. She made no mention of her "acquired son," who was merely five years her junior.

He smiled, too, the wiliness of his response concealed by his impeccable Dowling manners.

But Nancy's remark, influenced as it had been by eyes that looked upon Sara and him with warmhearted trust, disconcerted both of them. For the rest of that evening, Sara confined herself to the safe conventions of being Liam's dutiful wife. He, in turn, anchored his responses to Sara and to the

Flanagans within persuasive surfaces of courtesy and camaraderie.

Nancy's mention of Liam had, however, cast a pall upon the dinner party—at least, as far as they perceived it. The guilt that had held them in its chains during these many months hovered near them once again. As soon as the dinner party was over, though, and he and Sara had parted amiably from the Flanagans, the rebellious spirit that sometimes compelled his darker actions drove his responses with hardened energies. He resisted soul-searching. He resisted his uneasy conscience and the stark truth that he was betraying his bond with his father. When they returned to the privacy of Sara's apartment at the Dorchester, he pressed his lips against her lips, his passionate kiss drawing her deeper into his desire.

Roused by his touch and by her yearning for him, Sara gave herself completely to his kiss. It was a long kiss that left her breathless and that fired his ardor with new impatience.

"This is wrong," she told him, when at last he released her from the kiss. A tremulous fatalism informed her words. "Yet you are the man that I need. You are so like the husband that I lost. You do not look like Craig. But you are Craig in so many ways. You are as young as he was when I fell in love with him. You are athletic, you are confident, and—yes—sometimes you are a bit arrogant. You are sensitive, too. That is a nice surprise. Most of all, you are dangerous. With you, I am crossing into territory from which there is no way back."

"Why would you want to go back?" he asked. "We need each other now. That is the important thing. It is what makes everything right."

That was the first night when he shared her bed. Many

other nights were to follow. Their lovemaking was a mutual pleasure, her moaning sighs and nearly serene smiles intensifying always the vigor of his sensuality. Sometimes, as they climaxed together, she would scream out a name. But her voice, in spite of its jagged emphases, sounded far away. As he stroked her faster and faster, he drove himself more deeply into the wildness that was firing him, the heated ecstasy of their entwined bodies a perceived flare of colored and flickering lights and, at the crest of his fury, a vague awareness of his shuddering breath falling away from him.

One night, he did hear the name that Sara cried out.

"Craig!" she cried. "Craig!"

He did not tell her that he had heard her. He did not need her to explain what he already knew. She was still in love with Craig, three years after he died. If she loved Liam, whom she married because she felt abandoned and lonely, she loved him without the passion that her love for her first husband had inspired within her. Nor did she love *him*, the Dowling who was as young as Craig was when she first met him and who brought back his self-possessed manner for her apprehension and for her wishful thinking. She did not love *him*—Gavin Dowling—for himself. She loved him because he was Craig's ghost, reincarnated and made visible to her eyes alone. The thought did not anger him. It teased his sense of irony. Even during the most intense copulation, he often regarded himself as someone else, a stranger whose urgent sensuality stirred his primitive instincts and drove the experience of love toward a thrilling suggestion of violence. Sex, even when it was consensual, seemed an act of aggression. For him, copulation subverted his often understated and shrewdly calibrated responses to other people. The wildness that overtook him when he was in bed with a woman belonged even now, fifteen years after his first carnal experience, to the savage nature that lay dormant within him. In that year of 1964, when he was eighteen and had come to be Sara's lover, his body wakened in new ways to its vigorous sensuality.

She loved this wildness within him and the hint of savagery. But, even though their desire for each other intensified, they took care not to be discovered by Liam or by the security guards that, undetected even when they were in plain sight, ferreted out the adversaries who were betraying him. They did not know when Liam, if roused by suspicion, would set his guards on their trail. Aware of his father's hardened nature and his ingrained distrust of people, he devised intricate plans that allowed Sara and him to disappear casually, without drawing the alarm of their friends or goading the anger of his father. Always, Sara traveled on the pretext of researching material for her latest book. He, in turn, convinced his friends and his professors that he was making trips into the out-of-the-way cities and towns of Europe, so that he could study, close up, the architecture of different periods. Away from their friends and familiar locations, they each became someone else, their fictionalized biographies defining them either as a married couple from Boston who taught mathematics and science at a private secondary school or as newlyweds from Melbourne who worked for a renowned architectural firm there.

Whenever he was on recess from his studies at Cambridge, Sara and he managed to meet discreetly in remote locations that eluded the notice of Liam's watchmen. One time, in November of the first year of their affair, they skied on the steep, afternoon slopes and long downhill runs of the Shilthorn

Mountain in Mürren, Switzerland. At night, they made love in a chalet within the nearby village of Lauterbrunnen. During a week together the following February that they had not anticipated, they went scuba diving in the Andaman Sea, within the Beacon Reef of Thailand, where underwater mountains and coral gardens sparkled like indigo jewels and where batfish, lionfish, and moray eels swam around them. At night, they swam in moonlit waters and, with new and prolonged intensities, made love on the white sands of the beach. In other years, they kayaked in Tahiti, they rode Arab bays on a horse farm in Provence, and they co-piloted a Cessna 206 from a private air base outside London.

Sometimes, they spent days in semi-seclusion. After he completed his studies in the Department of Architecture at Cambridge University and when he was enrolled in a graduate program in The Royal Danish Academy of Fine Arts in Copenhagen, they reveled in their few stolen days together within a secluded townhouse in the Douro Valley of Porto, Portugal. Later, while he was involved in another graduate program in École des Beaux Arts in Paris, they spent an early autumn weekend, sequestered and sensual, in a picturesque stone cottage in Fontainebleau. In the following May, after being away from each other for several months, they met in Cordes-sur-Ciel, a beautiful hilltop village in southwest France. There, within the Cérou Valley of Tarn, they revived the love affair that Sara's marriage to his father had compelled them, at least temporarily, to abandon. There was a special reward in being away from the crowded cities that knew them and from the many friends who, on the rare occasions when they saw them together, perceived them in uncomplicated ways as a gifted young architect and his demure step-mother. In all the places that did not recognize them, they cloaked their identities with the mystery that attends even casual newcomers to a scene. They played their parts so well, that they grew comfortable with their ongoing betrayal of Liam.

On two occasions, though, during the fourth and sixth years of their trysts, Sara wept uncontrollably. Each time that remorse overtook her fragile will, she awakened with him beside her, naked and surfeited, in a comfortable bed within the glamorous privacies of secluded hotels near St. Tropez and Venice. Their night of love had brought each of them thrilling pleasures. He had, afterwards, slept eased and contented. Sara (so she admitted later) had also slept easily. But, when morning light streaming through the panoramic window revealed the sensual reality of their naked bodies, the rumpled bed linen, and the evening clothes strewn across the needlepoint chairs not far from their bed, Sara, as if with new eyes, felt shame. The guilt that she suppressed every day since their affair had begun rose up now to accuse her of treachery and self-deceit. A few minutes later, when he, too, awakened, he saw first of all her pale, haunted face and, right after that, her blue eyes that were peering at him with fearful apprehension as though he were a stranger.

"What is wrong?" he asked.

Whether she had heard his words, he did not know. Enclosed within her silence, she kept staring not merely at, but right through, him. Her troubled gaze saw beyond him, as if she were reviewing the many episodes they had navigated with self-willed and culpable abandon.

"Tell me what is wrong," he urged her once more. "Let me help you."

His words brought her back into the moment that held them now, caught and wary.

"I can't go on like this," she cried out. "I don't want to be two persons. I don't want to disguise who I am and what I feel when I am with Liam. I can't love him the way a wife should love her husband. I love only you in that way. I want to be done with this scheming. I want to tell Liam the truth about us."

"You must not do that," he told her. "You know the rules that we made when we started. We agreed that we were going to keep everything a secret. In that way, nobody will get hurt."

"I'm hurt already. I am being torn apart."

"Don't give in to the hurt. Enjoy what we have together."

"It isn't enough. I want so much more of you. I want to be your wife."

"You are thinking like a schoolgirl. You are not being realistic. We can't afford to make an enemy of my father. We need his good will."

"You want his money."

"Of course, I do. I have a right to it. I am his son. But I want more than that. Some day, I want to lead the Dowling Corporation."

For a moment, his words made her pause. Her gaze held him even more firmly in its keen-eyed awareness.

"It is more than the money with you, isn't it? You love your father, yet you resent his hold over you. In spite of your ambivalent feelings toward him, you need his approval."

He hesitated before he answered her, so guarded was he about his feelings for his father.

"Yes."

"You are not willing to give up this life of wealth and privilege—not even for me."

"It isn't necessary to give it up. We would be fools to give it up. Besides, we have everything we want."

"Maybe you have everything. I do not."

"Don't want too much, Sara. We'll lose everything if you want too much."

"I don't want everything. I want myself back, without the lies and the scheming. I want to stand with you without any pretense, so that the world can see who we are together."

"Don't spoil things between us. This is all we can have together. Keep remembering that, if we were to tell the truth about ourselves, the world will judge us harshly and my father will become our enemy."

"I know. I know all of it. I have told myself so many times. But what we have now is not enough."

All the while that she was explaining how it was with her, she studied him with a new intensity. In spite of the sadness that touched her face, her beauty glowed. Now, weary of the words they had shared and resisting, still, the influence of her rankled spirit, she turned from him and hurried out of their bed. Morning sunlight caressed her supple body as she made her way to the bath that would solace her. Her nakedness thrilled him. He did not want to end their secret relationship. At the same time, he did not want to lose his bond with his father. He wanted even more of the privileges of being a rich man's son. Yet he did not want his sexual need of his father's wife to push him off the path that was surely going to lead him to greater wealth and power. Sara and he needed to stay apart for a while. He sensed that she felt the same way. He was not surprised when, during their flight back to London, she whispered her feeling about this need for a separation.

"Let's see what happens when we are away from each

other," she said. "Maybe I have to learn all over again not to ask for everything. Maybe I want too much. Being away from you may teach me to be satisfied with the secret hours and stolen days that we do share."

Shortly after those few days they shared in Venice, they did not see one another for three months. Though he contented himself with various nightclub girls and two or three of the promiscuous young women from his own class, he missed Sara. At night, especially, he missed her. During this period, he saw her occasionally with Liam at charity balls, Wall Street soirées, and New York after-theater parties. Always, they exchanged cordial greetings and polite anecdotes while they were part of a group that included his father, as well as the girl that he was escorting for that evening. On these evenings, there were no furtive glances between Sara and him. There were no intimate meetings in out-of-the-way alcoves or behind the marble columns of skyline terraces. They had agreed to stay away from each other. Reluctantly, he had remained true to their pact. Yet, knowing her as he did, he told himself that it would be merely a matter of time before she came back to him.

When, after the third month of their separation, she phoned him, she arranged to meet him in Paris. She was there, doing research for another of her popular books. Liam was away on business in South Africa.

"I cannot really be happy with you, and I cannot be happy without you," she told him after their first night of love in this new cycle of secret meetings. "But I am less unhappy when I am with you."

Sara and he continued to be lovers whenever chance allowed them to be. When he could not be with her, he contented himself with one-night stands involving chorus girls and ambitious starlets and, sometimes, with casual affairs involving university girls and warmhearted socialites. Sara never mentioned the many women with whom he was sharing his bed. Nor did she speak of her sex life with Liam. About Liam, she did not need to explain anything. He knew his father well. Liam Dowling had loved his first wife completely. The love or carnal interest he showed to his second wife was yoked to his guilt-laden and usually repressed desire. Though, in his perverse way, his father loved Sara, he could not love her completely. Their copulation involved (he imagined with bitter antipathy) his father's swift, thrusting dominance. It was a frenzied display of his prowess. It was a vigorous proof of his desire. For Sara, it must have seemed like a lover's ambiguous and possibly thrilling assault. But their lovemaking was not a collaboration of desire. Sara did not love Liam. Nor did he love her. Not profoundly. Not honestly. How could he? The ghost of his first wife haunted him. She had not set him free. He had not willed her to do so. Liam must have guessed that Sara was offering him the same stinted feelings that he, as her second husband, shared with her. Sara loved Craig, her first husband, with the same kind of passion that Liam brought to his memory of his first wife, his beloved Mary. But Liam did not know the whole truth. He did not know that Sara's passion for his son Gavin had nearly displaced her yearning for her first husband.

Chapter Six
Betrayals

In the seventh year of their discreet affair, Gavin and Sara began to take risks, heedless of the consequences. In retrospect, he wondered whether he and Sara wanted Liam to discover them. There would be reprisals. Liam might disinherit them. He might banish them from his life. But they would then be freed of all the strictures that he now placed upon them. During these careless times, he and Sara did not inhabit their usual fictions or devise new schemes that made their being together seem both natural and appropriate. Nor did they surround themselves with other couples whose gregarious presence would have deflected the attention of spectators from the extraordinary fact of their appearing together once again. Now, journalists took notice of them. They photographed them when they were skiing in St. Moritz, for example, and when they emerged from the tea salon of The Schlosshotel Kronberg near Frankfurt, Germany. The newspapers portrayed him as an international playboy who occasionally escorted his young and glamorous stepmother to tony ski resorts in Switzerland and Colorado, on a luxurious voyage to the Bahamas, and to lavish parties in Manhattan, London, Hong Kong, and Berlin. Reporters writing for the leading newspapers and magazines acknowledged that, as the scion of the Dowling fortune, he was filling in for his father, whose obligations to his partnerships in globally-empowered oil and steel corporations, to a finance committee that he chaired for the United States government, and to a wide array of architectural commissions often sent him and his senior staff to locations as disparate as Washington, D. C.; Melbourne; Madrid; and Johannesburg. The journalists were subtle. They avoided incendiary words that could bring Liam Dowling's wrath upon them and rancorous lawsuits. There was no need for outspoken words. The photographs, with their romantic implications, carried their own suggestive narratives. Gavin Dowling, paired as he often was with beautiful Sara, might be filling in for his father in more intimate places than ski slopes, banquet halls, and theater premieres.

In the spring of the eighth year, Liam did discover their betrayal of him. Or, rather, the security guard in his employ discovered them *in flagrante delicto*, when he quietly entered the master bedroom of their townhouse at The Dorchester in London. The boom of thunder and the flare of lightning had overtaken the rain-swept afternoon. Whether it was the howl of the wind or the blare of thunder or the jagged streaks of lightning outside the panoramic window or the intensity of his and Sara's copulation that prevented him from hearing the security guard entering the room, he did not know for certain. Whatever the case, the guard entered the room without attracting his or Sara's notice and quickly photographed their naked bodies in the heated ecstasy of their passion.

He was pulling out of Sara when he saw a flash of light rising over the languorous haze that had overtaken his senses. He was vaguely aware that, two or three minutes earlier, a similar light had flashed three or four times in swift succession from a distant corner of the room that was out of the range of their accurate seeing. He had thought the flashes belonged to the lightning. Now he heard Sara's startled scream, and he saw fear in her blue eyes. A big-boned, corpulent man with a flashcube camera was hovering by their bed. His six-foot, corpulent frame; his shock of steel-gray hair and his beady eyes; and the scar that twisted across the left side of his face and cut through his upper lip made him look menacing.

For a split second, their eyes met. His own stare was influenced by his surprise and by his anger. The intruder's stare was filled with malice and contempt.

"There's no need to be angry," he said, his clipped words imparting a blunt taunt. "You put on a good show."

The intruder retreated and began swiftly making his way out of the room.

"Bastard!" he heard himself cry out as he leaped from the bed.

As soon as he made contact with the carpet, he moved into a karate stance. He used his back leg to rotate his hip and shoulder, relaxed his arm and his fist, and, while targeting the impact with his second and third knuckles, made swift contact with the man that Liam had sent on their trail.

The intruder, with his massive girth, was lumbering toward the threshold of the door when he struck him down with a hard-driving punch into his back. The man keeled over, reeling in and out of consciousness as his massive frame went sprawling upon the carpet. He was about to grab hold of the intruder's camera, which had fallen a few feet away from his prostrate body, when he felt something or someone striking the side of his head. The room spun away from him, as he struggled to keep himself from falling. Vaguely, as if it came from a place that was far away, he heard Sara screaming and saw her pointing a snub-nosed revolver at a red-haired youth with a blackjack in his right hand. After that, he heard the sounds of a pistol being fired. A man groaned in angry protest. His reeling senses guessed that the guttural rasp belonged to the red-haired youth whose hard-bodied leanness was wavering before him. Whether the youth keeled over, he had no way of knowing. In that instant, the room hurled itself upward, and he himself was plunged into darkness.

When he saw the light once more, Sara was kneeling by him, comforting his bruised head with a cold compress.

"They've gone," she whispered. "They've taken the camera with them. I could have killed both of them. But killing them would not have helped us. The police would become involved. "

There flashed across his awareness both an ambivalent pleasure and a muted sadness that his father would know for certain that Sara and he had betrayed him. When he tried to respond to Sara's news, he could not find the words that would convey his conflicted feelings.

"Liam," was all he could say.

"It's too late for regrets," Sara said. "What's done is done."

Her voice, though steady, was fraught with a melancholy not unlike his own.

Now she helped him to stand up and make his way to the edge of the bed. For a few minutes, after they covered their nakedness with bathrobes, they sat together in silence while she adjusted the cool compress and also dabbed his face with an even cooler washcloth.

"I don't regret any of it," he answered her. "His knowing about us doesn't change things between you and me. My father will make plenty of trouble. He is a hard man. Things are finished between him and me. But it can't be helped."

"No," Sara said, echoing his bitterness, though hers carried, still, a tremulous edge. "It can't be helped."

His senses were reeling again, and, in spite of the cold compress that Sara had placed upon his head, the pain of the blow that his father's henchman had inflicted felt raw and stinging. Nevertheless, he offered Sara words that meant to solace her.

"We'll soldier through," he said. "We'll make a life together without disguises or secrecy."

"It won't be easy," Sara said. "I know your father even better than you do. He is not going to make a big scandal. The newspapers will not have a field day. Your father will keep everything out of the newspapers. But he will probably tell a few of his most powerful friends. He will make certain that all the 'right' people turn away from us."

"We'll have new friends. We'll make a new life in Europe or in South America. Companies will hire me because I'm a good architect. I know my way around. I'll make things work for us. Besides, I don't need my father's money. My mother left me money. That will be more than enough to keep us living in style."

He noticed her studious regard of him. She was searching his face for the truth that his words had concealed. She did not believe the words that had casually dismissed the pain that they were inflicting upon his father and the ingrained love that he felt for him.

"But what about your bond with your father?" she asked, still searching for the truth that he was withholding from her and from himself. "I know how important he is to you. I know that, even when you have resisted his influence over your life, you have always sought his approval. And what about your plan to share his power?"

He paused, as if he needed to steady himself while standing at the edge of a precipice. One step forward and he would enter a reality that was going to drop him a long way down. He felt his voice tightening. An eerie stillness overtook him until her searching glance induced him to speak, though not before he found the matter-of-fact words that might disguise his unease.

"I'll have to get used to his not being there for me. I'll have to tough it out. I'm not going to have some of the things that I expected to have."

"We'll have enough," she said, caressing his broad shoulder as she encouraged him. "There's the half-million dollars that my parents gave Craig and me as a wedding gift. There is also an equal amount that I received from Craig's estate after he died. You must remember, too, that my books have brought me a small fortune."

Her words brought him no comfort. Her millions of dollars could not mitigate the kinds of losses that he was calculating.

"Things will be different for us, no matter how much money we have."

Sara knew how difficult everything was going to be for him. Once again, with her sorrowful voice, she accused herself of wrongs that could not be undone.

"I'm to blame," she said, her eyes filling with tears for the years of infidelity that could not be undone. "I started this thing between us. You were too young to realize what you were getting into."

"I knew," he said. "I knew even then. I have no regrets."

She took hold of his right hand and, bringing it to her lips, gently kissed it. Her voice was a plea for his understanding.

"I couldn't help myself. You made me feel alive again. I am so sorry. Remember that I told you so, when you begin to hate me for what I have done to you and to your father."

Understated and cool-headed, he resisted the path onto which she was leading him. He wanted no more of her recriminations.

"There is nothing to forgive," he said. "The important thing is to fight our way through the trouble my father is going to make for us."

"I'll do my best," she said, "as long as you stay with me."

But Liam did not make trouble. Nor did he disinherit them, or banish them from his life. He did not even confront them with accusations and threats. He never mentioned the photos of their lovemaking or the security guards he had sent to gather proof of their betrayal. His henchmen had delivered a warning to them. They must end their romantic relationship. They must stay out of each other's bed. They must repair their tattered bond with him. He was going to help them. He was going to make certain that they stayed away from each other.

"You need a change," his father told him in their first meeting together after the henchmen had caught them in bed. "You have grown too sure of yourself here. You need new challenges. You need different locations that will test you further. I am sending you to Berlin and, after that, to Rio de Janeiro. You are a man who needs to go forward. You want to climb to the top of the mountain. Here is your chance. Use it well. Treat your staff with patience and kindness, but hold them to the highest standards. Always be hardest with yourself. Remember. The world may forgive you a first failure. But, if you fail a second time, not even your closest friends will forgive you."

That spring of 1972, his father sent him away for two years. There was no sentimental departure from this man whose trust he had betrayed. Nor was he allowed a private farewell with Sara. How could there be any private moment between them? Sara was not his mother, and she was no longer his mistress. She was his father's wife. She was the jewel that added luster to his father's wealth. Except for their public relations meetings during fashionable occasions that took place around the globe, he did not socialize with his father or Sara. He did not see them even privately. But his father was keeping an eye on him. Flinty and ambivalent, his father despised him because of his betrayal. But, because they shared the same blood and because he remembered all the years when he had been a loyal son, he was going to forgive him his first offense. At least, he imagined that his father was willing to forgive him. He was, after all, Liam Dowling's son. He was the heir to the Dowling fortune. His father wanted him to succeed. He was willing to forgive him his carnal indiscretion if, as a young, enterprising man of the world, he became a tremendous Dowling success.

He made a success with the Dowling team in Berlin. He stayed in Germany for a year and then, at his father's behest, moved on to Rio de Janeiro. During this two-year period, his father kept sending him memos about the strategies that he must invoke to win important clients and to consolidate the positive relations that the Dowling Corporation had built with other companies. Occasionally, his father sent him words of praise, via cablegrams and airmail correspondence. But never did he telephone him, or send him a handwritten note of congratulation. They shared conversations only when they met during business meetings in various parts of the globe and when they joined convivial guests at lavish parties and at stately ceremonies. For the time being, at least, Liam chose not to express any new words to him face to face.

Then, in the third year of their strained relations, his father suffered a heart attack at the Dowling corporate office in New York. After a team of renowned cardiologists saved him, his father relented and called him home.

"I won't last much longer," his father told him, with no evidence of self-pity or regret and with the face and body of a rangy man gone pale and gaunt. "That is why I want you here. I'm going to show you how to fit in with the best minds in this organization. I am going to test you even further. You have always been spot-on. You know how to be ruthless—a little. Now my team and I will show you how to be more tough-minded than you have ever been. With me at your side, you will learn how to wield and expand your power and how to keep it."

The sight of his father startled him. There, in his hospital bed, propped against the white swell of pillows and tethered to a network of tubes, he appeared vulnerable and even finished. Now the memory of the strong bond that he had shared with his father flashed before him, like a ghost that had come there to watch him as he moved closer to his father and touched his hand. For a moment, while he looked with wary regret upon his father, he clenched his jaw and held his face very still to keep from crying. Penitent though he was, he understood that his father wanted many things from him. But he did not want a show of emotion. When he found the words that he wanted to tell his father, however, his husky voice broke a little.

"I'll do whatever you ask of me," he said. "I'll be whoever you want me to be."

His father was studying him carefully. Perhaps, he recognized his grief as genuine. But his father's eyes did not mist. Nor did he bid him to move even closer so that he might hug him. Instead, he grew very still. The morning sun softly touched his enervated features and, just for an instant, his father's face looked like an apparition or a death mask. When, at last, he spoke, he summoned brisk and matter-of-fact words.

"Well," he said. "I see that you are learning how to be a good son again."

Still he went on observing him with penetrating gaze. The hint of a sneer, yoked as it was to muted disdain, touched the right corner of his mouth.

"Now you will have to learn something even more important. You will have to become a craftier leader. Thus far, you have done well enough, in your way. You have a gift for concealing your arrogance. You are honing skillfully the deviousness that will push you to even more formidable success. Keep on learning. Keep remembering that the corporate world gives no quarter to hesitation or failure. Ride roughshod over all your competitors, without the self-recrimination that weakens the will and makes folly out of your ambitions."

His father's harsh words stung at his conscience. He had not forgiven him his betrayal. Yet, in spite of this sudden flare of his father's bitterness, he would stay the course. He wanted his father's love. He wanted his forgiveness.

"I thought that you liked the way that I have been

making things work for me," he said. His voice was low, yet husky with nearly repressed emotion.

"Of course, I like what you have accomplished. You have made a favorable impression. You have earned the respect of my team. But there is so much more that you need to learn. There is so much more that you need to do before you earn your place with the champions—with all the men and a few women who would crush anyone who gets in their way."

His father refused to give him his due. He was determined not to recognize his son's merit. This was part of the punishment that he was meting out to him because he had broken the bond between them. He was no longer a loyal son. He was a stranger disguised as a son.

So he perceived, while his sorrow-laden awareness compelled him to defend himself. This time he did not hold back his own bitter feelings. This time he expressed his otherwise hidden disdain for his father's knavery. Wily even in his protest, he harnessed his anger to a taut control. His words carried, as well, the vague self-hatred that sometimes burned through his soul because he so readily deferred to his father's will.

"You say that I am not devious enough. Don't I have any other choice? What ever happened to fair play? Isn't there a place for honesty and for collaboration?"

"Not if you want to be Number One," his father shot back. "Not when you are fighting to stay at the top."

"I'm no innocent," he answered him. "You already know that. I've kicked plenty of adversaries out of my way. I've lied to well-meaning executives who have trusted me. I've hoodwinked jaded CEOs who thought that they might climb onto my bandwagon and reap the spoils. I haven't liked myself for doing so. But chicanery and deviousness come with the territory. They are part of the game. Nevertheless and in spite of what you are telling me, I do not care to be devious all of the time. There have to be moments when I can be truly human. There have to be days when I can be the real Gavin Dowling again."

"Ah, but there is the puzzle. Who are you, really? You admit that you are no longer innocent. The unblemished man that you imagine you are no longer exists. You have entered an unforgiving battlefield. You can't afford to hold back or to flinch when you are striking at the brutes, thugs, and other primitives who wear custom-tailored suits and expensive watches. You know all these things. You have won a battle or two. Stop thinking that you can return to untested innocence and unblemished honor. Once you have made your pact with the devil, you have to live with him."

His father's harsh words, rendered with even-tempered calm, further provoked his resistance. He did not want to relinquish the ideal self that he still carried within the secret recesses of his heart. He did not care to make his pact with the devil irrevocable. Was he condemned to live with the devil forever?

"Maybe," he said, answering his father's blunt appraisal with clear-eyed willfulness. "Maybe not."

His father noticed his resistance. Ambivalent and judgmental, he goaded him further.

"Your cousin Aaron will win big far more easily than you. He has a cruel streak. He is rough at the edges when it suits him. He is greedy for success. He will stop at nothing to get what he wants. He even knows how to pick the right woman. He's teamed up with Lauren Winters because she's rich and because he can use her to push himself forward. You can learn a great deal from Aaron. Keep your eye on him. He is your main competitor. He is a callous man who is moving to the top."

This was not the first time that his father tried to stir his envy of Aaron. Envy can become hatred. Hate leads to all kinds of dissension. His father had chosen Aaron as a second son. Possibly, he regarded Aaron as a substitute for *him*—the son that had forfeited his bond with the father who had always loved him. It was, in fact, altogether plausible that Liam Dowling would make Aaron his only son. He imagined, though, that, after he— the biological son and in his mind the only authentic son—slept with Liam's young, second wife, his father had no affection for sons, biological or makeshift.

To maintain his peace with his father, whose acceptance he still craved, he met his praise of Aaron with cool-headed irony.

"You are right," he said. "Aaron is a devious man. He is a master of disguise. I can learn so much from him."

His father smiled, pleased at his seeming acquiescence. Even tough-minded young men have to learn the art of parrying remarks that bruise one's spirit, if not the soul.

Despite this unsettling encounter with him, he worked even harder to win his father's forgiveness. He drew the most prominent clients away from his father's competitors. He won international praise for his new building projects in San Francisco, Chicago, Brazil, and Hong Kong. Then, quite unexpectedly, as though the wall between them tumbled away or a truce had been signed by each of them, his father drew closer to him. Whether it was a realistic awareness of his frail health that influenced this new surge of forgiveness, he could not tell. Possibly, it was his recollection of all the favorable years that they had shared as generous father and dutiful son. Or, maybe, a weary impatience with brooding and bitterness had reawakened his need to be once again the father who regarded his son with untrammeled affection and with genuine pride.

It was during these early months of 1975 that he, Gavin Dowling, the scapegrace son who had hurt his father so deeply, came to believe that Liam Dowling had consented to love him again. These were months in which he felt reborn as the rightful heir and deserving recipient of his father's acceptance. He clung to the happiness that derived from this new cycle of their relationship, understanding nonetheless that happiness is tenuous and fleeting.

For more than a year, his father rallied. He appeared well. He gained a bit of weight. He led the Dowling Corporation with newfound stamina. He drove himself, once again, with the fierce tenacity that had always accompanied his venturing through the world. Rigorous and discerning, his father continued to mentor him, the son he used to call "Gavin Will-Be-Great," devising tests that challenged his capacities and that sharpened his insights. Working with his father and with a team of senior executives, he reaffirmed his early promise as a man who was moving up the ladder not merely because he was Liam Dowling's son, but especially because he anchored his wily energies to steel-true self-possession and charismatic persuasiveness.

On those days when his father appeared to have recovered much of his lost vigor, they sailed in Nantucket waters, fished in Nova Scotia, and co-piloted a Cessna Skyhawk from New York to Maryland. Sara was never with them. The *raison-d'être* of these excursions was the strengthening of their bond as father and son. This was to be their "year of alterations," his father told him at the start of this new cycle in their relationship—this cautious *rapprochement*, this restoration of discarded loyalty and broken trust. He must work to make their new time a solid reaffirmation of the original bond between them that, until his affair with Sara, had remained unsullied. The veracity of his filial conduct would lend more than a borrowed conviction to their new alliance.

"You have found your better self," his father told him on a later afternoon when they had met for lunch at The Hotel Pierre in New York. "Your discipline and your ambition bring me much pleasure."

He answered his father in kind, his controlled inflections melding with the soft rhythms of a distant piano and the *sotto voce* conversations at the tables around them.

"I am proud to be your son," he said. "I will never again let you down."

True to his promise, he stayed away from Sara. No longer did they meet in countryside hideaways in Vermont and Provence or within the glamorous privacies of hotel rooms in Paris, London, and New York. Whenever he happened to see her—at a concert in London's Albert Hall, for instance, or at a Dowling *soirée* in Buenos Aires—he noticed that Sara looked more beautiful than ever. His father was often at her side, his ingrained self-possession complementing her well-calibrated demureness. Always, dutiful and guilt-racked son that he was, he willed himself to exchange polite and even casual remarks with her and with Liam. Always, he was aware of the melancholy in her blue eyes whenever she glanced at him. Always, for days afterward, he yearned for her, his memories of their lovemaking intensifying his desire and leaving him bitter and bereft. But never would he try to renew their intimacy. His guilt at having betrayed his father was more powerful even than his desire for Sara.

Instead, he continued to make amends for his wrongdoing. He brought to his father's corporation new, prestigious clients from Boston, Chicago, and San Francisco. He mentored poor African-American youths from Brooklyn ghettos; he raised funds for cancer research in New York, Philadelphia, and Helsinki; and he sponsored and arranged for the comfortable housing of a Chinese neurosurgeon and his family in Philadelphia when they applied for American citizenship. He started to believe that he could make something worthwhile of his life. But, without Sara, he would never be happy.

In this third year of his unhappiness, his loneliness had become unbearable. Though his frequent copulation with debutantes, nightclub girls, and fashion models fed his lust, he avoided emotional involvement with his partners. He thought only of Sara. But, with self-denying aptitudes that left him uneasy and surprised, he did not seek her out. His fear that his father might, in some cruel way, bring his wrath down upon Sara kept him from her. Not only his apprehension for her wellbeing held him back. His angry fear that his father would disown him kept his rebellious inclinations subdued, as though by heavy prison chains. He did not go to her when, at a glamorous charity ball held in October 1975 within The Starlight Roof of New York's Waldorf Astoria, he saw her surrounded by a group of power brokers and their wives or their fiancées. He might have gone to her then, because Liam was in Texas, where he was negotiating lucrative business deals involving his oil fields. She was dressed in an ice blue gown, its close-fitting chiffon lace enhancing her statuesque body and the radiance of her blonde hair. Her appearance dazzled him once again, rousing his need of her and intensifying his destitution.

He did not go to her in the following December when their paths crossed in a five-star restaurant, where she was sharing lunch with her agent and her publisher while, he guessed, they were conferring about her latest book. He did not go to her then, or even in February when, from a distance, he glimpsed her fleetingly with his father's waterskiing party in Tahiti. Nor did he go to her privately in April, after he read in a New York society column that she was staying at the Pierre and granting interviews to reporters from newspapers and magazines about her latest book. In every season, his despair enfolded him like a dead man's shroud. Whatever spark of life ran through his veins quickened new self-awareness. Even when he was partying with a group of friends or copulating with a manufactured Hollywood starlet or with an authentic society girl, he was incapable of profound feelings. He might revel in the sensations of the moment and, without looking back, hurry on to the temporary flare of other vaguely familiar incidents and to the colorful flash of new, forgettable people. Yet, always, even when he attained a momentary reprieve from the punishment that his life had meted out to him, he thought about Sara. How could he forget her? She was his soul mate. She was his lifeline. She held the key to his happiness. Without her, he would be forever lost. Yet he did not go to her.

Then, quite unexpectedly in May of 1976, at three in the morning, Sara came to him. She had not asked her chauffeur to drive her to his apartment, for fear that the cadre of detectives whom Liam had set upon her every move while he was away in

China would follow her. Instead, while she was spending the weekend with friends in Connecticut, she borrowed their Bentley and made a smooth drive into Manhattan, all the while eluding any member of Liam's team who might follow her. She had entered his apartment with a key that he had given her years earlier. She found him sleeping alone in the bed that they had shared a few times. She shook him gently awake, her blue eyes filled with so much love that was haunted by melancholy.

"I had to see you," she said, as she sat at the edge of his bed. "I cannot stop loving you. I cannot be happy unless we are together at least some of the time."

To his eyes, her tense melancholy made her even more beautiful. Their mutual need of each other thrilled him. But they did not go to bed immediately. They reveled, instead, within the intimacy of their conversation at the bar in the living room of his richly appointed apartment and by means of the quick sting of their scotch whiskey.

"I'll find a way for us to be together more often," he said. "Let come what may. I'm done with self-recrimination and penitent soul-searching."

"This time, I am not going to be afraid or ashamed of our love," she promised him. "You and I are meant to be together. If Liam finds out, so be it. I would rather have you than Liam's fortune."

"If we play this game smartly," he said, "we can have each other *and* the fortune."

Their words, spoken defiantly, exhilarated them. Right after that, they went to bed with an eagerness that coiled its intensities around their renegade spirit. They went to bed often, though rarely when they were in his apartment. Usually, they met while Liam was traveling on the West Coast or out of the country. Random Chance was on their side. They always managed to conceal themselves from Liam's henchmen and from Aaron Dowling who, after that one dismaying time, had never again discovered them in bed. They concealed themselves as adroitly when they were in the company of Liam's friends and when they were partying with all the other persons who belonged to their privileged circle. Always, they disguised their intimacy. With a poise that melded its assurance with a nearly imperceptible cynicism, Sara brought genteel conviction to her role as Liam's dutiful wife. He, in turn—Liam's errant son—expressed a well-modulated deference when they appeared in public together. Never were they alone. Sara made certain that, on those occasions when Liam could not be with her, she was paired with married couples young and older from New York, Palm Beach, and San Francisco, or with the distinguished guests from Washington, London, and Melbourne who were being honored at a society ball or at the premiere of a Hollywood epic or at a government awards ceremony. As canny as Sara, he often appeared in public with beautiful, young women whom he did not love and who rarely expected more from him than a festive evening that he made even more palatable when he gave them a diamond necklace or an emerald brooch and when he made love with them that was as vigorous as it was cold-hearted.

Sara gave no evidence of being aware of his sexual escapades. He imagined that, because she was a bright and cultivated woman, she understood that his frequent partners satisfied his large appetite without winning his love. He was pleased that her separation from him increased the fervency of her desire. Although her experience of Liam and of him had taught her to be more knowing about love's various betrayals and depredations, she idealized nonetheless the passionate relationship that she was enjoying with *him*—the secretly rebellious stepson who was merely five years her junior. A happy Fate had brought them together, teaching her how to revise the narrow laws of love. She was learning to be a free spirit. She was more lighthearted now when she was with him. Her face glowed with the excitement of being completely happy.

No longer did she dwell upon the darker truth of their affair. Her happiness betrayed the bond that she had made with Liam. But, though that betrayal was a bitter indictment of her moral status, she had taught herself to turn away from the guilt that was shadowing her. He, Liam's errant son, had brought joy into her life. After so many years of grieving the loss of her beloved, first husband and after the long months and years of her loveless union with Liam, she had fallen in love again. He— Gavin Dowling, Liam's sometime dutiful son who became her lover—was, she told him, her rescuer. In her own way, she was the drowning woman that he saved. She was the sleeping, young widow who was wakened to new life by his kiss. It did not matter anymore that, for now, they would have to share their love in secret. In years to come, after Liam had lived out the natural span of his life, they would marry. She did not wish Liam dead. She was going to do all the right things that would help him to attain the rational happiness that he sought. In these same years, she would enjoy the passionate love that she had known only once before. She would be with him, Gavin Dowling, savoring the willfulness and the ecstasy of their rebellion.

"We'll have days and days together," she promised him, "and nights that are meant for us alone."

For the rest of that year, as though her words were a magical prophecy, they did enjoy their surreptitious love. Always, in these months, they were circumspect in their private meetings and equally disciplined in their conduct toward each other when they found themselves at the same social occasions. Appearing serene and self-possessed, Sara was most often accompanied by Liam. Sometimes, when Liam was away on business, she accepted as her escort a visiting foreign diplomat or a renowned poet or an inspired scientist that her glamorous dinners and her sumptuous dances were honoring. He, the Dowling heir, whose every move more than a few ambitious journalists and several inquisitive members of their circle carefully observed, invariably attended these occasions with one of his temporary girlfriends. Reflecting afterwards on all that was to happen, he was surprised that both Sara and he had accepted, as if it were the natural order of things, their careful betrayal of his father and their wild gambling with the chance that he might uncover this second cycle of betrayal that was even more pernicious because it expressed their subtle contempt for his forgiveness of their earlier transgression.

At the close of these seven months—to his mind quite suddenly because he was not expecting it—his father died. While he was sleeping, his heart stopped. He died a peaceful death. At least, his cardiologist thought so. But he—the wayward son who had slept with his father's young wife—thought differently. The knowledge of his wife's infidelity and of his son's deception had weighed heavily upon his father. Though he suppressed the outward show of his feelings, his father grieved his way through sleepless nights and equally unhappy days. Had his father become aware of Sara's and his new betrayal? He wondered, understanding nevertheless that the gravity of their first offense was sufficient cause for destroying his father's peace. His father could have ruined their prospects or even devised their murders. Instead, as if subverting his ruthless disposition, he chose never to mention their transgressions. His silence in the face of their betrayal was a grueling experiment that he willed himself to endure. Finally, the experiment, with its fabricated scenario, was too punishing. The burden of silence that it engendered sealed his fate. He did not murder his unfaithful wife and his wily son. But, by means of their various deceptions, they murdered him. They stole his peace. They tarnished his self-respect. They cut into the secret recesses of his heart and drained away the life-blood of his self-belief, his arrogance, his unscrupulous ambition, and his very existence.

So Gavin told himself, imagining that his treachery and Sara's had breached some fault line in his father's authority, some hairline fracture in his power.

Liam's funeral was a stately occasion that took place at Saint Thomas Episcopal Church on Fifth Avenue in New York. Jaded CEOs from the leading, global corporations were there. Many other power brokers were there, too: slick Wall Street wheeler-dealers; well-honed athletes who had become celebrity hucksters; movie studio moguls who peddled comic book epics and the glossy superstars who appeared in them; renowned architects, musicians, and playwrights whose work Liam had supported; and equally famous surgeons and lawyers. An Anglican bishop, whose popularity derived from his television show and his best-selling, inspirational books, presided at the memorial ceremony; and his uncle, the Reverend Ryan Dowling—the Spartan and understated missionary who was

Liam's brother—flew in from Northern Rhodesia to recite a moving eulogy and to express his gratitude for the generous financial support that Liam had lately made to several charities and building projects that were a part of Reverend Dowling's mission in South Africa.

Guilt-racked and remorseful, he—the son who had failed his father's trust—remembered even now, as though they were happening for the first time, all of these things that were part of his father's funeral. He recalled, as well, the sounds of weeping from the upright matrons and loyal secretaries who had admired his father's ingenuity and his gallantry. He heard the choir singing "Amazing Grace," "Lift High the Cross," "A Mighty Fortress Is Our God," and "All Things Bright and Beautiful." He studied, uneasily once more, the pensive stillness of his cousin Aaron, whom his father regarded as his "second son." He saw again, on a table near the chancel steps, the gold urn that contained his father's ashes. But eclipsing all of these images was the beautiful face and perfect figure of Sara, her blonde beauty even more striking in a black chiffon dress and a black cashmere coat. She, too, was pensive, but her melancholy worked like a fuse igniting her radiance. That her parents were flanking her was all to the good. Their staid presence deflected the sensual implications of her glamour.

Two weeks later, after returning from a business trip to California, he sat next to Sara in their lawyer's office during the reading of Liam's will. The intricacies of that will reflected his father's decision to forgive Sara her infidelity. At the same time, the will revealed Liam's ambivalence toward him and his calculated endorsement of Aaron as his rival. Meticulously drawn up by a team of shrewd lawyers, the will gave Sara access to five hundred million dollars, which was a third of his estate. It also bestowed upon him an equal share. His father left the remaining third of the estate to Aaron, with an important condition. Aaron would not receive his share for fifteen years. Should either Aaron or he die before that time, or even afterward without a wife or children, his portion of the estate would be divided between Sara and the surviving male heir.

A superficial assessment of the will suggested that, without reservation, his father endorsed him as a worthy son. His treatment of Aaron was another matter. His father had left Aaron a great deal of money. But, as though it were a perverse way of reminding Aaron that he was not, after all, an authentic son, the will teased Aaron with an inheritance to which he had no claim for fifteen long years. He was not a son at all. He was a second-class individual. He was the poor nephew that Liam Dowling had decided to bring into the big money, eventually.

There was more to the will than that surface information. Beneath its careful apportioning of Liam Dowling's wealth, the language of the will, with its secret malice and dangerous motives, meant to ignite Aaron's hatred of him as the only son and inveterate rival whose existence stood in the way of his attaining the immense wealth that Liam had left him. Only if he died soon could Aaron instantly claim his inheritance. His awareness of the dark implications of the will left him brooding for weeks after the lawyers had read its intricate terms, as if they were reciting them with hushed and raspy inflections in a Hall of Justice. Filled with remorse because he had failed his father's trust, he began imagining that, in spite of its generous bequests, the will conveyed with cunning legality and equivocating language his father's hatred of him. His father had not forgiven him. In fact, even in death he was inciting Aaron to kill him.

So, during his most anguished days, he told himself.

He began carrying a snub-nosed revolver inside the secret pocket of his jackets. Always, at night, he placed the revolver beneath his pillow—a habit he had adopted ever since Liam had sent his henchman after Sara and him. For weeks at a time, he stayed unhappy. He was a stranger to himself, falling down and down through a bottomless well.

After that meeting in the lawyer's office, he did not see Sara for eight months. He was racked by guilt and by nightmares in which his father rose from the grave and entered his bedroom to cry out his curse upon him. Whether it was his guilt that held him back from seeing Sara or whether it was his contempt and hatred of himself, he could never fathom in those uneasy nights when he confronted over and over again all the occasions in which he had betrayed his father. Eventually, because his will to go on living exceeded and eclipsed his self-recriminations, he stopped having nightmares. His season of grieving was over. Once more, he began to think of his love for Sara. Once again, he admitted that, without Sara, he would always be lost. He had to see her.

So, at last, he arranged a meeting with her.

Now, on this early afternoon in September 1977, when his recollection of their complicated love affair had confirmed the rightness of his decision, he joined her for lunch in the main dining room of the Ritz-Carlton. The plush ambiance of the room subdued, at least a little, whatever tension he and Sara were feeling as they experienced the first hour of their reunion with each other. The room and all of its careful amenities smoothly accommodated the urgency that lay at the heart of this first encounter between them.

Sara, as much as he, wanted this luncheon to be very special. She suggested, as it was her habit, that he order lunch for them, and he was pleased to do so. They began with glasses of Dom Pérignon and afterward enjoyed a spinach-and-ham quiche and sea bass with mushrooms and cream. About them, waiters moved with deft subtleties and attended their every need.

In the distance, a young and good-looking pianist was bringing melodic interpretations to Cole Porter, Jerome Kern, and George Gershwin. Nearer than that, at meticulously arranged tables, business colleagues as well as husbands and wives appeared by turns to be self-assured, convivial, and altogether contented. At the table next to theirs, a stylish middle-aged couple occasionally looked up from their meal and observed them with studious interest. Perhaps, he thought, they recognized Sara and him. Pictures of them, sometimes paired together but usually partnered with other well-regarded companions or with groups of world-renowned guests, often appeared in newspapers and magazines because of the Dowling name and because they were involved in the glamorous social occasions in New York.

Sara and he began by conversing about many things. She spoke briskly of the new book that she was writing. She described with accurate details and with genuine appreciation the places that she saw and the people that she met during her recent travels to Argentina, Hong Kong, and New Zealand. She summarized with assured brevity her work alongside the expert New York team that Liam had chosen to carry forward the goals of his philanthropic foundation. He, in turn, told her about his most recent and still ongoing architectural commissions in Chicago and in Santa Barbara. He mentioned playing polo in Argentina and kayaking in Finland. He talked of his piloting of a new Cessna 206.

Now two waiters were briskly around them, serving them souffléed crêpes flamed with cointreau. They merely nibbled at the crêpes. Nor had they eaten much of the delicious quiche or the excellent sea bass. The excitement of the hour had stolen away their appetite. Soon enough, though, he admitted to himself why Sara and he had no interest in the meal. Each of them was waiting to speak the words that had been on their minds all through the luncheon. No sooner had he begun to eat the crêpes, then he put down his fork.

"Things will be different between us," he said. "I am never again going to run away from what we mean to each other. I am finished with the nightmares and the guilt that has haunted me for so long. What's done is done. When two people fall in love, somebody else may get hurt. It can't be helped. You were meant for me, not for Liam."

His words pleased Sara. But their emotional intensity did not dispel her doubts about his readiness to leave behind him the wayward scenes of their past.

"Are you quite certain that you have conquered Liam's ghost? Can you trust yourself to go forward with me, even though we cannot really forgive ourselves for deceiving Liam?"

He answered her quickly, without hesitation or misgiving.

"I've never been more certain of anything. Nothing comes easy. Nobody is innocent. All of us are tarnished. All of us are guilty. That's the way things are. That is who we are. If there is a heaven, I don't want it if I can't be with you here on earth. Everything without you would be hell to me."

Sara beamed with a delight that she had shown him in only the extraordinary moments that they had shared. The quiet force of his words thrilled her. His words made her believe that, through profound loneliness or tough-minded determination or a newly acquired hardheartedness, he had exorcised his ghosts. So he imagined. Nor did her new words dissuade him from that thought.

"You and I are going to have a grand life together," she said, while modulating her elation with her genteel voice. "Everything will be in the open now. There is no need for disguise or deception. We are free to tell the world that we are in love with each other."

They decided to tell the world in this very instant. They drank champagne. He brushed her lips with a gentle kiss. They hummed along while the pianist sang a ballad about the love that lasts forever. Their faces beamed with the new happiness that they were claiming for themselves. The sophisticated couples and the adept businessmen looked up from their lunches and smiled with varying degrees of nostalgia, surprise, and good will. For that moment, at least, the world appeared to be on their side.

Only when they were leaving the dining room did a cloud loom over them, drawing them back into the harsher subtexts of existence. There, in the proximate distance, at a table in the north corner of the room, his cousin Aaron and his girlfriend, Lauren Winters, were engaged in a tense and unhappy conversation. Aaron, as wily as ever, was resisting whatever petition Lauren was making. She, in turn, looked worn down and fearful. The two of them did not see Sara and him. Nor did he and Sara care to intrude upon their unhappy scene. Instead, they made their way quickly out of the dining room. Neither of them mentioned afterwards the emotional turmoil of Lauren's expression or the arbitrariness of Aaron's detachment. To do so, he felt, would have blighted the romantic glow and the idealized expectations that the hour had granted them. Nevertheless, his witnessing that unhappy moment between Lauren and Aaron left him uneasy. With blunt emphasis, the sight of Lauren's sorrowful and nearly desperate face brought him back to the real world that he and Sara had eluded for that one, extraordinary hour in the dining room of the Ritz Carleton. He wanted to believe that he and Sara, together, had won the golden cup. He wanted to believe that Sara and he were going to be happy forever.

But he could not convince himself that Lauren would ever be happy. He knew enough about human nature to read correctly its ambiguous dispositions. He felt that, in that moment when she was imploring Aaron to listen to her, he—Gavin Dowling, who had met her only a few times—understood Lauren Winters very well. Fear had overtaken her, and bitter desperation was burning through her soul.

Chapter Seven
Schemes, Disguises, & Traps

Bryce pointed his snub-nosed revolver at Lauren's head, as she lay sleeping uneasily against the soft pillows of her bed. The revolver's polished-blue barrel gleamed inside the light of the moon that, with sinuous tentacles, entered the room from two large windows that flanked a reclining nude woman in a Renoir canvas on the wall and overlooked the autumn-speckled night colors of Central Park fourteen stories below. Lauren, he knew, welcomed the light—not only the light of the moon, but also the light that, with more reliable capacities, shone from the lamp on the table beside her bed. Often, though not always, the light from the moon, as though it were a hastening motion, pushed away the darkness, unless a lingering cloud dimmed its radiance and then concealed its light. On those nights, the moon suddenly vanished, a guardian power that betrayed its promise of safety. But the lamplight seldom failed her. It served as an ally, a loyal sentry that revealed familiar objects and the trusted surfaces of things. On this night, the moon and the lamplight collaborated. They suggested, even as they disguised, the accurate dimensions of the room and its luxurious components.

He knew this room well. For nearly a year, he had shared Lauren's bed and all the other amenities here that solaced his angry spirit, if only intermittently. Upon entering, he quickly scanned the rose-dust walls with gray window trim and the pleated silk draperies. The upholstered walls created a cocooned effect that quieted the sounds of midtown Manhattan and offered the illusion of safety. He noticed the scaled down cornice moldings, the shallow tray ceiling, and the Beauvais carpet. Once more, situated as it was in the proximate distance near a southerly window, he recognized the Regency center table, a vase of fresh red roses, and the Swedish neoclassical armchairs. He and Lauren had often breakfasted at that table, rather than on the terrace in the east wing of the penthouse that looked out upon Fifth Avenue. They had enjoyed the painterly view of the park, and Lauren had savored the feeling of being enclosed within a privacy that kept the world away in the early morning hours. As his glance took in the north corner of the room, he saw the 1890 Dutch table on which Lauren had usually placed her gifts to him: a gold Swiss watch, the keys to a Maserati, airline tickets for their trip to Rio de Janeiro, and checkbooks for a bank account that she had opened for him and that held the fifty thousand dollars that she had placed in it. The Dutch table was much more than an ordinary table. With its steady supply of gifts, it was an emblem of Lauren's favor, a sign of her generosity, and a symbol of the intimate bond between them. More lately, though, as a continuing repository of her gifts to him, the table was a telling proof of her fear. Implicated so deeply in his conflicted relationship with Lauren, the sight of the table displaced at least momentarily, there on the upholstered wall above it, Matisse's 1942 canvas of a young woman with flowing dark hair and swanlike neck who was wearing a sleeveless evening dress of gray chiffon that had a plunging neckline. Though she sat leaning into a chair, somnolent and reflective, she could not suppress her sensuality, which was vivid and palpable.

All these things—the lamplight and the light of the moon, the Regency table and its vase of roses, the silk draperies and upholstered walls, the cornice moldings and the Beauvais carpet, the Renoir and the Matisse—he noticed while, with quick yet furtive movements, he hurried into the bedroom after making his way through a flowing array of spacious rooms that also revealed themselves within the watchful glow of soft lamplight and the gleam of the crescent moon that sent its light through and beyond the panoramic windows. With the key that Lauren had given him a year earlier, he had come into the building from the private rear entrance. Another key gave him access to the elevator that brought him, two hours after midnight, to an equally private hallway, and a third key opened the main door of the apartment. Because of his familiarity with the apartment and because of his quick pace, the rooms hurried past him like a busy montage. Only when he arrived at the door to Lauren's bedroom did he allow himself to pause. The possibility that she might not be alone did not deter him or even alarm him. With the Colt Cobra .38 Special in his hand, he was prepared to meet any adversary who challenged him.

As far as he knew, Aaron Dowling had boarded a nine-thirty flight on the previous evening that was bound for Palm Beach. But Dowling's plans could have changed. He might be in the bedroom with Lauren. If that were so, if Dowling's plans had changed and he was, instead, sleeping beside Lauren or making love to her, he—Bryce Thompson, the man that Lauren had casually loved for nearly a year and, just as casually, had betrayed—would kill both Dowling and Lauren. Then, he would kill himself. Until last night, he had been waiting for Lauren to marry Dowling. Once that happened, he was prepared to wait a few months longer—maybe, even a year—before he killed him. He had willed himself to be patient. When so much money was involved, he could be very patient. Only in that way could he and Lauren win two fortunes. Only by playing the waiting game would their schemes and traps work.

But, early that morning, *The Herald Tribune* published a front-page story that told him what he had long suspected. Lauren and Aaron Dowling were married. They had been married for five months. The reporter who made the discovery had traveled to Rhode Island to research Newport's public records for an unrelated story. Only by chance did he come upon the information that told him of the marriage. Years earlier, Lauren's father had sued this same reporter for writing stories that portrayed Lauren as self-centered and promiscuous. Lauren's father won the lawsuit, and the reporter lost his job. Now, while working for a different newspaper and without fear of being sued because he was providing his readers with the facts, the reporter drew from those facts damaging innuendos and ambiguous subtexts. The main text of the newspaper article told of Lauren's painful rehabilitation and her continuing struggle to stay drug-free. But the headline anchored the story to Lauren's scandalous past and to her problematic mating with an ambitious architect from a conservative corporation: "High society nightclub girl flees troubled past and marries rising Dowling executive."

That headline, he imagined, had cost Lauren and him a fortune. It had rendered their schemes null and void. It had uncovered her recent disguise as a demure woman. This newspaper story had brought her past scandals into the present. By marrying Aaron Dowling in secret and without her brother Calden's approval, Lauren had destroyed her chance of claiming the forty million dollars that her brother and his lawyers had been willing to grant her on the condition that she enhance, rather than scandalize, the family name.

Maybe, her brother and his lawyers would applaud her marriage to a man who was making a success as an architect. Maybe, they saw in Aaron Dowling not only the husband who could tamp down Lauren's wildness, but also the inheritor of one-third of Liam Dowling's fortune.

Maybe not...

What was certain was Lauren's betrayal. She had fallen in love with Dowling. She had married him in secret because she had no intention of going through with the trap that they had set for him. Aaron Dowling was going to be a wealthy man. Lauren did not need her family's money. With Dowling, she would have a life of luxury.

Once more, this thought infuriated him. She was closing him out of her life. She was leaving him behind, the ne'er-do-well who was always reaching for the brass ring and coming up short. For the past fourteen hours, he kept his fury at bay. At first, right after he learned that a business assignment had drawn Dowling to Florida for a week, he planned to wait until Dowling returned, so that he could kill him and Lauren at the same time. But by early afternoon, inflamed as he was because of her betrayal, he changed his mind about waiting until Dowling returned from Florida. If Dowling was really in Florida, he was going to leave him out of the picture. Dowling was a hated adversary. But Dowling had not betrayed him. It was Lauren who had messed with him. It was Lauren who had shut him out, casting him away as if he were a self-deluded outsider or an embarrassing intruder. In her eyes, he was a clueless failure who invited her secret contempt and whom she did not care to have in her life. Though she still feared him, she believed that she could safely trick him. She had found in Dowling an unwitting partner in her trickery. Without knowing his importance in her scheme, Dowling had become the agent of her escape.

He would not allow Lauren to escape. Nor would he wait to move against her. He did not want to endure a week of angry regret and brooding. He did not want to be hounded any longer by the murderous thoughts that, for much of his life, had made him a stranger to himself. Nor did he intend to seek out a wealthy, young divorcée who could be very generous to a romantic and dangerous bed partner or to find a rich, glamorous widow who was willing to pay for a vigorous lover smart enough to make her believe his lies. He wanted to be through with it. He wanted to be finished. But he did not want Lauren to run free of him. The hatred that he felt for her and for himself was so intense, that he decided to act swiftly. He would kill her tonight, and—right after that—he would kill himself.

All these thoughts, shrouded as they were with bitter images, had hurried him through room after sumptuous room that carefully modulated their opulence. They were rooms that he and Lauren might have shared. They would not be borrowed rooms. They would be rooms that, had she carried out her part of their plan to do away with Dowling, he might have called his own.

His anger did not diminish his incisive awareness of things or relax his hold upon the Colt .38. With wily stillness, he had opened the door to Lauren's bedroom. He had quickly scanned the room, his tall and rugged frame poised to shoot Dowling or any of Lauren's occasional boyfriends, should they happen to be standing before him with pistols of their own. He was prepared, as well, to shoot Lauren right away, if she hurried toward him with her Enfield revolver or her Smith & Wesson pistol. She might be expecting him. Her fear would have warned her, once *The Herald Tribune* published the news of her marriage, that he would pursue her. That same fear would have prevented her from changing the locks on the doors. Had she done so, she would have instantly alerted him about her betrayal. She must have believed that she could handle him. She would devise a story meant to convince him of her loyalty. The marriage, she would tell him, was a ruse. It was an important part of the scenario that they had planned together. There were reasons why she had kept the marriage a secret even from him. He must trust her. He must not act in haste or in anger. He must stay clear-headed. He must be detached. Only in that way could they succeed. Their game was still on. Their plan to kill Dowling was moving forward. They were going to win the great treasure, the bank vaults filled with gold, the hundreds of millions of dollars.

She was playing him for a fool, of course. She was making a big mistake. Now there was no way out for them. There was no way to salvage their relationship. They were ruined. They were all used up. Or, rather, he was used up. Not Lauren. She was already running free of him. But he was not going to set her free. He was not going to let her get away. He was going to take her down with him.

Standing beside her bed now, while she lay sleeping on her back, he noticed (as he had so many other times in the year when they were often together) the exotic beauty of her face, with its olive complexion, turned-up nose, and full, sensual lips. Her head, with its flowing dark hair, was resting against an array of cream-white pillows. An azure blue nightgown, with delicate lacework, covered her firm, round breasts and her long, slim body. Apparently both restless and fearful even while sleeping, she had tossed aside the fragrant sheets. The nervous motion of her sleeping body had raised her shapely legs, as well as her nightgown. Even asleep, with her raised legs spread apart almost casually, she looked carnal and seductive. The memory of their copulation suddenly flared its vivid intensities, but only for a moment. All that was in the past. He had not slept with her for three months. In those final weeks, he had been as rough with her as he could be. Their copulation became ambivalent and fierce. But she never screamed in protest, though her vague grimace hinted at the pain that his brute thrusting and his crude handling of her breasts and her arms were inflicting upon her. She welcomed his aggression. She wanted him to bring her pain. If the pain drove her to the edge of a scream, she brought to her parted lips a gleaming, twisted smile that distorted her beauty even as it held back the scream. He did not really enjoy being rough with her in bed. He felt like a killer animal or a rancid sub-human that does not know how to love.

Yet, as reluctant as he was to admit it to himself, he loved Lauren Winters in his perverse way. He, Bryce Thompson, who treated love with wily disdain, had given at least a corner of his heart to this careless and devious woman. Until he lived through these months without her, he had concealed that ambivalent love even from himself. It wasn't only the sex that he missed. He missed all the occasions that their being together made exciting and even adventurous. He missed being with a woman who perceived the world as he did. He missed the clever ways that she resisted her vulnerability and the resourceful ways that she expressed her tough-mindedness. At first, he had merely wanted to use her. She was a means to an end. With her as a partner, he could plot his way into the wealth that his fate had always denied him. She would get her share. She would reap a fortune. Why not? She would earn it. She was going to set up Dowling. Then, he—the street-wise hustler who knew how to grab hold of a good thing—would step in and do his part. He would kill Dowling and get his share of the Dowling fortune. Because Lauren agreed to marry him after Aaron Dowling was out of the way, he was going to win even some of the Winters' money. At that time, because of the volatile subtexts of their relationship, he was not conscious of loving her. She was a promiscuous and narcissistic woman that he could use. She was his ticket to a comfortable life. If things did not work out between them, they would go their separate ways, with no hard feelings to complicate their freedom.

But, after she started seeing Dowling, he began missing her. It wasn't just the sex. He could get that from any one of the nightclub girls who enjoyed his company. He missed the fragrance of her body. He missed her dark eyes that teased his inquiry and that gave him a jagged rush of pleasure. He missed the tint of melancholy that gave her beauty a special poignancy and that suggested that she was as lost as he was. He began to regard her differently. More than a sentimental shift of his perception, his feelings for her became anchored to a need that only her presence could satisfy. He had fallen in love with her. His was not a conventional love. It was a love entangled by jealousy, domination, and brutality. Its ambivalence matched Lauren's feelings for him. But, because of their ambivalence toward each other, the love could not appease his angry heart. His realistic hold on things told him that, after the first year of their relationship, Lauren both loved and hated him. Yet in all of their secret meetings, after she started carrying forward the plot that involved Dowling, she suggested a genuine and even obsessive need for him—for *him*, Bryce Thompson, the outsider that she also feared because he was both hardhearted and devious. He did not really want to love her at all, not even in this ambivalent way. To love someone was to betray a weakness within himself. It was to let down his guard. It made him vulnerable.

He could not help himself.

It had cost him these past three months to fathom the truth. Dowling had taken his place. Lauren had married Aaron Dowling because she loved him. There would be no murder of Aaron Dowling. She was running away with him. If he—Bryce Thompson, the lover whose dangerous undercurrent she had enjoyed most of all—gave her trouble, she might be willing to pay him off. Or, maybe, she would pay someone to kill him. Possibly, while keeping herself in the clear, she would persuade the police to hunt him down as a blackmailer or a swindler—a con man who harbored murderous tendencies. In all these ways, by paying him far less than he expected or by spurning him or by setting him up to be killed or thrown into prison, she could betray him.

He wasn't going to give her that chance.

An eerie stillness overtook him now, as he stood beside her bed and aimed his revolver at her heart. The danger that she had often discerned in him rose up to overtake his more temperate will. His throat tightened. His body stiffened with hair-trigger tension. If Lauren had wakened then and, noticing him as a hovering menace, had screamed in fear or swiftly reached for the Smith and Wesson pistol that she kept in the top drawer of a bedside table, he would have fired into her all but one of the bullets from the revolver that he went on pointing at her. Suddenly, for a split second, he shivered. His ghost must have paused to observe and then touch him. The slight tremor surprised and angered him at the same time. He regarded the tremor as a weakness. It did not put him off his guard. On the contrary, it roused his furtiveness. Quickly, he recovered himself. Whatever happened in this room tonight was going to determine whether he and Lauren lived or died. He clasped his revolver even more firmly as he held it pointed toward Lauren's heart. He continued to glare at her. He could hear her uneasy breathing. He watched her restless movements. Her occasional moaning did not push her out of sleep. Her unhappy dream held her in its chains. Guilt-laden (at least to his eyes), she was her own prisoner, there in her unquiet bed. Yet, even in her troubled sleep, she appeared wanton and lascivious. All during these moments when he was observing her restlessness, she lay against three or four soft pillows with her spread legs lifted sensually, as though she were inviting a man to enter her. He wondered how often she took Aaron Dowling inside her. The thought of their copulating maddened him.

With rough impatience, he leaned over her and tapped her forehead with the muzzle of his revolver. Instantly, she wakened. Her brown eyes opened wide with the surprise of his standing over her as he pushed the muzzle against her forehead. She did not move. Nor did she permit herself to draw back in fear against the quilted headboard or to lean further into the soft comfort of her pillows. She held herself taut and waited. If she believed that he was going to press the trigger of his revolver right then and fire the bullet that would kill her, she gave him no evidence of her apprehension. Shrouded within her stillness, she went on watching him, her eyes holding him in her silence without making any appeal or protest. A vague fatalism attended her. She was accepting her death as inevitable. There was no way for her to alter or escape it. What the Fates had decreed must be. In this moment, she believed that he was going to press the trigger. Or, rather, *he* imagined that Lauren believed he would shoot her. If that were so, if in this quickened moment she was telling herself that she was about to die, she was prepared to meet death without whimpering. She was finished with the weeks and months of fearing him. The games between them were over. She had come to the bad end that she had been anticipating. The wayward lover, whom she had never really loved, was now her executioner.

But he did not press the trigger. That would make things too easy for Lauren. He wanted, instead, to tease her into believing that he could not go through with the killing. He wanted to prod her ambiguous trust in him. He wanted to hear her lies. He wanted her to believe that she was outwitting him. Only then, after he persuaded her that he believed her lies, would he press the trigger.

He began baiting her.

"You married him," he said. "You married Aaron Dowling without telling me."

He continued to press the muzzle of his revolver against her forehead.

She did not move. She did not avert her gaze. She looked him straight in the eye. But she did not speak. He guessed that she was not certain whether he wanted to say more. Only after she understood that he was waiting for her words did she speak.

She answered him calmly, binding her words to matter-of-fact and stoical understatement.

"I had to marry him. I had to act quickly, before he hooked himself to one of those rich debutantes who had been sleeping with him before I met him. Tracy Holt was one of those girls. She had nearly convinced him that they were meant for each other. She had convinced her father. Her old man was very willing to buy her a street-wise Dowling who was on his way up. I had to do a lot of talking before I persuaded Aaron Dowling that his marriage to me was going to bring him much more wealth than he could expect from the Holt family. They are well off, but they cannot compete with the forty million dollars I'll collect because I've married a Dowling."

While she spoke, she met his hardened gaze with clear-eyed matter-of-factness. Her words made him pause, but they did not resolve his suspicion. She wanted him to believe that she was leveling with him. She wanted him to believe that she was playing the game the way it should be played. Closing him out of any contact with her increased her assurance that Dowling would not discover her continued relationship with *him*, Bryce Thompson—the smooth con man and cynical user of women and of any other persons who were foolish enough to league themselves with him.

No, he could not trust her. But he was willing, for the moment at least, to suppress his murderous regard of her. It was his turn to play games with her. He baited her further. He withdrew the muzzle of his revolver from her forehead and returned it to the inside pocket of his jacket. While he kept his brooding gaze fixed upon her, he backed away from the bed. She would imagine that his angry distrust of her had relaxed its hold upon him. His placing his revolver in his pocket signaled his willingness to listen to whatever words she might devise as an explanation.

Sensing her moment and all the while maintaining a careful poise, Lauren slipped out of her bed and moved toward him. With the feminine delicacy that had, in their best days, never failed to soothe his rough temperament, she tried to embrace him. He pushed her away. But the gentle nature of the push would, he was certain, convince her that he might be willing to make peace with her. Her eyes softened now, and her bare arms reached out to him in petition. She hurried back to him and, as though it were the most natural gesture, caressed him.

"Love me," she murmured. "Love me as much as I love you."

Even against his conscious will, her touch stirred him. It recalled for him the pleasure that her touch had often given him. Still, he resisted her petition. He pulled away from her embrace. His bitter wariness of her was like a wildness burning through him.

When he answered her, his tightly controlled voice—raspy from a bout of heavy drinking during the past week—carried an undercurrent of menace. But, though he imagined that the grimace overtaking his face must have made him look sinister, Lauren did not back away from him. She continued to gaze upon him with affectionate brown eyes that disguised her fear. He, still resisting her, spewed through his teeth low-pitched, muted words that were blunt with accusation.

"You hid your marriage from me," he said. "You are leaving me out of the picture. You are double-crossing me."

She inched her way closer to him. She chose words meant

to comfort him. Her artifice made her solicitude sound almost genuine.

"I'm doing everything that you want me to do. I've got Dowling in the palm of my hand."

Still he resisted her.

"You are in love with him. He's your Mister Right. You have no intention of setting him up to be killed."

She lowered her voice so that, intimate and murmurous, it sounded warm with love for him. At the same time, she touched his right arm with the tips of her fingers. The touch was delicate and felt like a caress.

"I tell you nothing has changed between us. You have to be patient. We can't make this thing happen too fast. We have to keep ourselves in the clear."

She imparted her words with such conviction that everything she said seemed true. Yet he felt that she was still lying. Now he threw out a new challenge.

"Why didn't you tell me that you married Dowling?"

Almost imperceptibly, she paused before his question. Her careful eyes still held him in her soft regard. But now a slight frown creased her brow.

"You would have killed him right away."

"Maybe. Maybe not."

She hurried to say more, with words that were more voluble and quickened with conviction. She wanted him to understand how it was with her.

"Your killing Dowling too soon would have placed me in a bad light. The police would have used my past against me. They might have found out about you and me."

The energy with which she imparted her remark

impressed him. She might be telling him what was true. She might be play-acting. His instinct told him to spurn her careful words.

"You are making excuses. You are lying."

For an instant, silence overtook the room, hovering uneasily near them. She studied him quietly, as they stood there together, face to face. When she resumed speaking, her expression was nearly serene, and her voice was even more assured. It was as though she recognized in him a vague hesitation or a fault line in his animosity. Or, perhaps, he alone detected the flaw. Perhaps, he was not yet ready to be rid of her and of himself.

"You don't really believe that I am lying," she said. "How could you believe that, when you know what we have been to each other?"

Tenderly, she touched his face. She brushed her lips against his lips.

This time, he did not resist her touch. Nor did he deny that her kiss had roused him. But, though her kiss abated for an instant the wild anger that was burning through him, it did not subdue the impulse that had brought him here to kill her and then kill himself. He waited for her to say more, even as he weighed the next step that he needed to take.

"I'm doing everything for you and me," she said. "You need not worry about my brother. He won't make any trouble. He regards Aaron Dowling as a man who is on his way up. Aaron's recent commissions have pushed him into the big time. His new assignment in Florida means that he is one of the big boys in architecture. That commission is going to make a fortune for him, as well as for the Dowling Corporation. My brother and his lawyers are prepared to be very impressed. That's when he will really accept the idea of my marriage. That's when I'll collect the forty million dollars. A few months after that, you can make your move. You can kill Dowling."

Her smooth words incited his anger. With brute and rancorous swiftness, he grabbed the back of her hair with his left hand and pulled her toward him. Then, with his right hand, he took from his pocket his Colt revolver and pointed it at her temple.

"You are not leveling with me," he snarled. "You are feeding me lies. You don't want me to kill Dowling. You are in love with him."

The fear that she had kept at bay rose up now to trap her. If she struggled to be free of his hold upon her or if she uttered the wrong words, the wildness that was churning inside him would push him forward. He would kill her and then kill himself. Instead, she consented to his rough handling and, with a voice turned tremulous and urgent, she pledged her loyalty to him.

"You are the only man that I love. Aaron Dowling is a means to an end. He's our ticket to big money and a great future."

Her petitioning manner wasn't enough. He needed to punish her even more. The cruelty that his bleak experiences had sharpened pushed his finger close to the hammer of the revolver, as if he were ready to cock it and then squeeze the trigger. She did not move. She held her breath inside her taut stillness. For two or three minutes, he kept her in his vise-like grip, while the barrel of his revolver pressed against her forehead. Only when he believed that she had lost all hope of staying alive and because he accepted her silence as a humbled acquiescence to his will did he release her from his rough handling and return the revolver to the inside pocket of his jacket.

She was trembling now. Her eyes were cloudy with her terror of him. But she did not scream.

Her fear appeased him even as it ignited his self-hatred. Nevertheless, he found new, abrasive words to threaten her further.

"Don't play me for a fool. I'll make you sorry, if you do."

She pulled herself together. The danger was past, at least for tonight. So, he imagined she was thinking. Now, clasping her hands as if in new petitioning, she approached him with the feminine grace and demure inflections that were her stock in trade.

"Believe in me," she said. "None of this will be any good if you don't believe in me."

"You are good at your game, baby. You are really good. I like that hint of sadness in your eyes and the slight tremor in your voice. Try them on Dowling. Maybe he'll believe in them."

His show of disdain did not stop her. They had played out scenes of this kind two or three times before, though never with these murderous underpinnings. As before, she plied his good will with her well-calibrated sensuality and with her cruel irony.

"I've missed you. I want you inside me. I want to see the magic lights again when you make love to me."

His street-wise realism told him she was lying. Yet, way back in the most secret recesses of his mind, he wanted to believe that she loved him. He wanted to admit to himself that he needed her and that the rage that might push him to kill her was anchored to his chaotic love. The grudging words he now offered her revealed his ambivalence.

"Maybe I've missed you, too," he said. "Maybe I want to be inside you. But that doesn't mean I trust you. I know you. You and I are alike. Only a fool would trust either of us."

Her eyes gleamed, as if she were delighted. He was permitting her to hope in their future, such as it was. Once again, she brushed his lips with a kiss.

"Take a chance on me. I won't let you down."

"I told you that I'll go a few more rounds with you. Let's see what happens."

He kissed her lips lightly, and then he kissed her even more passionately. She returned his kiss, this time touching his tongue with her lips and entering his mouth. The sheer pleasure of the kiss thrilled him. That, as well as her soft skin, with its perfumed fragrance, and her firm breasts that he gently cupped, roused his perverse need of her. He tore her lingerie from her body and carried her to her bed. Just as urgently, he pulled off his clothes. For him, this act of disrobing was equivalent to gambling with death. It was a form of Russian roulette. While he was shedding his clothes, Lauren might grab her Smith and Wesson pistol from her bed table and shoot him. There was a dark part of him that did not care whether he lived or died. Tonight, he was very aware that, by shedding his clothes and disarming himself of his revolver, he was placing himself in the hands of Fate or at the mercy of this woman whom he had occasionally beaten and frequently threatened. His consenting to be open to attack made vivid and palpable, to his mind at least, the death wish that was surfacing more often in this bleak aftermath of the university scandal that, years earlier, had wrecked his life.

But Lauren did not make a rush for her pistol or,

grabbing it from the secret drawer in the bed table, fire its bullets into his heart. Instead, she lay propped against a galaxy of soft pillows, waiting for him. Her face still wore a serene smile, and her arms reached out eagerly to him. He did not believe in her serenity. Nor did he attribute to deep-seated love her refusal to kill him. True, Lauren could be a frivolous and narcissistic woman. But she also had a cynical understanding of her situation. If she killed him, the ensuing scandal would not only cost her the fortune that she was about to inherit from her parents' estate. It would also wreck her chance of inheriting Aaron Dowling's money. Nevertheless, Lauren's not reaching for her pistol quickened his need of her.

He was not surprised that, on this turbulent night when he made love to her, she was different. There was no longer between them the longed-for symmetry, the smooth and natural rhythms of their bodies together, their teasing and constant momentum, and the protracted joy of their climaxes. Their intercourse had become a shared and enigmatic tension. Whatever pleasures remained were part of an unsentimental biological act. Gone was her roused elation when, naked and erect, he entered her—vigorous, spermatic, and adept. Gone, too, was his belief that she belonged to him alone. When he was finished, he pulled out of her and turned away, feeling sated yet strangely hollow. He did not caress her, as in their happier times he had always done, or, while holding her body close to his, whisper the words that told her how much he loved her. They had gone past the solacing conventions of lovemaking. Their copulating merely filled an animal need. More than that, it gave them the illusion of solidarity. It made credible the possibility that, in spite of their discord, they would maintain their partnership. No, he did not caress her or soothe her with endearments. Instead, believing that he had lost her to Dowling and bitter that this acrimonious night had not resolved his distrust of her, he turned away from her and fell into a tentative and troubled sleep.

He awoke an hour later, at two in the morning. His conscious awareness was stirred by the light of the moon streaming through the French doors that opened out to the solarium and to a terrace on both sides. The sporadic rays of the moon as well as the muted light from the lamp on the bed table shimmered fitfully, casting a haze upon the objects in the room even as they revealed them only partially. The dark of the night kept pushing away the light, concealing the accurate identity of the room and disguising with shadows the palatial appointments even when the light touched their surfaces. Occasionally, the light reached the bed and streamed across the soft pillows and across the rumpled sheets that he had tossed away from the heat of his naked body. Lauren was not lying in bed next to him. Tethered to the rim of sleep as he had been, he had heard her slip away three-quarters of an hour ago, drawn by her restlessness and by her anxiety to a room where she could be free of what she must have regarded as his willful and menacing presence.

He hurried from the bed and quickly found his place in the shower that he had often used when he and Lauren were first together. The warm spray revived his spirit, cleansing his body and bringing to his skin the sheen of newness. The next hours would bring a different day that, prodded by his skillful manipulation, might work for him. He dressed with a swift energy that pleased him, and then he hurried to join Lauren in the living room. He saw her before she noticed him. She was seated at the bar, withdrawn to a pensive stillness as she sipped on one of her favorite escapes: bourbon straight up.

"I'll have the same," he said, while invoking a casual manner to dispel at least some of the tension that still lived, adamant and mysterious, between them.

Hearing his voice, she looked up, wary and furtive. His being there when she had not yet expected him left her momentarily startled. She was calculating his motive for hurrying toward her. With the cold and penetrating eyes of a sentry, she watched him cautiously as he came toward her from out of the recessed light of a distant hallway. Then, more certain now that he had not come to harm her, she summoned a bright smile. So warmly did she extend her arms to greet him and with such enthusiasm did she rise from her seat to brush his lips with a kiss, that he nearly consented to her careful radiance. Whether his ingrained distrust prevented him from believing in her or whether it was his abiding self-hatred, he did not know. His brooding nature notwithstanding, he had not learned how to fathom accurately the darker regions of his heart.

"You and I need to talk," she said, as she moved with graceful poise behind the bar. She found other useful words to say while, with equal grace, she poured him a drink. "You want us to move faster than I expected. We'll have to review our plan carefully, if we want to make it work for us."

Her lavender fragrance and her gleaming skin told him that she, too, had bathed. He imagined that she wanted to wash away his scent and to douche herself as a way of detoxing her body of his sperm. His negative interpretation of their relations stung at his pride, even as it fed his self-loathing. As abruptly as his bitterness had summoned this thought, his determination to win a share of the fortune that Lauren stood to inherit pulled him into the unresolved subtleties of the present moment. His swaggering confidence, yoked to his rugged masculinity even while it disguised his uncertainty, carried him forward.

"You are setting up Dowling for a fall," he said. "You have been setting him up for more than a year. Now it's my turn to make the plan work. Everything will move into place after I kill him."

Taking a seat next to him at the bar, she touched his arm affectionately and planted a kiss lightly upon the right side of his face. Then, with a calm voice that meant to soothe him, she guided him onto the path that she was already treading.

"The time has to be right. You have always told me so. If we move too fast, we could ruin everything."

"You are stalling."

"Of course, I am. Stalling is what we need to do. We need to wait a few more months. By then, I'll have been married to Aaron for a year. I can play the grieving widow with far more conviction if I've been married to him for a year."

"What happens to me, in the meantime?"

"You can be the playboy that you enjoy being. You will still have the apartment that I have leased for you and a hundred thousands dollars from the recent sale of some of my jewels. You can have a good time. Then, in five or six months when the time is right—after I have been married to Dowling for a year—you can kill him."

He pondered her words. They made sense. Yet the words stirred his protest.

"I don't like it. I don't like the thought of your sleeping with him. I don't like all the waiting that I'll have to do."

She kept her steady gaze upon him. She clasped his rough hand with her soft, feminine touch. Her voice became more intimate now and even seductive. Its excited inflections were alive with the thrill of anticipation.

"It will be worth the waiting," she said. "For the rest of our lives, we'll have everything that we ever dreamed of having."

"That's what I like to hear you say, baby. I'll like it even more when I really believe you."

They were moving to the sofa now and taking their places next to each other. Her brown eyes still gleamed with affection, and her smoky voice modulated its enthusiasm so that her low-keyed words became a shared secret between them.

"You *will* believe me. I am going to help you make our plan work. When the time is right, I'll give you a key to Aaron's apartment. Remember, Aaron and I are living in two apartments. Sometimes, each of us needs to be alone in our own space. His apartment often becomes a second studio for him. He is often at his drawing board late into the night, and his fellow architects are usually there working with him. From time to time, I invite the right people to share my apartment when they are in town. Everyone from best-selling authors to the CEOs of international corporations has been my guest. They bring their wives and their debutante daughters. Their being here enhances my image. My friendship with them pleases my brother and impresses Aaron. I enjoy making fools of all of them. I especially enjoy making a fool of Aaron. He thinks that he is a charmer. He really believes that I'm head over heels for him. When the time comes for you to carry out our plan, I'll let you know when Aaron is going to be alone in his apartment. After you kill him, you can mess up the apartment a little. Make things look like a robbery. Recently, during the city blackout, three robberies have occurred within neighboring penthouses. It is very likely that robberies will occur there even six months from now."

He challenged her certainty that they could make the plan work.

"The police will want to know how a burglar got hold of a key to the apartment."

She confronted his doubt without hesitation.

"If they question me—and I am certain that they will—I'll tell them that Aaron had lost the key or had been robbed of it. He was supposed to have a locksmith change the lock. He must have forgotten to do so."

He probed further.

"I wonder whether the police will believe you."

"I'll make them believe me. I'll be the grieving widow."

He imagined that she had rehearsed this scene of interrogation right after she met Aaron Dowling. But he could not imagine that she envisioned the scene once she fell in love with Dowling. Still, she might be on the level. Her inbred perversity could push her to be his accomplice to the murder.

"Maybe the plan will work. You are good at make believe."

His cynicism did not inhibit her show of enthusiasm.

"Think of it, Bryce. We'll have everything we want."

"I'll drink to that. But, keep remembering, baby, that I'll be watching you every step of the way. You'll be sorry if you cross me."

Once again she caressed his arm and then leaned closer to brush his lips with a kiss.

"Believe in me, Bryce. Believe in me. Can't you see? I love you all the way. I am going to do everything that I can do, so that we'll always be together."

"You are sweet-talking me, baby. I don't mind. There is a part of me that likes to hear your sweet-talk. But the other part is waiting for you to come through with your promises."

"I'll come through," she said. "I'll always come through for you."

She kissed him again, this time more passionately.

He returned the kiss, a subtle melancholy subverting his pleasure.

"Tell me again," he said. "Tell me that you will always come through for me."

Her eyes were misty now, as though her entire being were filled with the happiness of his needing her.

"I'll come through for you, Bryce. "I'll always come through for you."

He smiled at the thought. He acted as though he believed her.

"That is a big promise," he said. "Let's drink to it."

He swallowed his bourbon quickly, its cedar flavor stinging his palate a bit, and then he made a hurried departure, though not before reminding Lauren of what he planned to do.

"I'll wait a few more months before we get rid of Dowling. I'll stay away as long as I can. But remember, baby, I'll be watching you even though you won't see me."

She was studying him intently. She had never taken her gaze from him. Her face appeared serene.

"I'll be a good girl," she said. "We are going to get everything that we want."

For a moment, her words echoed beyond the doorway where she stood. Lost inside the echo, the words sounded eerie, as if they belonged to a woman in another world. He turned to verify her being *here*, on the threshold of her apartment. But, when he looked, nobody was there. She had disappeared to somewhere behind the door. Yet her echoing voice still filled his ears.

Brooding and uneasy, he hurried away.

With the wily movements of an infantryman or of a forest creature, he took the private elevator that brought him to the dimly lighted northeast corner of Fifty-Ninth Street. He did not retrieve his car from the underground parking facility where he had left it. Instead, he headed for a pub on Sixty-Fourth Street that stayed open all night. At first, no car or bus hurried by. There were no sounds of whispering or chattering pedestrians or of brisk crowds of confident New Yorkers and carefree tourists. Tall buildings, shrouded by thin cloaks of darkness, stood like ghosts observing him. Everything about the street looked ghostly, even after trucks making pre-dawn deliveries to hotels, department stores, and markets appeared, and after taxis, Cadillacs, and Bentleys began moving along the street. Except for the occasional, low hum of a truck's motor or the fleet cacophony of an automobile's horn, no sound broke through the stillness. An autumn breeze stirred the foliage and the bronzed leaves of the trees that, with decorous precision, lined the well-paved curbs that he kept passing and lined, as well, the edge of a well-lighted park across the wide street. He maintained a brisk pace while he walked to the pub. He savored the cool air at dawn and the sense of freedom that these solitary moments were granting him. But the walk solaced him only for an instant. His awareness of the world weighed heavily upon him. Freedom was merely an illusion. Nobody was free. Each of us makes the chains that bind us. So he told himself once more, before he reached the pub and as he reflected upon the dangerous game that was stealing his soul and his humanity.

His bitter wariness of Lauren kept him in this ambivalent game they were playing with one another. As often as he had played it and as knowledgeable as he was about some of its secrets, it was for him never the same game. It was a game of intricate plots and devices. It was a game of dangerous chance that anchored its impetus and its power to well-crafted schemes, disguises, and traps. The game could bring the player tremendous rewards. But, because it kept changing its rules, the game could—with swift and irrevocable reversals—destroy the player. More than an ordinary game, his and Lauren's capacity for scheming was a dark pocket of reality. Though to all the persons that came into his life he was an inveterate liar, he did not lie to himself. He knew who he was. Sometimes, though not very often, he permitted himself to remember who he had once been.

On those days, when on his way to meet at a New York corporate office or at an upscale bar a business acquaintance that he was duping, he might happen to sight a clean-cut university student emerging from a library with his armful of books or to cross paths with a young, gifted musician in a rehearsal hall on the same floor as the office that he shared with his shady partner. Then, he would recall the self that was lost to him. As if he were viewing the hastening imagery of a filmed montage, he saw his younger self in training with his high school boxing team, studying for a university exam, and playing jazz-mellow riffs on his saxophone. Just as vivid, the cragged face and patient voice of Irwin Baxter flashed before his private seeing and his private hearing as, with mentoring care and an aged man's solicitude, he advised him about the proper way to behave in the world. Now, more than at any other time, he—the makeshift son whom Baxter had rescued from poverty and degradation and afterwards wisely nurtured—stood grimly aware of how far he had fallen away from his best possibilities. He was a huckster, a swindler, a flimflam man, and potentially a killer. Yet, he told himself, he was not beyond regeneration. If he were, he would not regret his misdeeds. Remorse would not be burning through his soul. But anger was also burning through his soul. His anger, which was the wildness that had ignited his murderous plan, was not going to be stifled by self-recrimination. He had made anger and bitterness his brute friends. The game, with all its murderous implications, rankled his conscience. Yet he could not let go of it.

Chapter Eight
A Double Plot

"I haven't told you everything about myself," Lauren said. "There are things you need to know. There are problems that I should have told you about before we were married."

Aaron rose from her bed now. His naked muscularity gleamed inside the light of the moon that was cascading from the terrace of her apartment through the French doors that opened into the expansive surround of the room. The light sprayed its radiance upon the elliptical imagery of richly upholstered sofas and chairs, the Dégas on the south wall, and the French Provençal table below it that held the delicate vase of red and yellow roses. The same moonlight streamed across the Aubusson carpet and glowed upon the ample bed, where she lay, poised and intimate, as though she were lolling in carefree afterglow against a galaxy of soft pillows. From her furtive perspective, the light illuminated Aaron's body most of all. His dark-haired handsomeness and tall, limber body dominated the space he inhabited, as he walked confidently to the French doors. Her words did not persuade him to pause, nor did the brisk October air disturb him when he opened the doors onto the terrace and allowed the midnight radiance to cast a more enveloping sheen upon his athletic stature. Stepping onto the terrace, he peered down upon the quickened life of the city below. The familiar promise of Manhattan never ceased to excite his attention. It stirred his need to be in it again. It roused his desire to be at the center of things.

So she imagined, understanding him better than he knew, because they were both ambitious and self-centered.

She watched him stretching his rugged arms outward and then raising them, as if he were reaching for a fistful of the sky or of the moon or contemplating an equivalent appropriation. She did not call out to him, so intense was his withdrawal to his private thoughts and to the clarified awareness that imbues one's body and spirit after an hour of vigorous and solacing copulation. Whether she was part of his thoughts, she could not guess. Even in their closest moments, Aaron always seemed to distance himself from her. He had, she observed, taught himself to stand nearly outside the experiences that he was sharing. Perhaps it was his way of judging more keenly the persons and the circumstances that anchored themselves to the reality unfolding around him. He refrained from sentimental interpretations and from softhearted responses. In matters that pertained to his wellbeing and to his dealings with new adversaries and potential rivals, he gave quarter to no one. This hardened part of his nature intrigued her, even as it sometimes frightened her. Aaron Dowling was nobody's fool. To take him for granted or to cross him in even subtle ways was to destroy whatever trust he permitted himself to accord her.

In his company, she worked sedulously to conceal the kind of woman she was. Her various disguises yoked themselves most of the time to natural-seeming spontaneity and to discreet self-possession. Yet, in spite of her efforts to personify a feminine ideal that adequately represented young women of her class, she had occasionally revealed to him the hidden currents of her identity. On these occasions, he witnessed with carefully modulated cynicism her flares of anger, her anxious hesitation, and her unbridled sensuality. These characteristics made plausible all the stories that he had heard about her scandalous past. Yet, as far as she could tell, he tolerated her flaws with the same, casual manner that he brought to his praise of her merit. He calculated shrewdly the implications of her persona. Because he was sophisticated and levelheaded, he knew—in his relations with her and with the world—when it was in his best interest to call a spade a spade. He knew, as well, how to win the game by temporizing his judgments of ambiguous situations and of tarnished human beings.

When he did not answer her words, she busied herself with apparently casual gestures. She reached for the gold cigarette case on her bed table. Placing one of her French cigarettes in the corner of her mouth, she then took the gold lighter from the bed table. After igniting the tip of the cigarette, she lay back against the soft pillows and inhaled the fumes of its tangy tobacco. She exhaled and studied the vaporous smoke rings rising around her. So methodical were her movements and so subtle was her manner, that she might have been an actor in a play who had learned how to stylize her performance. The smallest gestures, craftily rendered, concealed her artifice. The fictive landscape that she inhabited on this imaginary stage melded smoothly with the equivocating real world where deeds and consequences altered their capricious meanings every time that she imposed her will on a scene.

She waited quietly, understanding that Aaron would turn back to her only after the autumn chill had further quickened his still-excited blood and after the flashing motion of the streets below had intensified his anticipation of all the days and nights that would become more than ordinary because he was a part of them.

When he did turn back, Aaron did not really turn to her. He was, she felt, not aware that she was here. He had withdrawn to the privacies of self-reflection that, at least temporarily, had eclipsed not only her familiar presence, but the entire room as well. He had shut her out of his thoughts. Whatever held his attention did not include her, poised as she was, devious and ensnaring, against a swell of pillows. Nor, she guessed, did it include the memory of their copulation, still vivid and palpable to her senses. When he paused at the French doors, a hint of a smile creased his enigmatic face. He stood very still, as if he were held spellbound by the private world he had entered and had forfeited the power to hurry, agile and proprietary, back to the bed on which she lay. Only gradually did his reverie set him free. Only then, as if the spell had lifted the scales from his eyes and allowed him to see the room once more, did he speak to her.

"I love this city"' he declared. "I love being in it and making it work for me."

He came back to her bed now and casually sat on the edge. He peered at her with no show of emotion other than the satisfaction that his terrace-view of the city had brought him. Then, with the quicksilver movement and sleight-of-hand gesture of a thief, he took hold of her cigarette and brought it to his lips. Inhaling its tangy flavor became another pleasure for his senses.

"I'll be thinking of this city at least some of the time that I am working in Florida," he said. "This city is in my blood. It's an adrenalin rush. It's my stock in trade."

She received his words as a cue to tell him what he needed to hear.

"New York might not work for you," she began. "There are important reasons why it may turn against you."

Her words made him pause, though his wiliness muted his surprise and banked the hostility he felt toward any words that threatened the future he was devising for himself. When he responded to her cryptic assertion, he chuckled. He appeared to be amused and a bit perplexed. He wanted her to believe that he wasn't about to take her words seriously.

"What makes you think that, baby? What are these big reasons that might ruin New York for me?"

"Bryce Thompson, for one."

"Him again," Aaron said, dismissing the name with blunt and disdainful arrogance. "I thought that you had decided to get him out of your system."

She made her voice more urgent now, its smoky inflections both matter-of-fact and insistent.

"You need to take him seriously. He is a problem that we need to face. He is not going away."

He eyed her with penetrating gaze.

"You told me that everything between you two was finished."

"I didn't want you to become involved. I thought that I could handle him myself."

Still he gazed upon her, determined to fathom the plot she was weaving. Impatient to discover the answer, he threw out a blunt question.

"What does this guy have on you? What secret from your past is he holding over you?"

After a moment's hesitation, she spoke the plausible words that, hours earlier, she had chosen to tell him.

"Everything," she said. "He knows everything about me. He knows all the things that you do not know. He knows that my parents never loved me. They merely tolerated me, and they betrayed me. They've kept back the forty million dollars that was my rightful inheritance. Bryce knows that I will get that money if I marry the right man."

"He thinks that *he* is the right man."

She pondered his remark and then, with carefully measured words that calculated their influence upon him, she told him a little more about the man whom she once perversely loved and who now loomed as a threat to her inheritance.

"The right man? No, Bryce knows better. He understands that my brother and his lawyers will never accept him. He is a realist. He is smart. Every important lesson that he's learned comes from his life in the streets."

"He still wants to be part of the score. That's it, isn't it? He wants his take. He wants to be there for the big cash-out."

"He knows that is impossible. My brother and his henchmen will keep their eyes on the ways that money is being used. The will gives them the power to do so. But Bryce thinks that he is still in the driver's seat. He's convinced himself that he can prevent me from getting the money. All he has to do is to involve me in a public scene or to feed some tabloid the information about the years when I was traveling with a fast crowd and doing drugs."

She saw the shadow of unease touching his face. Because he wanted to hide his dismay, he rose from his place at the edge of the bed and grabbed his robe from the needlepoint chair a few feet away. Only after he gathered its cobalt blue fabric about him did he allow her to see his face. He had closed off every emotion except the nearly rigid calm that gave to his handsome features an understated willfulness.

"Then you don't have an inheritance. Bryce Thompson has lost it for you."

She had drawn him to her mantrap, her words like steel springs there to bind him with their snares and chains. Formidable though he was and—in nearly imperceptible ways—dangerous, she led him to the rim of her trap.

"I'll have the forty million if he's out of the picture," she said. "I'll have it if he's not around to make trouble."

He was more certain of the way she was going now. He was even wilier than she had imagined. He recognized the trap, and he did not take it. He avoided the pitfall. He turned onto a different path. Yet he hovered over her with understated menace as he stood by the bed in which she still lay, propped against the galaxy of soft pillows with promiscuous carelessness.

"I'll be around to take care of you," he said. "Bryce won't give *me* any trouble."

Her words were more urgent now. Fear, or its wary simulation, was altering the sound of her voice.

"He is planning to kill you. He's slapped and punched me more than a few times. He wants me to understand what I'm in for if I don't go along with him. He wants me to give him the key to your apartment. He is going to shoot you and make everything look like the work of a thief. If I don't give him the key, he has made up his mind to kill me."

Still he avoided the trap that she was setting for him.

"Go to the police," he said, his manner as curt as it was militant. "Tell them everything. They'll take care of Bryce legally."

She made her voice more tremulous. She summoned bitter melancholy to alter the dark beauty of her face.

"My name will be smeared all over the newspapers again. I'll lose the forty million dollars."

Aaron grimaced. Within an instant, the expression transformed his identity. The lighthearted persona he had always so artfully devised, layered as it was with irony and sophistication, disappeared. His gaze bore into her, incisive and vigilant. The corners of his mouth twisted even more decisively into a sneer. His husky voice deepened. He might have been a relentless prosecutor, hostile and accusatory.

"You want Bryce dead," he declared. "You want me to kill him."

She held herself steady, with no betrayal of her uncertainty on this path that they were treading. She met his gaze with clear-eyed assurance. She wanted him to believe all the words she chose to draw him into her trap. Treacherous and tough-minded, even while she invoked a subdued tension like nearly repressed fear, she worked to convince him that they needed to save themselves from Bryce.

"Your killing Bryce would be foolish," she said. "Once he is dead, the police will find out about the year that he and I lived together. They will, in some way, find out about all the secret meetings that brought Bryce and me together. They may draw me into the scandal. They will, most certainly, push you into it. You will be in the spotlight. They will try to pin the murder on you. They will say that you had a motive. You saw Bryce as your rival. You wanted to be rid of him."

His wary face tightened. His voice turned raspy, and his words chained their anger to ingrained and hard-won disciplines.

He took another drag on the cigarette he had scooped out of her hand and, after crushing its remnants in the solid-gold ashtray on the night table, he confronted her with questions that coiled their implications with criminal charges.

"What do you plan to do? Hire a killer?"

She reached out and touched his arm. She wanted him to keep in mind the pleasures that they had shared not only on this night, but also for nearly a year. They had shared pleasures, as well, beyond the bed. The world could be their life-long adventure, if they wove their plots together and if they claimed the rewards that were theirs for the taking. Cautious and adept, she met his harsh questions with a softer, matter-of-fact explanation.

"We need a killer," she said, "but not a hired one. Even after he was paid, a hired killer might come back to blackmail us."

His brooding features studied her for another instant and then turned away. He needed his own space to calculate the trajectory of her plot. He walked over to the terrace window and peered once again upon the busy city that flashed and sparked its life fourteen stories below the place where he was standing.

She rose from her bed now, enclosing her figure within a delicate blue floral lace nightgown. She hurried to join him at the terrace window. Once again, she softly touched his arm. This time, though, she brought her body close to his. They belonged with each other. He was her partner. He was her collaborator.

With sinuous poise, he moved out of her reach. He wanted a better view of her. He needed to study her face while he threw out another question.

"How do you propose that we get rid of your Bryce?"

She did not answer him at once. It was, she felt, necessary to measure with cunning precision the apparent calm of her reply.

"We lead him to Gavin."

He glared at her as he fired back another question.

"What does Gavin have to do with it?"

"Gavin is standing in your way. This is the perfect setup for getting rid of him and Bryce at the same time."

"Why would Bryce want to kill Gavin? He doesn't even know him."

She took hold of his arm again. Her brown eyes met his gaze directly. Her voice, with its smoky textures, was more urgent now.

"He *will* want to kill him. He will believe that Gavin is you. The Fates have been working for us. They made Gavin resemble you. Thus far, Bryce has seen you only from a distance. He could easily mistake Gavin for you."

Her words did not dispel his grim expression. But she had, she thought, roused his interest. He was auditioning her. Skeptical though he was, he was allowing her to pitch her scenario of murder.

"The police will involve me," he said. "My apartment is right next to Gavin's."

She hurried to convince him that her plan was going to work. Her words became more excited now and carried with them her breathless inflections.

"You will not be in your apartment. You will be away in Florida, and I'll be there with you. When the police question you—in Palm Beach, perhaps, or after we return to New York—you can mention that your cousin Gavin recently lost the extra key to his apartment. The killer may have even stolen it from him in a restaurant or a gym or a nightclub. Gavin intended to have the lock changed, but apparently he had delayed making the change."

Her words did not persuade Aaron to alter his grim expression. Pensive while he calculated the realism of her plan, he waited a few moments before telling her why her plan was not going to work.

"Bryce might get rid of Gavin. But he will still be around to make trouble. He'll still be looking to kill you and me."

She hurried to dissuade his doubts.

"I'm going to set the police on Bryce's trail. I'll identify Bryce as a former boyfriend who had probably mistaken Gavin's apartment for yours. It will not be difficult to convince the police that Bryce had come there to kill you and me. His sordid past will give him the look of a guilty man. The rumor of his ties with petty thieves and small-time gangsters will work against him. Once I set the police on his trail, Bryce will be a dead man."

He grew very still. She wondered whether she had misjudged his willingness to flout all the essential laws to get what he wanted. Never before had she regarded him as especially high-minded or overly scrupulous. Always, he had appeared to be a man who made his own rules. Even now, she preferred to regard his stillness as another form of his wiliness. His kind of man—ambitious, devious, and altogether charming—would not hesitate to carry out the cold-blooded scenario she was putting before him. But he would require some surety that his risk came with big rewards. He was going to have to win everything that he wanted.

She drew closer to him. She caressed his rugged shoulder. When he did not resist, she lightly brushed his lips with a kiss. His blue eyes kept their steady gaze upon her without revealing what he was thinking. Nevertheless, she was not surprised when he challenged her with two more questions.

"What about you? How will the police regard you?"

She answered him without hesitation. She brought a contrived assurance to her voice. She wanted him to understand that she had figured out every aspect of her plan.

"I won't be a suspect. I'll run free of this scandal. Even my brother and his lawyers won't perceive it as my scandal. They will regard me as an innocent. I showed good sense. I recognized Bryce for what he is, and I broke free of him."

Anger and contempt brought stern lines to his face. His voice, subdued though it was by rigorous self-control, was sardonic and probing.

"You are good. You are really good. You've been planning this for weeks, haven't you? Ever since I told you that I'd get my inheritance far more quickly if Gavin didn't live very long."

She would not allow his words to stop her. She pushed harder.

"This is our chance to get everything that we want. You will have your share of the Dowling fortune, and I'll have the forty million dollars that, even in death, my wretched parents have been holding back from me."

He studied her face for an instant and then withdrew from the perfumed touch of her hands. He walked back to the bed and took an imported cigarette from her gold case. Quickly, she followed him. Only after he had ignited the cigarette with her gold lighter did he turn to her. The anger and contempt had drained away from his face. In their place were a muted melancholy and a nearly imperceptible hint of self-disgust.

"This isn't going to work, baby. Even if we fooled the police, we can never fool ourselves. We'd be catalysts for Gavin's death. I'll admit that, lately, I've had an uneasy relationship with him. We haven't always seen eye to eye. But it's only after his father set us up to be rivals that our friendship cooled."

She kept her voice steady. She wanted him to regard Gavin as an enemy.

"He's shoved you aside. He worked with his father to see to it that you have to wait fifteen years before you can call yourself a real Dowling."

"You are wrong. Liam Dowling hated both of us equally. He hated me for being the son of a poor man, who happens to be his brother. He hated Gavin for sleeping with his wife."

His words caught her by surprise.

"Gavin and Sara? Are you certain?"

"I'm certain."

"Even so, Gavin stands in your way as long as he stays alive."

Once again, anger and contempt were altering his features.

"I am not killing him. Nor will I set him up to be killed."

His caustic words did not hold her back. She held herself steady. She brought an even-tempered clarity to all that she was telling him. She wanted to convince him of the danger that awaited both of them.

"I won't mind waiting all those years for you to get hold of your inheritance. But, unless we get rid of Bryce, everything is finished for us. He'll kill you and get away with it. The police will believe it is the work of a thief. Then, he'll come after me and after my money. I won't tell the police that he killed you, because Bryce will say I planned your murder. I goaded him into it. If I want to stay alive and out of prison, I'll have to marry him."

His eyes stared at her with new comprehension. He took hold of her now, his big hands pinioning her arms so that she could not get away from him.

"You did goad Bryce. You wanted him to murder me."

She began struggling to free herself from his stronghold of her. The pressure of his hands brought jabs of pain to her arms. She felt herself panicking. With tremulous voice, she cried out her protest.

"No, you are wrong. I never did that."

With his left hand and arm still holding her captive, he used his right hand to slap her.

"You planned it before you really knew me," he said, his husky voice tight and unforgiving."

"No! I never did!" she screamed.

He slapped her again, the force of his hand against her skin even stronger.

"You planned it for the thrill of it."

"You're crazy," she said, her broken voice no longer a scream. "You've got it all wrong."

Her jaw ached, and her face was burning from the sting of his slap. She started to kick him in his right ankle.

He punched her now, the force of the blow throwing her head and her body backward. Her body went limp. But he would not allow her to fall away from him. His rough hand held her even more firmly as his prisoner. His face was wild with hatred.

The room was spinning around her now. For a split second, she was not certain of where she was. Slowly, the fragments of the room reassembled themselves. She saw her bed with its soft pillows and its embroidered coverlet. She saw the painting on the wall, the gold cigarette case and the gold lighter on her night table, and she knew the room once more. Then, she heard Aaron's angry voice and saw his hostile face.

"Maybe you and Bryce were snorting cocaine when you planned to murder me. Or maybe you were jabbing yourselves with a heroin fix."

She would not give in.

"It's not so," she said. "I never planned anything with him."

He hit her again, his clenched fist punching her in her ribs until her body wavered and sank as he held her painfully in his grasp. For an instant, her breath went out of her. She felt herself spinning and spinning and then making the fall into darkness.

Her legs gave way, and she slumped beneath his grasp.

He threw her onto her bed. She felt that he—or some force that she could not clearly ascertain—was throwing her out of consciousness.

When she became aware once more, she saw him standing before her. He had showered and shaved and was dressed in a burgundy turtleneck sweater, gray slacks, and a navy sports jacket. With his weekend travel bag in his hand, he was ready to leave, but not before he told her what he felt was happening between them.

She began whimpering. She did not want him to say the words that would end their marriage. But she did not move. Nor did she raise her voice in protest, weary and weak though her protest would have sounded.

He was pitiless. The cruelty that he had carefully suppressed through all of this year of their being together flared its powers before her. In spite of the pain that he had inflicted upon her body, he threw out new, snarling words. His voice stayed low and dangerous, while his tall, athletic frame hovered by her as she lay there on her bed, battered and tossed aside.

"Just the thought of being involved with a murder gave you a high," he told her. "Admit it! It made you feel powerful. You liked playing God. You liked deciding how long I might live and in what way I was going to die."

She tried to rise from the bed, but pain was shooting through her arms and face and stomach. But the stabs of pain did not keep her from sitting up. She pushed herself to persuade him that she was innocent. She imagined that a sickly pallor was covering her face. She must have appeared vulnerable. To his eyes, she was fragile and defeated. She would make his beating of her work in her favor. Her anguished expression might conceal her lies.

"It wasn't me. It was never me," she said, her voice a painful whisper. "You've got to believe me. It was Bryce. He planned everything, and I talked him out of it. But that was months ago. Now it's too late. He's not listening to me anymore. He's going ahead with his plan. He wants to kill you."

"I'll take care of Bryce, and I won't have to kill him. I'll get the police involved, and I'll run free of this."

She went on imploring him. She anchored her petition to subtle taunting.

"You'll ruin things for us. There will be a scandal. We won't have my forty million dollars. My brother and his lawyers will see to that."

"I may not need your forty million. I'll make a success on my own terms."

Still she taunted him. She made her words sound matter-of-fact and reflective. She might have been a seer imparting her ruthless message without qualms or reticence.

"Fifteen years is a long time to wait for your inheritance to kick through," she said. "You'll be working with high rollers and power brokers. You may even make a few millions. But you won't be in their league. For fifteen years, you'll be an also-ran. Oh, the big boys will give you your due. You are a Dowling, after all. But you won't be their equal. You will be a man who is waiting to claim his fortune."

He observed her with cold eyes that flashed with his quickened hatred of her. Yet he appeared otherwise calm. These violent moments between them that had unraveled their haphazard madness had sent his future scattering. Yet the thought that he would have to wait years before he enjoyed the immense success that he craved did not steal his assurance or condemn him to instant trepidation or regret. He stayed tough as he confronted his dilemma. With low-key words that must have suppressed his pent-up fury, he reminded her of how resilient he was.

"I can be very patient when I have to be."

His hardhearted answer impressed her, but she did not like it. With softer words now, she plied him with questions that were meant to stir his memory of the wealth and the adventures that were within his grasp.

"What about us?" she asked him. "What about the kind of life we've been counting on?"

His answer unsettled her. From this volatile evening, he had come to conclusions that disarranged her expectations. Their time for lying to each other was over. So she understood as his words burned into her bitter awareness.

"I'm not certain that there is going to be anymore *us*," he said. "My choosing to team with you in the first place confounds my better judgment. But, a year ago, I could convince myself that the choice was inevitable. You and I are alike in many ways. We are ambitious. We are devious. We are narcissistic. We have an insatiable appetite for exploiting other people and for betraying friends as well as enemies. The promise of your inheritance made my marriage to you a smart move. On the days when you did not allow your various neuroses to overtake you, you were fun to be around. But this is not a year ago. Too many things have changed since then. My being a successful architect isn't enough for you. Maybe it hasn't been enough for me. Maybe I don't want so much anymore. But you do. You want so much more. You don't even mind making me an accomplice to my cousin's murder. You bet I'm going to the police. You are bad news, baby."

Though pain was still shooting through her, she managed to lift herself out of her bed. She did not touch him. Her instincts warned her that her touch would incite new anger within him. Nor did she petition him. Her petitions, contrived from her fear and her insolence, would not work their influence upon him. Instead, she approached him warily and began reasoning with him. Her subdued manner made her words sound pragmatic and appropriate.

"Going to the police is not a smart move, Aaron. You do that, and Bryce will come after you. He'll kill you and your cousin. He may even kill me. He'll kill for the sheer pleasure of it."

"You never let up, do you? You are still making your pitch. You disgust me."

"It is not important how you feel right now. Feelings can change. I thought that I loved you. Even now, I think that I love you, as far as I can love anyone. I love you in spite of the beating. I love you because of the surprise and the perversity of my willingness to continue our marriage. Maybe it's better that everything is in the open between us. We don't need to pretend that we are capable of profound feelings for each other or for anyone else. On that score, at least, we can be honest. We can call a spade a spade and work together to get all of the things that we want out of life."

His keen eyes were studying her, as though he might be memorizing every detail of her expression. The thought that he was looking at her for the last time gave her pause. His new words dismayed her.

"We are finished, baby," he said. "We are not good for each other."

He turned from her now and began making his way through the reception room that would bring him to the main door of the penthouse and on to the private elevator.

Before he had reached the door, she called out to him. She made her tone confident and persistent.

"You will be back, Aaron. You are too smart to throw away a fortune."

He did not answer her. He was hurrying to get away from her now. She kept following him until he closed the door behind him. For a long while, she stood there alone, in the midst of her richly appointed reception room. She could not have moved, even if that had been her intention. She just stood there. Stillness, funereal and apprehensive, had come there to watch her. In these moments, she wondered whether Aaron had turned suddenly moral. She wondered, too, whether he had gone out of her life forever.

He stayed away for a week.

During that uneasy time, she masked her uncertainty by participating in all the public occasions that would have pleased her brother if, by chance, he read a favorable report of her activities in the society column of a premier magazine or a reputable newspaper. The watchmen in his service would have noticed, as well, the discreet manner with which she negotiated her public appearances. With Leah Cohen, she chaired a committee that, by means of a glamorous ball that took place at the Ritz-Carlton, raised more than a million dollars for the maimed veterans of the war in Vietnam. Aaron's absence did not invite suspicion. Everyone in their circle knew that his architectural commissions often drew him away from New York. On the next evening, with renowned artist friends who lived in Soho, she attended the opening of a new Broadway production of Eugene O'Neill's *More Stately Mansions*. At the after-theater party that was held at Sardi's, she invoked a demure radiance while she danced with the cosmopolitan and courtly mayor of New York. She chatted amiably with Wall Street bankers and brokers; with Hubert de Givenchy, the famous couturier who was designing her winter wardrobe; with the astronaut Buzz Aldrin and his wife; and with Ingrid Bergman, Arthur Hill, and Colleen Dewhurst, the gifted actors who had inhabited so well the leading roles in O'Neill's play. Later, with her lawyer and his wife sharing her table, she accepted, with wisely calibrated exhilaration, the salutary greetings of her brother's friends who had read about her marriage to Aaron Dowling.

Toward the end of that week, she spent two days with the Cohens in her aunt's country-style home in Vermont. That her aunt was travelling during this season in South America made the Vermont weekend less complicated. Her aunt was both intuitive and intrusive. She would have imagined all the right reasons why Aaron had not accompanied her. With insinuating questions disguised as a reflection of her concern, she would have discovered the chink in her armor, the hairline crack in her assurance, the nearly imperceptible fissure in her artifice. Her aunt did not bear her malice. She had always been on her side. But even a woman of fifty sometimes enjoys being made privy to the wayward escapades of an adventurous niece. Without her aunt there in Vermont to meddle, the weekend provided the refuge that she required. Every morning, punctually at seven, Mr. and Mrs. Conway, the middle-aged couple who served, respectively, as the groundskeeper and as the housekeeper and cook, drove in from their home in a neighboring village to make her visit with Leah and Paul unfold with no untoward incident and within the bracing montage of varied and quickened activities. The days were filled with sailing and hiking, as well as with shopping in the quaint stores of Stowe, visiting a pristine art gallery, picking apples in an autumn orchard, and dining amidst rustic and unpretentious settings. The windburn that brought a glow to her face concealed the pallor that her sculpted features might otherwise have revealed. Leah and Paul gave no evidence of noticing the melancholy that occasionally touched her face or of perceiving in her responses to their occasional mention of Aaron a slight tremor in her inflections.

At night, restless and anxious and unable to sleep, she thought of the steps that she would have to take if Aaron had really turned away from her. She loved Aaron as much as she could love anyone. But that love was leagued with pragmatic conditions, self-aggrandizing motives, and ruthless calculations. She knew Aaron too well to believe, except in those moments when her anxiety overtook her tough-minded realism, that he would expose her murderous plot to the police or even to her brother. He had too much to lose. His involvement in the scandal would cost him his position with the Dowling Corporation. The newspapers and the television reports would accuse him of being a partner in the scheme to murder Gavin Dowling. The news media would soon find out that Aaron stood to gain more than a hundred million dollars if Gavin died early. Television anchors and newspaper reporters would suggest that it was he who had actually initiated the plan to kill Gavin. They would insinuate that only at the last minute had he backed away from the plan, because she had begged him not to carry his plan forward. These same reporters and policemen would say that, even though Bryce had committed the murder on his own, Aaron had—until the night of the murder—acted as his accomplice. If the police came after her, she would convince them and the news media that, at the last moment, Aaron had fabricated a story that made him appear innocent because he feared that she was going to divulge his murder plan to the police. Even if his lawyers dissuaded the police from arresting him for lack of tangible evidence, the adverse publicity would bring him down. The power brokers and the other wheeler-dealers would keep him at bay. He would be finished. He would have to return to the drab charity life his father had prepared for him in South Africa.

So she imagined during the unforgiving hours when she believed that Aaron was not coming back to her.

This bleak scenario, in which she abandoned and betrayed Aaron to save herself, robbed her of sleep and stole, as well, the fragile respect for herself that she had salvaged from her disreputable past. But her nightmares did not end there. A variant nightmare scenario leaped up to taunt her, igniting new self-contempt and revealing blighted corners of her nature that, before this weekend, she had rarely perceived. In this scenario, Aaron was not coming back to her, even though he remained silent about the plan to murder Gavin. Always now, they remained apart, yet his silence stayed with her. It hovered about her like an executioner watching her every move. In her nightmare, there was no place to run from this specter of silence to which Aaron had condemned her, this ghost that was as mute as it was unidentifiable. There was no place to hide and no chance to retaliate from it until she pushed herself out of the nightmare, moaning and anguished and screaming. Her black-hearted dream left her exhausted. Her assurance fell away from her, tattered by its jagged confusion and void of the energy that had always driven its powers. The light from a bed lamp became a sentry that quickly dispersed the wretched images that had leaped out of her nightmare. Scotch and cigarettes revived her willfulness, without suppressing the contempt that she felt for herself. Propped against an array of pure white pillows, she took frequent drags upon her cigarette and, as it was her habit, watched the rings of smoke rise, vaporous and floating, around her.

This latest of her nightmares had invaded her sleep like a messenger from hell. Spawned from the cavernous murkiness of her fear, the message was clear. She would have to rid herself of the threat that Aaron posed. Once again, she would have to league herself with Bryce and move against Aaron. She and Bryce must activate their original plan to kill Aaron. As his widow, she would collect the hundred million dollars. But she needed to act swiftly. She and Bryce would have to initiate their murder plan before Aaron divorced her and before he changed his will.

Not even the busy schedule through which she moved with lighthearted camaraderie and athletic agility during this four-day respite from the city could dispel her self-disgust. Nor could it diminish the ambivalent love that she still felt for Aaron. Caught though they were inside her nightmare, her murderous impulses that drove their fury against Aaron made her a stranger to herself.

"You will come to a bad end," her mother had warned her.

Even now, eight years later, the words of that disapproving woman still burned inside her soul. Maybe her mother was right. Maybe she was hastening her way to that bad end.

Maybe not.

If Aaron did not return, she would have to let him go to his death. She wanted the hundred million dollars that would be his widow's to claim upon his death. With that money, as well as with the forty million dollars that she was about to inherit from her parents' legacy, she would devise many happy endings for herself. Whenever she thought of her mother, she could scoff at the brittle prophecy that the hateful woman had flung at her.

But, in spite of the murderous thoughts that were propelling her sinister plot, she did not want Aaron to die. Nor did she want Bryce to kill Gavin. If Bryce killed Gavin, believing that he was killing Aaron, she would still lose Aaron. Even if Aaron did not tell the police about the plan to murder Gavin, because he feared that he would be implicated in the killing and because he wanted that hundred million dollars, he would leave her. He would not want to live with a woman that had become the catalyst for his cousin Gavin's death. But, if Bryce did not kill Gavin, she would have a chance to win Aaron back. They could live very comfortably on her forty million dollars. She needed to dissuade Bryce from killing Aaron. She would tell him that Aaron was on to the murder plan. Bryce would probably still want to kill Aaron. But she would lie to Bryce. She would tell him that Aaron had written a letter that was held secure in a safety deposit box at his lawyer's bank. Should Aaron die unexpectedly, his lawyer would open the letter that revealed Bryce Thompson as the killer.

She would pay off Bryce. She would make certain that he had a comfortable life. From time to time, she might even sleep with him. He was very good in bed. His brute sensuality, anchored as it was to rough and prolonged copulation, gave her inordinate pleasures. But he did not belong to her class. Her brother and his business colleagues, as well as her gallery of well-born friends, would always perceive him as an intruder. He had not moved up to their circle. His cunning and his secret plots had been merely self-defeating. In retrospect, she saw that her teaming up with him was an act of rebellion against the rigid codes invoked by her ambitious and class-conscious family. Now, her turning away from him became absolutely essential, if she wanted to claim the wealth that was in her reach. She would not let go of Bryce completely. She did not love him. But she needed him. Her desires to be punished, to be treated cruelly, and to be intimidated and even threatened—all these desires yoked themselves to the perversity of her will. In her sporadic flashes of profound awareness, she hated herself. Without recognizing the subtexts of his powers, Bryce was an agent of stern justice that some avenging angel had set on her path. With Bryce by her side, she could never be happy. His brooding presence would compel her to pay for her sins. She would accept the moments when, through a pitiless tirade or a threatening word, he turned his violence upon her. He was the unwitting Nemesis that the Fates or the avenging angel or his own wayward impulses had driven into her life. Their narcissistic schemes, their inability to love deeply, and their bitter self-regard had drawn them to each other. Someday, maybe, Bryce would even become her executioner.

All these things she told herself during the hours when she could not sleep. It was at night that she thought she would run mad from the fear that she had lost Aaron forever. But, in the first hour after dawn, she pushed that fear way back inside the hidden recesses of her mind. She told herself that she would devise some plan or scenario that would bring Aaron back to her. Believing so, she willed herself to meet each new day in Vermont with an even-tempered disposition and with the tough-minded resilience that had always been the armor that protected her in her battles with the world.

Then, quite suddenly and just as unexpectedly, the hoped-for rescue arrived. On the morning when she and the

Cohens were preparing to return to New York, Aaron telephoned her. His husky voice sounded as it always had—calm and self-assured. He told her that he had been thinking about her and about the two of them together. What he was thinking, he did not say. Nor did she ask him to explain his words, because she was apprehensive about breaking whatever spell had induced him to call her. Besides, she needed no explanation. The significance of his call came with the message that he was imparting to her. That evening, he wanted to have dinner with her right after she arrived in Manhattan.

The Starlight Roof of the Waldorf Astoria provided the glamorous environment for their meeting. The ballroom had frequently provided the setting for other auspicious evenings. She imagined that Aaron had chosen this particular setting for that reason. The Starlight Roof smoothly melded emblems of a ballroom, a nightclub, and a restaurant. The plush ambiance of the place—with its capacious room of nearly six thousand feet, its gilded ceiling that soared eighteen to twenty-four feet, and its Austrian chandeliers—might very well subdue whatever tension they might be harboring as they experienced their first hour with each other. The room and all of its glamorous surfaces could, in fact, dispel the business-like inquiry that lay at the heart of this new cycle in their conflicted relationship. Its plush setting could also reinforce for Aaron's astute appraisal the life style that would be his to keep the moment that he acquired the hundred million dollars that his uncle had left him.

Aaron, she perceived, wanted this evening to be very special. His navy Armani suit enhanced his image as a Dowling who was on his way up. Her Dior evening dress, with its delicate blush satin, and her Tiffany diamond strands identified her as the daughter of a wealthy family. Together, they appeared to be a most compatible married couple. She well understood the importance of their wardrobe. Clothes were the costumes that lent conviction to the personas that she and Aaron assumed. They were the props that defined the roles that they were playing. They were the emblems that identified the class to which they belonged or that implied the rank to which they aspired.

Many of their friends, who were dining at tables nearby, smiled amiably after noticing them. In the proximate distance, within the central surround of lavish banquet tables, two hundred guests were celebrating the visit of the French ambassador to the United States. Farther than that, inside the east wing of the lavish room, Hollywood film executives from Columbia Pictures and seventy-five international guests were celebrating the premiere of Steven Spielberg's science fiction thriller *Close Encounters of the Third Kind*. A wedding party of a hundred American guests enhanced the glamour of the room's south wing.

She suggested that he order dinner for them, and he was pleased to do so. They began with glasses of Dom Pérignon that she merely sipped, wary of allowing the wine to exhilarate her senses. Afterwards, Bryce ordered a cheese soufflé, poached salmon with herbed mayonnaise, and a saffron-yellow sorbet served with slices of green kiwi fruit and sprigs of fresh mint. About them, waiters moved with smooth precision and attended their every need. In the distance, on a stage located a hundred feet beyond the celebration for the French ambassador, a young and handsome pianist was bringing melodic subtleties to Irving Berlin, Rodgers and Hart, and Harold Arlen. Nearer than that, at meticulously appointed tables, young lawyers and seasoned politicians as well as their wives or mistresses appeared by turns to be self-possessed, exuberant, and pleased. At the table next to theirs, a lovely Asian-American woman and her equally impressive husband occasionally looked up from their meal and observed them with musing interest. Apparently, she thought, the couple recognized them. Pictures of them, together and alone, often appeared in newspapers around the world because she was the daughter of Leonard Winters and because Aaron was a Dowling heir.

The evening began well.

"We are in it again—you and I," Aaron said. "Our brief separation gave us enough time to reignite our marriage. We'll do well together, because we understand each other."

He raised his glass of Champagne in salute to her.

She lightly touched his glass with her own.

"This time will be even better for us," she said. "This time we'll get everything that we want."

Her words brought a smile to his lips. It was a man-of-the-world smile. It was a knowing smile that was slightly jaded, vaguely enigmatic, and probably unsentimental. She liked the smile. It withheld more than it offered.

While they were in the ballroom, he made no mention of the double plot that she had devised. Instead, he spoke of his current work in Palm Beach and a future assignment that would bring him to California. He mentioned his having been invited to play soccer with a team of Wall Street executives in a tournament that was scheduled to take place the following summer in Rio de Janeiro. He also spoke of a Jackson Pollack canvas that his uncle Liam had bequeathed to him, with the stipulation that he could not sell the painting for fifteen years.

She, in turn, spoke about her charity work and about the blue chip stocks that she had recently bought.

They danced with poised assurance to the music of Cole Porter, Jerome Kern, Franz Lehar, and George Gershwin. They continued to drink their Dom Perignon discreetly, and they ate small portions of their delicious food. Wary even at the rim of exhilaration, they invoked new disciplines that kept them agreeably sober and fully aware of their surroundings. They needed to stay in perfect control of each remark that they made and of the idiosyncrasies that informed their behavior. They could not afford to slip up. They had to maintain with plausible ease their disguise as a happily married couple. There could be conveyed between them no whispered talk of the plot to murder Gavin Dowling. Nor could they mention, while vengeful frowns creased their brows and while a sadistic pleasure altered the rhythms of their voices, the ways that the double plot would very likely bring down Bryce. All manner of eyes were observing them casually or studying them carefully. On this night especially, they needed to play their devious games with apparently authentic naturalness for the many friends and acquaintances that stopped to chat with them at their table or on the skyline terrace or at the bar.

Their evening at the Waldorf was an immense success. The friends who had always regarded them as an ideal couple were pleased to have their original impression validated by the smooth rapport that informed her relationship with Aaron. The new acquaintances that the evening had brought into their lives and a few acquaintances of longer duration that had often observed them skeptically now found them charming and unpretentious.

Later, after she and Aaron had left the Waldorf and when Aaron was behind the wheel of his Bentley, driving them to their apartment in Sutton Place, he spoke of their success.

"Tonight, we played the game well," he said. "You and I do make a good team. We are inveterate schemers. We wear our disguises well. We put on a convincing show. We could fool the devil himself, if we had to."

He did not mention the plot to murder Gavin until after they had gone to bed together for the first time in more than a week.

She reveled in their copulation. The sight of Aaron—naked and erect—roused her desire as it had during the first weeks that he made love to her. His touch thrilled her in a new and insatiable way. Often, with his big, skillful hands, he caressed her breasts and, from time to time, bent down to kiss her neck and lips. There was a brute energy to his every move. Tonight his brooding face and his rough kisses brought an edgy ambivalence to his passion. There was a reckless and even sadistic power in his thrusting. He wanted to hurt her. He wanted to punish her. She wanted to be punished. Even as she moaned with pleasure, she saw in his flushed, handsome face the mounting lust, the contorted expressions, and the angry joy that were overtaking his senses. Every so often, while he was inside her, his cold blue eyes stared upon her face, as if he were deciphering a puzzle that she had devised for him. His steely gaze looked just as sharply into her eyes, searching for clues behind the enigmatic smile that crossed her lips and the dark, twisted sensuality that rose out of her expression.

Even after he pulled out of her and leaned into the galaxy of soft pillows, she noticed Aaron studying her with brooding attention. The surprise of his nearly suppressed ambiguity brought her abruptly back to the reality of the lavender-scented bed where he had mounted her. Nevertheless, she summoned a sweet-faced smile that, she felt, must have appeared as somnolent as it was satisfied.

"We *are* right for each other," she murmured, as she echoed the words that he had spoken an hour earlier and while she reached out to caress his face.

But she had barely touched his face, when he turned away from her without uttering a word. He grabbed his Italian black velvet robe from the needlepoint chair that stood near the bed and, at the same time that he covered his nakedness, hurried to the bar. With the manly poise that was a trademark of his character, he poured himself a shot of scotch and quickly swallowed it. Without a pause, he poured himself another drink and opened the French door that allowed him to walk out to the terrace. It was not the first time that she had observed him standing there, peering upon the muted lights of the midnight city. It was foolish to call out to him. He would pay her no heed. Though he had never apologized for his closing himself off from her or explained the cause of his brooding, she knew him well enough to surmise the reason behind his dilemma. Tonight, whatever troubled reality he perceived after their copulation was closing in upon him. He needed to inhabit open space. He needed the sight of the city and its promise of wealth and adventure.

The autumn breeze was crisp and even chilling. It tousled his sandy hair and rippled across his robe. Yet Aaron chose to remain standing there, pensive and silent by the white granite column that gave to the terrace a classical ambiance. Five minutes later, after he had swallowed the second shot of scotch and after he had dwelled alone within the privacy of his unease, he left the terrace and returned to the bar. He poured himself a third shot of scotch and, once again, swallowed it quickly. After that, he came back to the bed. He stood there with stern authority and, while peering upon her dark and naked seductiveness, positioned as it was against a medley of soft pillows, he told her what was on his mind. The scotch had released him from the mandates of his devious persona and from the subtle discipline that informed his worldly assurance. Once again, as it had on the evening that he had apparently walked away from her life, he spoke words that were as blunt as they were truthful. The timbre of his voice was melancholic, and bitter regret was casting a shadow upon his handsome face.

"I'm no good, and neither are you," he said. "We are made for each other. We have lied about many things—to each other and to many of the people who trusted us. But we won't be able to lie about the murder of Gavin. We won't be in the room with Bryce when he shoots Gavin. We won't be the one who is pressing the trigger. But we are killers, nonetheless."

Cool-headed and matter-of-fact, she resisted his accusation.

"I don't believe that," she said. "Whatever happens in that room on the night of the murder will involve only Bryce and Gavin. Bryce was born to kill Gavin. On the night that he does kill him, he will be living out the fate that has always pursued him."

"You are lying to yourself, baby. I wonder how long it will take you to believe your lie."

"I am not lying," she answered him. "I don't need to lie. I see things as they really are."

He smiled a sardonic smile.

"You are good, baby. You are really good. You are a cold-hearted liar. That pretty face of yours conceals a killer's disposition."

She stifled her anger. She did not want to lose him again. She did not want him to back out of their plan.

"Thanks for the character description," she said, her words almost playful in their irony and their carelessness. "Thanks for nothing."

Silence overtook him now, while his cold blue eyes went on studying her. He took an imported cigarette from his gold case on the night table and, with his gold lighter and a casual gesture that belied his tension, quickly ignited it. He took a long drag on the cigarette and, after exhaling, watched the smoky vapors shrouding his face. Then he sat on the edge of the bed, and—still harnessed to tension and bitterness—told her how it was with him.

"Just now, over there on the terrace, I was thinking of my father," he said. "My father is a good man. Many have called him a true man of God. I was remembering the special words that he told me more than a few times. 'There is evil in the world,' he said. 'There is violence. But you must never allow evil and violence to tarnish your goodness. Nor must you league yourself with a killer.'"

This display of his conscience left her uneasy. Only in their most recent meetings had he made her privy to his soul-searching. She perceived it as a weakness that surprised her and as a hairline fracture in his hardness. Nevertheless, she affected a natural empathy and allowed her hand to caress his broad shoulder.

"It can't be helped," she said. "It's the only way that will work for us."

For a moment, withdrawn as he was into the privacies of his brooding sorrow, he said nothing. He was studying her with a contemptuous edginess. He was toughing out this moment when he was sealing his bond with her. Even though a suppressed sorrow held him in its chains, he spoke with a matter-of-fact realism that was devoid of sentimentality or self-pity.

"I used to be a good human being once. You would have thought so, if you had met me then."

She hurried to placate the anger and the sorrow that were yoked to his dark mood.

"You are good enough now," she said. "You are just fine the way you are."

He scoffed at her words.

"Sure, I'm fine," he said, his inflections thick with disdain. "I fit the bill. I am willing to become involved in a murder."

"We won't be at the scene of the crime. You and I will be in Palm Beach. Keep remembering that Bryce wants to kill you. I'm giving him the key to Gavin's apartment. He will not know that your apartment is next door to Gavin's. He will enter Gavin's apartment while intending to kill you. Once he kills Gavin, Bryce has two options. If he is as smart as I think he is, he will ransack Gavin's place and make it look like the scene of a robbery. He will steal Gavin's forty-thousand dollar watch, a Monet canvas, and the thousands of dollars that he keeps in a concealed wall safe that, you told me, is located in his bathroom. Afterward, I'll pay off Bryce. I'll send him to some far away country. He'll be all set.

If he gives me any trouble, then his days will be numbered. Sooner or later, the police will be on his trail. I'll see to that."

She spoke in a spate of words and with clear-headed enthusiasm. She wanted him to see how easy it was going to be. Once Bryce initiated the murder plan, everything was going to fall into place.

At first, Aaron said nothing. He took another drag on his cigarette and peered upon her with a stillness that made her apprehensive. There was a raw menace in him that she must not waken.

Now she switched gears. She invoked a petitioning manner. She brought a crease to her brow that suggested a deep-seated concern for his wellbeing. She reached out to touch his left hand. Smoke wafted in vapors from his cigarette and shrouded part of his face. With the cigarette dangling from the corner of his mouth, he had the look of a steel-hearted broker or a jaded detective.

"Don't you see, Aaron? Everything will be all right for us. We'll be in the clear. We can have the lives that we have always wanted."

Upon hearing her words this time, he did not wait to witness, with a cursory glance or a judgmental stare, the artifice of her expression. He rose abruptly from his place at the edge of the bed and returned to the bar for his fifth shot of scotch. Tonight, he wanted to get drunk. He wanted to forget the trap into which he was falling. With drink in hand, he walked back to the bed once again and, with the cold-hearted detachment that he had made his stock in trade and with a vague sneer twisting the right corner of his mouth, he spoke the quiet words that told her about the man that he used to be.

"There was a time when I would have found your murder plan repugnant. Even now it disgusts me."

He had not accepted this new stain upon his character. He was being defensive. He was struggling to retrieve his lost honor, even while in the back of his mind he understood that there was no going back. He had already made his choice. From this time forward, he would have to live with the knowledge that he was an accomplice to the murder of a cousin who had never wronged him. He would learn to be all right with it, eventually. Prodigious wealth and formidable power brokering would make it all right. Still, she thought it best to remind him that he had already chosen his path.

"You are playing the game," she said. "You are helping me to put the plan in motion."

He glared at her. For an instant, she believed that he was going to slap or even punch her. An eerie stillness hovered by him, as if it were watching him. Then, summoning the grim detachment from his feelings that had always enabled him to push his way forward, he willed himself to speak the hard word that she wanted to hear.

"Yes."

"What made you change your mind?"

"Fifteen years is too long to wait for anything."

"You are smart to come back to the plan. Apart from these eleventh-hour recriminations, how do you feel about that? How do you really feel now that you have accepted the plan that I was selling you?"

He paused before he answered her. Then, as if he could no longer avoid the other word that condemned him, he answered her with an honesty that was as caustic as it was bitter.

"Sold," he said.

Chapter Nine
Death Trap

Bryce awoke snarling his protest. With raw and furious instincts and with reflexes as taut as they were swift, he reached beneath his pillows for the Colt Cobra .38 revolver. Not completely awake, startled and defensive, he saw his enemy standing before him. Ian Templeton was right there, standing by the bench at the end of the bed and aiming his Beretta pistol at his heart. His shock of white hair; the ghostly pallor of his face; his furious, brown-eyed glare; the twisted sneer of his mouth; and his clenched jaw—all of these emblems of identity intensified the formidable six foot, four inch hulking figure that was pressing his finger against the trigger of his pistol.

"You killed my daughter," Templeton was shouting to him. "You were the death of her."

"No! No! It wasn't like that," he heard himself crying out, his raspy belligerence disguising his guilt even as it concealed his remorse. "I had nothing to do with it. She killed herself."

"You brought death to Meredith," Templeton insisted, his grating voice sounding not quite human. It sounded hollow and sepulchral. It was the voice of a father crazed with grief. It was the voice of a vengeful spirit. "You were a trap. You were her death trap."

"She killed herself," he shouted back. "She was a romantic fool. She was in it over her head. She was her own worst enemy."

"She's gone forever," Templeton said. His words were a soft lament now. In spite of the pistol that, willful and murderous, he was brandishing, he was a broken man. "She will never come back. Never. Never. Never."

Ian Templeton was also a man who wanted to kill him. He had tried once before. Only by random chance had he failed. Now, on this storm-turbulent night while thunder boomed, lightning flared its yellow claws, and winds howling their powers lashed thepanoramic window with driving rain, he was going to try once again to kill him. He was not surprised or even shaken while Ian Templeton held his finger near the trigger of his pistol. But he was shaken nonetheless by the accusation that this lost man, this grief-stricken father hurled at him.

"You were her trap," he said once more. This time, his voice was as bitter as it was rancorous. "You are Mister Death. You are a death trap."

Templeton began pressing his finger against the trigger of his pistol.

He, Bryce Thompson—the street-wise huckster whose primitive instincts had, always before this moment, served him well—raised his revolver with the wily swiftness of a man who was ready to kill this gaunt-faced menace standing by the bench at the foot of this oversized bed.

Propped against a cadre of navy-blue pillows as he confronted his murderous enemy, Bryce held his revolver with steady precision that belied his angry tension. With his rugged arms stretched forward, he had wrapped the thumb of his strong hand around the middle finger that he had placed on the grip. In nearly the same instant, he had rested the thumb of his support hand parallel with and just under the pistol slide. His index finger pressed the trigger, and the revolver fired two of its six bullets at the enemy who was firing at him. As soon as he fired his weapon, Ian darted away to a darker corner of the room. He fired again, and Ian returned the fire. But no bullets ripped through his own body or, on impact, threw him backward before blood spurted up from his chest and his legs gave way as he slid downward with a finality that surprised him, overcome and dying. None of that happened. In spite of the bullets that Ian had fired upon him, he remained untouched.

The first bullets rushing from his revolver slammed through Ian and hurried onward into the southerly wall behind his assailant, shattering intricate moldings, beveled edges, and fillets. The third bullet nicked the pale gray finish that melded with the exposed old gilt of a richly upholstered chair near the fireplace in that same corner. Still tracking the swift movements of Ian Templeton, he fired the fourth bullet into his chest. Blood spilled across his chest and rushed out of his back. Yet he did not fall. Instead, he hurried toward the north part of the room, still firing his Beretta. None of Ian's bullets hit him. He returned the fire. The bullets exploded into Templeton's head, and thick globules of blood rushed out of his forehead and ripped away the top of his head. His left eye popped out, the viscous fluid dripping down his cheek while the chiseled contours of his face collapsed. The bullets cut through him and flew behind him, disarranging and damaging the furnishings in the east corner of the room. The nineteenth-century French mirror above his dresser cracked, and the flickering light bulb from the overturned lamp there on the same Louis XVI dresser hissed and blew out its glow.

But Ian Templeton stood before him, unwounded and still firing his Beretta.

At that moment, the light of the moon, with will-o'-the-wisp proclivities and the nimble motion of a thief, hurried through the panoramic window and shimmered its radiance across the Aubusson carpet and upon the burnished gray of walls and cabinets and plasterwork that, Lauren had once assured him, lent an old-world air to this master bedroom. The shimmering light touched, as well, the Louis XVI-style bed and the mahogany bench in front of it. The light of the moon also incited his new awareness. The moon and its radiance showed his eyes that no one was here in his bedroom—at least, not within his seeing.

He had wakened into his nightmare. Chained to the murky surfaces of his sleep, he had struggled to escape the phantoms from his past that, with implacable hatred and murderous powers, were pursuing him. Through the sheer force of his will and a brute guardedness before all the persons whom he had wronged that were now haunting his dreams, he had broken the chains of his sleep without being freed from it. His dark memories would not let him go. Even broken, the chains weighed him down. On this uneasy night, only one night away from the quiet hour when he would kill Aaron Dowling, he struggled in vain to escape from his punishing dreams. But he could not easily elude them. The unforgiving phantoms of his past had leaped on this bleak night nearly upon him. But he kept pushing himself out of his dreams. He had escaped from nearly all of his phantoms. Yet, caught at the rim of sleep at the same time that he was pushing his way into wakening awareness, he had brought one of those phantoms into this room with him.

Ian Templeton was that phantom. He had come to haunt him in the name of justice. He had come to taunt him in the name of revenge. He had come with words that were meant to burn in his soul. He had come to remind him that, when he was Professor Bryce Thompson, he had been the catalyst in the death of a beautiful, innocent girl.

From a faraway corner in his awareness, he heard a doorbell ringing. Someone was not only pressing his index finger against the doorbell. He was also banging against the door. The sounds, muffled by distance yet insistent nonetheless, rose in waves and echoed their urgency all the way through the long hall that led from the living room to his bedroom. The sounds pushed him, at last, into full consciousness of his surroundings. He could hear, as a vague signal of intrusion or trespass or danger—perhaps, all of them at the same time—a key being twisted inside an intricate door lock. The signal, as grating as it was metallic, called him into swift action. With the wily agility of a panther, he sprinted from the bed and grabbed a burgundy robe to cover his nakedness. His revolver never left his grip, not even as, by means of his sleight of hand, he covered himself with his robe and as he placed the revolver in the oversized pocket of that robe, while keeping his finger near the trigger.

When, in that instant, a grim-faced security guard was running along the hall that led to the bedroom, he was ready for his questions. Though the dimly lighted hall concealed his face, he saw that the guard was pointing his Browning handgun in his direction. As the guard approached the threshold of the bedroom, he recognized him as Brendan Fitzgerald. He was well acquainted with him. Once inside the room, Brendan quickly glanced at him and, just as quickly, gave his attention to the entire surround of the scene. His probing eyes were scanning the room for an assailant, and his big hands were pointing his handgun in all the places where, he may have been imagining, a thief whose crime he had interrupted was hiding. Because there was no thief to be found, Brendan looked at him with quizzical and suspicious gaze.

A tall and brawny man in his late twenties, he was a hardened combat veteran who had recently completed two tours of duty in a Special Forces unit assigned to the war still raging in Vietnam. He had killed many enemies. Three or four of those same enemies had fired bullets into his rugged body. Brendan Fitzgerald carried shrapnel in the left side of his head and an inch away from his heart. His mane of red hair and freckled face gave a fleeting suggestion of boyishness, but the cold gaze of his blue eyes, the gritted teeth, and the tightened jawline revealed the dangerous impulses that were churning, repressed and malignant, inside him. His Army training had taught him to harness those impulses to the lawful surfaces of conduct and to the unrelenting pursuit of criminals upon whom he often inflicted savage beatings before he brought them, handcuffed and bleeding, to the nearest police station. His cynical view of the world's nearly casual depredations and his distrust of even benevolent-seeming individuals made him a younger brother-in-spirit with a soul as damaged as his own.

Brendan had lived through a wretched childhood in Rhode Island ghettos and had suffered undeserved beatings from his foster father and coldhearted indifference from a promiscuous foster mother. Tough-minded, in his boyhood and afterward, Brendan had survived not only all the rescue missions he captained in Vietnam. He had also survived drug-addicted parents who often forgot who he was, so lost were they inside the murky hell that they had made for themselves. He had survived, too, though not without visible wounds, the gang of killers that pursued him in the dark, narrow alleys and deserted night streets of South Providence. His blighted childhood in Rhode Island had left scars that were deeper than the ones that remained like ugly welts behind his left ear, across his chest, and beneath his throat.

When he was fifteen, on his own initiative and with the thick-skinned mentoring of a former heavyweight fighter who never made the big time, he learned how to box at a local gym. A year later, he knew how to fire a Remington rifle, a Smith & Wesson semi-automatic pistol, and a Magnum revolver. At seventeen, he persuaded his foster father, on one of the many nights when that jaded and twisted bastard had fallen into a drunken stupor, to sign the papers that would gain him entrance into the Army. He never regretted the Army. It was the only real parent that he came to know. Harsh and forbidding and protective, the Army always leveled with him. The lessons that it meted out to him confirmed what he had learned from a volatile household and from angry, unforgiving streets. In ways that were even more profound than his experience of the ghetto, the Army acquainted him with his fierce capacities for combat, his tremendous will to go on living, and the darkened areas of his soul that had closed themselves off from sentimentality and compunction.

Brendan and he had never met until a year ago. Yet they had shared many similar experiences. Those experiences had left them bitter, pugnacious, and dangerous. In many ways, their lives mirrored each other's. But there were differences. Though both of them were survivors, Brendan—because he was ten years younger and, possibly, because he was even more tough-minded—had maintained his fierce desire to go on living at any cost. He could not imagine that Brendan had ever thought of killing himself.

Brendan held him in his steely gaze. Then, he threw a blunt pair of questions his way.

"Where is he? Where is the thief?"

Perverse and unyielding while hovering at the rim of their friendship, he met Brendan's inquiring eyes with matter-of-fact attention, even as he withheld the truth of things.

"Your guess is as good as mine," he said.

Right away, Brendan was on to his game.

"Maybe my guess is better than yours," he said, with the sardonic inflections that often spiked the meaning of his words.

Brendan was all right. He was not going to make trouble. But the official part of him—the meticulous part that kept him wary and vigilant—drove him to do the thing that needed to be done. Because he wanted to validate his guess that no thief was hiding in any other room of this penthouse, he hurried down the hall that would bring him back to the living room and to all the other rooms that, with stealthy gait and brandished handgun, he was going to investigate.

While Brendan was gone to his guard duties, he—Bryce Thompson, the world-weary hustler who was going to kill Aaron Dowling within the next twenty hours—poured himself a double shot of scotch from the gold-rimmed flask that sat upon one of his bed tables. He swallowed the scotch fast, savoring the sting of it and the cedar taste. The scotch appeased his apparent restlessness and his muted apprehension. But, unlike cocaine or marijuana, it did not allow him to become instantly lost inside a far-flung sanctuary. By the time Brendan returned, he had lighted an imported cigarette and was taking a drag on it.

Brendan noticed the emptied glass of scotch and the opened flask next to it. He noticed, as well, the hair-trigger signs of his brooding. He read those signs with honed-sharp awareness. There was no surprise to it. He and Brendan had been spawned from the same hell. Lately, Brendan appeared to have run free of it. He had survived the war. His stint as a security guard was nearing an end. His cosmopolitan edginess and his sexual prowess had won him the favor of a wealthy divorcée who lived in a penthouse on the eighteenth floor. Although she was ten years his senior, she was still beautiful, and—according to Brendan—she was good in bed. She wanted to marry him, and she was going to push him up to an executive position in her father's steel corporation. She had wanted him to leave his post as a security guard. But, savvy and self-assured, he used his Special Forces background and his job as a security guard to make a favorable impression upon her father. Her father was very pleased when he heard that Brendan had insisted on keeping his job until he joined the corporation. He wanted to earn money to pay his own way.

"That is a man who knows how to fight battles and win. He also knows the value and the honor that come from honest work," her father told her. "I can use a man like him in my corporation."

As guileful as he was ambitious, Brendan knew how to work things in his favor. He was flying high. Maybe, by means of random chance or of his shrewd playing of the cards that the Fates were dealing him, he really would overcome his wretched beginnings. Maybe. Maybe not.

Taking his full measure, all brooding tension and suppressed animosity, Brendan prodded him to explain things.

"What's happened, Bryce?"

"A bad dream."

Brendan tried to go easy. He did not want to make trouble.

"I have them all the time," he said, while he accepted one of his imported cigarettes. "But I don't shoot up my bedroom."

"It has never happened before."

"Do you want to talk about it?"

He met Brendan's question with a quiet terseness that concealed his surly disposition.

"No," he answered him.

Brendan was not displeased. He respected the adamant will that draws upon its own powers to resolve the problems that incited its energies. Brendan might have responded within the same willful isolation, had he been the ill-fated bastard who was trying to find his way out of his dilemma. Tonight, Brendan was really trying to be his friend. He was not going to make any trouble. He was all right. Brendan's instincts told him that this conflicted alter-ego standing before him in a burgundy cashmere robe and with an imported cigarette dangling at the right corner of his mouth—this con man and huckster, this devious business cohort and wily user of women, this incorrigible Bryce Thompson—was not about to make a wrong move or to take a false step that would draw the attention of the police or of any other adversaries.

Brendan turned to leave now. While making a quick exit and without turning back, he raised his hand in a casual salute to him, as he spoke with lighthearted panache the cautionary words that were meant to steer him to a safe path.

"Well, lay off the booze, friend," he said. "Too much of that scotch can get you into trouble."

Then, as swiftly as he had appeared, he was gone.

But his memory of Meredith Templeton stayed. Even against his conscious will, her imaginary presence was a palpable influence upon his senses. On this uneasy night, when his life seemed to be closing in upon him, her genteel beauty, enhanced as it was by her titian hair, blue eyes, and fair skin, was vivid and life-like. Her voice, nearly tremulous with her love for him, was calling out his name from a long ago evening while he sat, here and now, in the amply upholstered chair by his bed and nursed still another shot of scotch whiskey.

"Why can't you say it, Bryce?" she was asking him. "Why can't you tell me that you love me?"

They were sitting in a dimly lighted corner of a crowded Greenwich Village pub. He was enjoying a shot of ninety-proof vodka. Every so often, she allowed herself to sip her Manhattan. In the smoke-clouded distance, a jazz combo was exploring the sensual rhythms of a ballad about lost love, to which a young and nubile African American beauty was imparting poignant implications and dramatic shades of meaning. Even within the shadowy privacies of their favorite corner of the pub, Meredith's eyes glowed with love for him. The touch of her right hand upon his left shoulder was like no other woman's soft caress. The feminine grace that was her defining manner leaned into him, as she kept her hand upon his shoulder. Her Chanel fragrance, with its jasmine, rose, and lily of the valley subtleties, roused his carnal interest even as it recalled a montage of images in which they were in bed together, copulating and ecstatic.

Cynical and careless, he refused to placate her need to be told that he loved her. She was too needy. She was too vulnerable. Though he admired her fragile loveliness and the delicate manner through which she defined who she was, he disdained the neurotic intricacies of her persona. He preferred his women to be tough-minded and resilient. In the hurly-burly of complicated relationships, they neither whimpered nor asked for pity. Yet, in spite of these reservations, he found Meredith intriguing. He had never met anyone else like her. He had not, even after the six months that spanned the furtive undercurrents of their assignations, come close to fathoming her mystery.

Away from the university environment where they were confined by their roles as a well-regarded professor of American literature and an extremely bright student from a privileged background, he enjoyed many of the emotional territories they were free to explore as lovers and friends. But he met with casual repartee and a sly wit that subverted real intimacy all her suggestions that the bond they were creating with each other was meant to be both ideal and lasting.

So, on this remembered night when, with their pulses still quickened by the thrill of their unanticipated romance, Meredith asked him why he would not tell her that he loved her, he answered her with the same casual remarks that he had used on those other occasions when she implored him to say that he loved her.

"I don't have to say 'I love you,'" he said. "You can see in my eyes the love that is there for you. You can perceive that love in my smile and feel it in my kisses and in my touch. You can hear in my voice the love I have for you, whenever we are talking about all the little things or some of the important things that help two people to know that they are in love with each other. By now, if you need me to say that I love you, you are ignoring all the natural clues to the way I feel about you. They are extemporaneous signals that reflect my true feelings."

"Those are wonderful clues," she agreed. "All of them delight me. But, as wonderful as those clues are, I think that most women want something more. Each of them wants her man to say those three words. She wants to hear him say, 'I love you.'"

"I have never used conventional words or memorized phrases to court a woman. I could never make the words sound natural."

"Oh, they would sound natural, if you really meant them."

"You want too much, baby. I told you how it is with me when we began seeing one another. That first night, I asked you whether you wanted to play the game of love with me. 'This is just a game,' I reminded you. 'We can have a good time together, as long as you understand that.' You said that you understood perfectly. You promised not to be trapped by romantic feelings. You were in it for a good time, you said. 'Love comes. Love goes. I'll treat it lightly and have a good time.' That is what you told me. That is what you promised."

"I didn't really know you then," she said. "That was just the beginning for us. That was before I fell in love with you."

"You will get over it," he told her. "Nothing lasts forever."

"True love lasts," she said. "I won't get over it. That is a promise. I'll make you see how true I can be. Then, maybe, you will want to be true as well."

"You are a very romantic woman," he said. "Be careful. Romantic women often fall into traps. They don't recognize danger, even when it is standing next to them."

"I'll take my chances," she said.

Meredith's beautiful face had been wistful then. It was wistful now, ten years later—here, in this plush bedroom that was borrowed from Lauren's addiction to him and from her apprehension. That night, Meredith's face had been filled with love for him. Tonight, her face was radiant still with her love. She seemed so real. She seemed alive. But she was not alive. She was a ghostly apparition who had come here to prod the guilt that he held, as though with chains, inside the darkest corner of his mind. To dispel the memory of that long-ago evening in the pub, he rose from his chair by the bed and hurried to the bar, where once again he filled his glass with scotch. He swallowed the scotch quickly and walked barefooted across the Aubusson carpet onto the terrace. The brisk October air quickened his awareness, even as it diminished the influence of the scotch upon his senses. But the bright lights of the nearly deserted three o'clock city could not appease his conscience or displace his memory of Meredith.

Standing there, by the marble column on the terrace, he thought of other days and nights that he had spent with Meredith Templeton.

One time, during a winter recess from Columbia University, he and Meredith made a journey to Graubünden, a ski resort in Switzerland. For all the wrong reasons, Graubünden was a place he would not forget. Even now, the name called forth a memory of Meredith's uneasy soul searching and her intimate revelations. The name summoned, too, an echo of Meredith's tremulous voice and a vision of her petitioning manner, as she imparted to him an urgent message concerning their relationship, as though he were her religious confessor or, more likely, the one man that she had grown to love and to trust and that she wanted to marry. Even before their journey began, he was aware that Meredith regarded this holiday excursion to Europe as much more than an occasion for skiing, for sightseeing, and for meeting new friends.

In those years, he was flying high. He had recently been promoted to full professor, and his books about Fitzgerald and Hemingway had made the bestseller lists. Before he met Meredith, he had been sleeping with five or six other beautiful students. All of them had been born into wealth, and they regarded the privileges that their lives had bestowed upon them as both natural and inevitable. They were debutantes who did not mind displaying their glamour and their father's riches in photo shoots for upscale magazines and during interviews on primetime television. They were hard, promiscuous, and self-centered. They were adventurers willing to lavish big money and luxurious gifts upon him. For his jaded purposes, they were ideal mates—in bed and on bar stools, as well as at luxurious vacation playgrounds, on glamorous ballroom dance floors, and in tony Alpine ski lodges.

Meredith Templeton was altogether different. Sensitive, good-natured, and unspoiled, she revived his youthful belief in the virtuous disposition of some women. When he learned of the tragedies that had scarred her life, he was not surprised that Meredith was sometimes afflicted by anxieties and nightmares. When she was fourteen years old, her brother Austin, who was ten years her senior, had died heroically as a bomber pilot in Vietnam. Her mother, grieving over the loss of her favorite child and only son, died soon afterward of a massive stroke. Her father, the formidable Wall Street broker Ian Templeton, came to depend upon Meredith for emotional sustenance. He was not ready to go forward to another mate. Nor, at the age of fifty-four, did he care to sire another son whom the Fates might destroy and leave him, the once-happy father who had now become a hollow man, with dashed hopes and grieving heart.

Before tragedy destroyed their happiness, the Templeton family traveled widely. Each autumn or winter, they spent many exhilarating days in Graubünden. In that year when he was carrying on a clandestine affair with her, Meredith wanted to replicate the memorable experiences that she had known in Switzerland with her parents and with her brother. So eager was she to return to Graubünden, that she persuaded him to make a journey with him to this southeast area of Switzerland, which bordered on Liechtenstein and Austria to the north and on Italy to the east and south. They would be enjoying the freedom of their winter recess from university obligations, and they would be staying at a fine hotel. Every autumn or winter, from the time that she was six years old until she was fourteen, she spent some of the happiest days of her life there. That her return to Graubünden might recall that happy period intrigued him, even as it teased her expectations.

Graubünden did not disappoint her, and it pleased him, as well. He saw the same winter imagery that she was apprehending. Yet she saw something else, something more than its Alpine beauty. She saw herself with her parents and with her brother. Its folded landscapes of deep, isolated valleys, its sheer rocky summits, and its thick pine forests possessed, as an imprint on the landscapes which were visible now only to her eyes, the imagery of herself with her father, her mother, and—until he was eighteen and vacationing with university friends—her supremely athletic brother horse-riding or hiking or traveling in a Bentley all around the region.

"When I was six or seven years old," she said, "it fascinated me to see glaciers oozing from between the high mountains. Even now, I can hear my mother's voice explaining their importance. It was these glaciers that launched two of Europe's great rivers—the Rhine, on its way to the North Sea, and the Inn, hurrying into the Black Sea. On that trip, my father pointed out two smaller rivers that were watering pomegranates, figs, and chestnuts in secluded southern valleys. These rivers, he said, were en route to the Po and the Gulf of Venice."

Her voice trembled, and her smile wavered at the brink of weeping. Graubünden, he discerned, affected her more deeply than she had expected. Though it had given her glimpses of her parents and her brother and of herself as an innocent child, the recollection left her uneasy and sorrow-laden.

"I'll never have any of this back," she said. "I'll never see this place without the ghosts. I've lost the best of it. I've lost *them*. I've lost my mother and my brother. I've lost all the days here that were free of disappointment and tragedy."

They had gone skiing early that morning. Now, a few minutes past noon and alone in their snowmobiles, they were hurrying back to their chalet, where they would enjoy hot toddies and roast beef sandwiches. Two of his young colleagues from Columbia University, along with their even younger wives, had joined them in their vigorous hours of skiing. Everyone had had a good time. They would also join them for lunch, bringing to the gathering of a half dozen people the *joie-de-vivre* that kept friendship spirited and new.

Before they reached the pristine chalet that her father had bought for her Swiss visits, he chose understated words to persuade her to see Graubünden in a different way. His life, with its sudden upheavals and unforgiving betrayals, had taught him to disdain nostalgia as a self-defeating weakness. He prodded her now to see Graubünden without the emotional sub-texts that, against her conscious will, were making her believe that she had lost happiness forever.

"Try to see this place as a landscape of your happy childhood and not as a scene that invites you to calculate your current losses," he said. "You were happy in the years when you first visited this area. You can be happy now and even later, if you will yourself to be so. Your life is still in the making. There are no rules that require you to be unhappy. Make your own rules. Promise yourself that you will laugh your cares away."

He felt her soft, blue eyes observing him while he navigated their snowmobile with swift and steady momentum, as they made their way to the chalet. She moved closer to him and leaned her beaming face into his shoulder.

"You are good for what ails me," she said. "You know how to rescue a woman from her melancholy."

"You and I are here to have a good time," he said. "There will be no more melancholy. That is a promise. I'll push your melancholy away every time that it kicks you around."

His words drew from her a lighthearted laughter. Clearly, she was grateful for all that he was doing for her. Her eyes gleamed with love for him. Her gloved hand carefully touched his shoulder, as if by touching him she might gather unto herself some of his strength. The gesture pleased him. In the same moment, though, he felt surprised that he had not walked away when, weeks earlier, she first revealed the sorrow that was overwhelming her. There was something in her manner that profoundly moved him. He had never before felt this way about anybody. He wondered whether what he was feeling for her was genuine love. The thought quickened his unease. He did not trust it. Maybe, in spite of her unexpected influence upon him, he did not trust Meredith. Maybe. Whether the rancorous scenes of his past held him back or the mysterious aspects of her personality, he could not say. Whatever it was, he resolved to do everything that he could to make her happy for as long as they were together.

On the pretext that he was eager to see more of Graubünden, he persuaded Meredith to go forward to St. Moritz in the Engadine Valley, with its undulating ski runs and its tobogganing races on the challenging slopes of Muottas Muragl; with its polo tournaments on a frozen lake; and with its lilting music festival. Though contentment and even exhilaration often touched their days here, he sensed within Meredith a pensive stillness that was anchored to dismay and sadness. Not even when they joined other couples in a paragliding excursion that brought them in astonishing proximity to lofty Engadine mountains or when they went white water rafting on the Inn River—not even these extraordinary times could ease her troubled mind beyond the swift hours that activated her competitive spirit and her natural self-possession. Nor on the day when they joined their friends in a tobogganing race or during the evenings when they were dancing at the Grand Hotel did she seem herself. Some burden was weighing her down. A sorrow like remorse or dismay was clouding whatever temporary happiness this vacation had brought her.

"What is wrong?" he gently asked her one night after he had been awakened by her tossing and turning beside him in bed and by her hastening out of her sleep to cry her alarm and her hostility toward some remembered adversary.

"Don't do it!" she shouted as she flailed the air with her right arm and with her clenched fist. "Don't leave me!"

"Tell me what is wrong," he said, his voice hushed by his wary witness of her and by the gentle nature of his petition.

He had risen from his pillows right after she had sprung forward from her place next to him. Only then did he place his hand on her shoulder and speak his soft words to her.

She, in turn, had come fully awake. Glancing at him momentarily, as if she needed to be certain of who he was, she at first said nothing. Only when he petitioned her once more did she answer him.

"Tell me," he said. "Tell me so that I can help you."

"It's nothing,' she said. "It's nothing you need to worry about."

"But I do worry," he said. "I care about you, and I want to make everything easier for you."

By this time, she had tossed the covers away from her nakedness and was sitting on the edge of the bed. The curve of her young back and the taut energy of her graceful arms enhanced her nakedness. In this moment of apprehension, she appeared vulnerable and hesitant.

He hurried from his side of the bed and clothed his own nakedness with the charcoal gray robe that he had thrown over the arm of a nearby chair, which was stitched in needlepoint and complemented the sumptuousness of the room. Then he took hold of the azure silk nightgown and blue robe that she had thrown over the arm of a companion chair and found a sitting place beside her as he helped her to clothe her nakedness.

He could see her face now, alert and brooding and self-questioning. As she rose from her place, so that she could allow the nightgown and robe to envelop her frame, she looked frightened and unhappy. With the tentative strategies that must have brought her through other bad nights, she had escaped from her nightmare, but she was not yet ready to deal with the world on its harsh and uncompromising terms.

He believed that this was how it was with her, having attained more than a little knowledge of men and women whom the world had bruised with all manner of betrayals.

He invited her to sit beside him once again at the edge of the bed. Extending his hand to meet hers, he drew her fragrant body into his massive arms and to the warmth of his smile.

"Tell me," he asked her while softly echoing his previous request. "Tell me what has upset you."

"You would not enjoy hearing it," she said.

"I am not weak," he said. "Besides, telling me about it may help you."

She moved away to peer at him silently while she considered his willingness to become implicated in her sadness. Then, approaching him once more and holding him in her searching gaze, she began speaking the words that told him the news that she had suppressed for many days.

"I've been having nightmares in which you leave me."

"Why would I want to do that? You have become part of my team. We always have a good time together."

"I'm pregnant," she said. "I've been pregnant for two months."

He could feel his jawline tightening and the angry surprise rising within him. He held himself steady. He did not want to hurt her. Yet he wanted to keep his distance from her dilemma. He met her words with a matter-of-fact assertion. His voice, low-keyed and eerily quiet, sounded vaguely blunt and hollow.

"You will have to get rid of it," he said.

For a few moments, his words held her fast to their pitiless implications. Then, breaking free of their hold upon her, she spoke with inflections that were as matter-of-fact as his words had been.

"I came to St. Moritz with a plan. I was going to have an accident. It would be very easy, I thought, to stage a bad fall when I was skiing across the frozen snow of a hill or to slip on the hardened ice of the rink where we were skating. Surely, I would have a miscarriage because of the fall. But I couldn't go through with it."

Hearing her words, he withdrew to a grim-faced stillness. He offered her neither the caress of his hand, nor the soft words of empathy that she was seeking. He was without pity.

Now she began petitioning him. Her eyes were misty with tears, and her voice was tremulous.

"I don't want to get rid of our baby," she murmured, as though she were afraid to give any emphasis to her protest. "I want to keep it. It thrills me to know that I am carrying your son. I am going to be very careful. I want our son to have life. I am certain that he can make both of us happier than we are now."

"You are thinking like a schoolgirl. You are not thinking clearly. We don't need a kid to make us happy. We have each other."

"We'll have something more than ourselves. But the wonderful thing is that our son will be a special part of ourselves."

"You want me to marry you."

"Yes."

"I told you that I am not marrying anybody, not even you."

"Having a son will make a difference. You will see."

"I don't want him," he said. "I don't need any kid to make me happy. I like my freedom. I'm not giving that away to anyone."

"You can still be free. I promise not to get in your way. I'll be content to be with my son when you can't be around."

"It's not any good, Meredith. You are asking me to be someone else—a Mister Upright who follows all the rules and, after an honest day's work, comes home to safe conventions and dull habits."

"Our life together will be more exciting than that. My father has a great deal of influence. He will help you move to the top, whether your choice is a university setting or a broker's office on Wall Street."

"I don't need his help. I'm doing all right on my own."

"But I need your help. I want to keep my baby. I don't want to be disgraced or to bring disgrace upon him. I need you to marry me."

"It is not going to work, I tell you. I do not love you in that way. I love you because we have a good time together. I love you because we promised that there would be no strings between us. We can float free of any entanglement. We promised not to trap one another. How can we float free, if there is a baby around? The baby is a trap."

"I need this baby, Bryce. I need him almost as much as I need you."

The tenuous pity he felt for her pushed him to softer words.

"There you go again, leading with your chin. You will never win the game that way."

"This isn't a game."

"No, it isn't."

"Help me, Bryce. Please."

"I'd like to, baby. But it isn't in me. At any rate, you have your old man. Ask him to help you."

"I don't want to involve my father. I don't want to make him sadder than he is now. He's still reeling from the loss of my mother and my brother. It will break his heart if he finds out that I am pregnant."

"How can you be certain of that? Your bringing another Templeton into the world may be just the thing to snap him out of his sadness."

"I know my father. He will not be pleased to have an illegitimate grandson."

"Then you should get rid of your problem. Get rid of the kid."

"No. I won't do that. Please say that you will marry me. We won't even have to live together. But we can still be lovers. I'll never stop loving you. I'm willing to be whoever you want me to be. I won't make any trouble. But you have to marry me. If you have any real love for me, you need to give me that protection. Will you at least think about marrying me?"

"Sure I will, baby. That is a promise. But today, and for the rest of the week while we are here in St. Moritz, let's have a good time. We'll chase your blues away. We'll stop worrying about tomorrow."

With their university friends, they did have a good time. Each morning, before breakfast, they swam in the heated pools of the spa. In the afternoon, they kayaked once again across the swift waters of the Inn River. They went paragliding high above the sun-glowing blue lakes and close by the ample hills and high mountain peaks of the Engadine Valley. They sailed from St. Moritz to Lake Lugano, navigating their way across breeze-quickened waters and sighting all around them the alpine peaks that were stretching to the horizon and the red tile roofs of houses that were scattered across the town's hillsides.

There were times when he and Meredith were not together. No longer did she care to join him while he skied across the steep-sloping challenges of the Engadine Valley or when he played a furious game of polo on a frozen lake. She wanted to protect the child that she was carrying. Instead, she spent her time within the spa, cautiously exercising her limbs and skillfully swimming across a heated pool.

On their last night together in St. Moritz, she hosted a birthday party for him in the grand ballroom of the hotel where they were staying. He put on a good show for their friends who were dancing around them and for the friends who were dining at nearby tables while watching Meredith and him waltzing together with natural-seeming ease and with the romantic poise of lovers who were meant for each other. Though he had not offered Meredith the promise of marriage that she wanted to hear, she had—during these festive days and nights—regained her vivacity and her optimism. He enjoyed clasping with his rugged left hand the warmth of her delicate hand and enjoyed as much the press of his right hand upon her lower back. He noticed the intensity of her blue eyes, the radiant blush that had overtaken her lovely features, and the gentle smile that, in spite of their troubled relationship, she was smoothly maintaining. A demure brunette was singing ballads about the true love that lasts, while a band of musicians accompanied her. Their blue notes kept floating across the crowded room and mingling with the exhilarated voices of the guests.

He danced with her in silence, consenting to their proximity with a love for her that surprised him. So moved was he by this unexpected moment that he refrained from speaking any words that might break the spell. He felt deeply about her, and the truth of those feelings that he had been suppressing now awed and confused him. Still he accepted the spell. Over and over he gave himself to the whirl and sway of the dance with her.

Then, as the singer was ending her medley of songs about newly discovered love, Meredith spoke the words that broke the spell and hurried him into the darker reality that was his willful decision to leave her.

"I want it to be this way always, Bryce," she said. "I want us to be as happy as we are at this moment."

He recognized the tremor within the sweet textures of her voice. The feminine timbres could not diminish the emotional charge of her words. Lost inside his wilderness, he resisted her belief in their love. But he chose careful words that concealed his plan to turn away from her.

"We are happy right now, baby. We don't need to ask for anything more than that."

Hearing his words, she laughed lightheartedly.

"I shall always ask for more, Bryce," she said. "You have so much love in your heart. One day, you may decide to give all of it to me."

"There you go again," he said. "You are always leading with your chin. Don't you know that you can get hurt that way?"

"I'll take the risk," she answered him. "With you, I'll always take the risk."

The music ended now. The musicians had completed this set of ballads and were taking a break.

He led her back to the table where their friends were waiting to include them in quick-witted conversation and frequent Champagne toasting of everyone who was a part of their company. He felt relieved to be freed of his protective clasp of Meredith and of her searching eyes. But, for the rest of that evening, her voice, carrying for his ears alone the faint residue of her recent sorrow, persuaded him to look upon her with a furtive gaze that both pitied and loved her.

"Leaving her is the best thing that I can do for her," he told himself. "She can get rid of the kid. She can forget about me. She'll find some other guy whose love is the real thing."

When they returned to New York, he saw her less often, because he was involved with grading examination papers and working with several colleagues on curriculum planning committees. Meredith, who was completing the first semester of her junior year, was busy writing term papers and taking her final tests for the semester.

But, when the semester was over, he hurried away from New York. He sailed to England to begin a year's sabbatical that was supposed to culminate in his writing a book about the American novelist Nathaniel Hawthorne. In that season, he was planning to research the life that Hawthorne had experienced in Liverpool, when he was serving as the United States consul to England's most important commercial city.

He had left Meredith behind, even though she had planned to study in London as part of the requirements for attaining her degree. She had chosen London, so that she could live with him. Their plan would have worked well, if she had not got herself pregnant. Eventually, he found out that she was continuing her studies in New York. It did not take long to convince himself that he was better off without her. Within the first week of his arrival in England, he was living with a film starlet that he had picked up in a popular nightclub.

In March of that year, he learned that Meredith had died from an overdose of sleeping pills. The baby that she was carrying died with her. For the rest of that year, he was haunted by nightmares in which, through various disguises and by means of a hangman's knot, a Napoleonic sword, a Beretta snub-nosed revolver, a Springfield rifle, and a five-inch stiletto, he executed her. He began drinking heavily. He drove the narcissistic starlet away. He concealed himself from the American reporters who had hurried to Liverpool to interview him as the university professor who had destroyed the life of one of his students. To elude these reporters, he spent time in Paris, Berlin, and Rome. When he returned to England a few months later, he went on the wagon. Mentored by a retired prizefighter, he began training as a boxer. It was in London that Meredith's father—Ian Templeton, the famous Wall Street magnate—hunted him down and shot him while he was drinking at a seamy bar with a wealthy British divorcée who, from time to time, liked slumming with men that she regarded as sensual and dangerous.

Nearly deranged by his grief and very drunk, Ian Templeton was an unsteady marksman. Though he fired six shots while those onlookers at the bar quickly scattered, only three of the bullets managed to hit him, the infamous Bryce Thompson who had won the trust and the love of a beautiful young woman before he left her to die, abandoned and heartbroken. Even now, the surprise of Templeton's attack unsettled him. Looking gaunt and disheveled on that rain-swept night, the white-haired and wild-eyed man called out to him the words that, ten years afterward, were still troubling his sleep.

"You killed my daughter! You trapped her! You were her death-trap!"

He spent two months in a London hospital, recovering from grievous wounds to his left temple, his chest, and his spleen. On the day before he left the hospital, his lawyer informed him that he had been fired from his university post and exposed as a ruthless predator of young women in American and foreign newspapers and magazines and on world-wide television newscasts. His university life was finished. The man who shot him, the very rich Ian Templeton, spent a year in a sanitarium. The police, as well as the public, were on his side—not because he was wealthy, but because he was a grieving father who was justified in taking revenge against the ruthless man that had destroyed his daughter.

When he returned to the United States, he had a few good years as a boxer. In quick succession, he won ten bouts as a middleweight. But the cocaine and the booze began stymying his powers. After losing six fights, he was finished. Willful and bitter, he made a living off the rich. In different years, he was their valet, their chauffeur, their personal trainer, and their bodyguard. On several occasions, he fronted for them because they were in trouble with their wives or their business partners or the tax people. He even calmed their problematic mistresses by bringing them into his bed, while the privileged bastards that he served looked the other way.

Then, one evening when he was not anticipating her, he met Lauren Winters.

Chapter Ten

Phantoms

Now he, Bryce Thompson—a bitter alter ego of the man that he once thought he could become—was about to make a dark reality out of the murder plan that he and Lauren had devised. He doubted that they would stay together for more than a year or two after that. But he would be home free. He would have a pile of money to keep him traveling with the big leaguers. His chaotic life had made him many kinds of men. But he had never killed anyone. In spite of his capacity for toughing his way through territories unknown to him, the thought of his killing Aaron Dowling left him uneasy. All the promises he had made to himself to travel a better path would mean nothing after he killed a man that he did not even know. He would be a savage. He would be just another sub-human who had trapped himself in a nightmare of his own making.

But killing Aaron Dowling was his only chance for winning the comfortable life that he craved. Hardhearted and fatalistic, he pushed away the stirrings of compunction and the traceries of guilt that were already yoking themselves to his tension. But only until nightfall did he remain free of the guilt that was churning inside him. On the evening before he planned to go through with the murder, he sat alone in the richly furnished Manhattan apartment that he was leasing with Lauren Winters' money. He was careful not to drink heavily. He needed to keep his mind clear. He needed to keep a firm hold on the reality that was swirling around him.

Around midnight, the memory of Meredith came back to haunt him. He tried to resist the image of her face and her long, slender figure as they suddenly appeared before him, there in the proximate distance by the terrace door. Her ghostly voice was calling to him.

"I loved you, Bryce," she was saying. "I loved you so much. Why couldn't you have loved me the way that I loved you?"

"I did love you," he quickly answered her. "I did love you, without understanding what I was feeling. I did love you. You are the only woman that I will ever love."

A voice echoed in the otherwise silent apartment. The voice that he heard was a man's voice, gravelly and taut with emotion. It was the echo of his own voice that he was hearing, right after he replied to the words that he had imagined Meredith was speaking to him. His confession of the love that he felt for her filled him with a sorrow that he had never known. His sorrow was irrevocable. His fate was sealed. He had spurned authentic love. He had rejected his only real chance for happiness. Out of fear and because of his perversity and self-hatred, he had turned away from the experience of authentic love. From this day forward, to the end of his life, he would have to carry that burden with him. It was his own body of death that he carried upon his back. He had condemned himself to live with his loss and with this new knowledge that, even before he plotted to kill Aaron Dowling, he had activated his capacity for killing. Without firing a weapon or brandishing a sword or a stiletto, he had killed Meredith, and he had killed their son. He had spurned not only love, but also life. In that moment, he became not only a killer. He became his own executioner. He chose a slow dying of his spirit. He was his own death trap.

To elude these dark memories that might weaken his resolve to murder Aaron Dowling, he directed his thoughts to all the things that he must do if he were to succeed in his plan. First, he must drive Lauren's Bentley into the private underground garage of the building where Aaron Dowling lived. A sensor attached to the key chain that Lauren had given him would instantly raise the garage door. Right after he parked the car, he would walk a few steps to the private elevator, for which he had a second key. With the third key that Lauren had given him a week earlier, he would enter Aaron's apartment at exactly two o'clock in the morning. If he followed his usual habits, Aaron would be asleep in his bed. It would take only a few minutes for him to kill Aaron. Then, to leave an impression that a thief had entered the apartment, he must take from one of the night tables flanking Aaron's bed a gold Swiss watch that was worth twenty thousand dollars. While he was in the bedroom area, he must steal, as well, a cache of several thousand dollars that Aaron kept in the wall safe that was located in the bathroom adjoining the bedroom. From Lauren's description, he surmised that the safe door was made of thin metal. With a crow bar that he would conceal inside the businessman's valise that he had carried into the apartment, he would pry open the door to the safe and steal the money. He must also steal a small Renoir canvas that was hanging on the north wall in the reception room. Sotheby had recently valued the painting at five million dollars. He would need only a few minutes to cover the top part of the painting with foam, to place the canvas in a thick layer of bubble wrap, which he would also be carrying in his valise, and to secure the wrap with masking tape. Then, he would place the canvas in an art box that Lauren was going to leave in a hallway closet. No later than two-thirty, he expected to be making his way from the private elevator to Lauren's Bentley.

Three nights earlier, after Lauren had assured him that Aaron would be spending the weekend with her in Newport, Rhode Island, he had made a trial run of his plan at precisely two o'clock. Everything had gone well. On that evening, he had studied the layout of Aaron's apartment. More than a few times, he had simulated his passage from the elevator into the apartment. He had moved through the foyer and reception room with the agility of a soundless phantom or a nearly invisible spirit. The glow of the moon that flowed past the terrace doors into the reception room touched the Renoir canvas that was hanging on a wall just beyond the foyer. He imagined how swiftly he would remove the canvas from the wall and place it in the box that he would carry away after he had killed Aaron Dowling. In this trial run, he had also passed along the winding hall that was leading him to the master bedroom, all the while noticing to the right and left of that passage a montage of richly appointed rooms. In an alcove of the hall, about ten feet from the master bedroom, he had paused before a mirror that hung above a small French Provençal table. The recessed lighting in the hall partly illumined his rugged features, reflected as they were within the shadowed world of the mirror. For a split second, he thought he was coming face to face with a stranger—a thug or phantom whose vaguely brutalized face gave him the look of a villain.

"Bastard!" he snarled, while his primitive instincts yoked themselves to angry surprise and to the fear that was poised at the cusp of violence.

He almost pressed his finger against the trigger of the Beretta pistol that he was carrying in his hand and pointing toward the mirror. But something held him back. Perhaps, it was the wretched face in the mirror snarling out its protest at exactly the same instant that a muted, snarling cry had erupted from his throat. That face was his face. That thug, who appeared at first to be a stranger, was nobody else except himself. Caught inside the mirror, his face wore the expression of a lost and desperate man. As quickly as he had noticed himself, lurking there in the mirror with his bleak expression and his big-boned, hulking physique, he turned away from this ghastly self-image. He wondered whether his meeting this reflection was an omen that the Fates had compelled him to see, on this evening that was only a few nights away from his becoming a cold-blooded killer.

Maybe it was an omen, a message sent by random chance to serve him a warning. Maybe that moment before the mirror meant nothing. Whatever the case, he had already cast his lot with killers.

He felt easier after he turned away. He continued to do the thing that remained for him to do. He entered the master bedroom and checked the drawers of the night tables for money and for weapons. But the drawers contained neither money, nor weapons. He found in them merely packs of imported cigarettes, a gold cigarette case and a gold lighter, an address book that contained a handwritten list of persons and their telephone numbers, packets of condoms, and a key chain holding six keys.

This trial run of his murder plan left him feeling less assured than he had expected, especially since his secret visit to Aaron's apartment had gone well. During the three days that followed his surveillance of what would become the scene of the murder, an apprehension that felt strange to him hovered about his every move. The image in the mirror, which had shown him a repugnant face that belonged to himself, haunted his nightmares and the unforgiving memories that pursued him during his waking hours. Yet, despite this foreboding, he compelled himself to go forward with the murderous plan that promised to set him free from the world's rough treatment of him and from all the betrayals that had wrecked his life. There was no way that he could know for certain that the murder plan would unfold with the smooth precision that allowed him to run free of its consequences. But he was determined to cover his tracks. He needed to outwit the police, who might connect him to the robbery and the murder because of his checkered past and because of his previous relationship with Lauren Winters. The police could regard as a sufficient motive the fact that Lauren had spurned him in favor of her marriage to Aaron Dowling.

To anticipate this possibility and to provide an alibi for himself on the night of the murder, he decided to escort Rhonda Darnell, his occasional girlfriend, to The Blue Note, the nightclub where she was singing at Rockefeller Plaza. It was his habit to watch her performance for a while and then, for a half hour or so, to visit the casino that adjoined the club where a large crowd was watching her glamorous show. The casino people knew and liked him. He was one of their regulars, not averse to gambling and losing the thousands of dollars that Lauren had given him to stay out of her life for the time being. He would play a few hands of poker. He would make himself seen. Then, he would hurry to Rhonda's dressing room at The Blue Note. There, he expected to meet a few more of her friends, as well as the Texas oilman with whom she was carrying on a clandestine affair. His name was Owen Garrett. On the surface, Garrett was a conservative family man who followed all the rules. Secretly, he had been sleeping with Rhonda during his quarterly visits to New York. He was, according to a discreet remark she once made, a generous lover. He had bought her a Manhattan penthouse, a Lamborghini, and diamonds from Harry Winston and Cartier. He had also provided her with a substantial bank account.

Without realizing it, Own Garrett and Rhonda Darnell were going to be essential links in the alibi that would keep the police from apprehending him as Aaron Dowling's murderer. If the police questioned her, Rhonda would tell them that she had spent the night with him—Bryce Thompson, her loyal friend and passionate lover. She would never mention Owen Garrett. Nor would Garrett come forward to dispute Rhonda's testimony or to declare himself as her secret lover.

On the night of the murder, he would visit Rhonda in her dressing room after her midnight show. By then, Owen Garrett would have arrived to escort her to the luxurious penthouse he had given her. There, he would spend the night making vigorous love to her.

Around one-thirty, he—Bryce Thompson, former boxer and teacher, perennial con man, and occasional thief—would hurry to the garage where he had parked Lauren's Bentley. Right after that, he would drive to Aaron's apartment and kill him.

The trial run he had made to Aaron's apartment and the scenario for his alibi kept him on a steady course during these three days before he would become a killer. Yet his bitter awareness of how he had failed himself and failed other people continued to torment him. Whether he was awake or asleep, the phantoms of his past rose up to accuse him.

The sadistic cop from his childhood was the most formidable of the phantoms. He had broken his jaw when, with a crazed fury, he punched him, a thirteen-year-old orphaned boy. Right after that, he broke his left arm when he beat him with a club. Then he jeered at him, a gangly teenager slumped on the floor while he was bleeding and moaning with pain.

"Don't take it so hard, kid," he said, spewing through his teeth the taunting words that burned in his soul twenty-five years later. "The orphanage isn't such a bad place. They give you a bed and three meals. Besides, nobody in this town wants you."

Irwin Baxter was a different kind of phantom. For much of their relationship, Mr. Baxter had believed in him. He felt certain that, with proper foster parentage and with self-discipline, he could realize his capacity for doing the right thing. Now, so close to the night when, with irrevocable finality, he would fall away from goodness, he heard, once more, the counseling words that Mr. Baxter had chosen to tell him. The man whom he regarded as his father wanted to keep him out of harm's way.

"Always be true to your honorable word," Mr. Baxter had advised him. "Always follow the rules. Remember this: You identify the person you are through your actions. Strive to be good. Stay clean. Don't let the world corrupt you. Respect all human beings, and forgive them their trespasses against you. Never let anger and bitterness destroy your goodness."

"I'll be all right," he had answered him. "I'll never make you ashamed of me."

Now, many years later, during these last days and nights before he was going to murder a man that he did not even know, other phantoms rose, without speaking, before his waking retrospection and his nocturnal reveries. He recalled the delicious meals that Mrs. Baxter cooked for him and the maternal care that she brought to washing and ironing his clothes.

"You are a smart young fellow," she used to tell him. "You are going to be a fine leader. You will make us proud of you."

The Baxters' belief in him spurred him forward to solid accomplishments in his academic studies and in his athletic competitions. The phantom images of himself in a high school science lab, on a soccer field, and in a boxing ring seemed to belong to a world that was completely lost to him. His memory of that world left him with a sorrow for which there was no remedy.

He recollected, as well, his helpful teachers and his friendly classmates during the years that he was a student at New York University and during the equally happy period of his graduate studies at the University of Pennsylvania. He saw, too, in both reverie and dreams and as if they were in the room with him, the good-natured colleagues with whom he had established an easy camaraderie during the period of his university teaching.

Often, in reflective moments while he was drinking his favorite scotch or bourbon, alone at the bar in his apartment, he saw this apparition of his younger self. That ghostly image seemed light years removed from the imperfect man that he had become. Yet he saw his youthful face and athletic body, nonetheless. Not yet twenty, he was standing before a bathroom mirror, while he shaved and while he spoke to the agreeable image in the mirror that had a healthy, ruddy complexion and a well-honed assurance.

"You have it made," his young self was telling his mirror image. "You are going to have a wonderful life."

During these final three days and nights before the murder, Lauren Winters also haunted his brooding thoughts and his troubled dreams. Her raven-black hair and olive skin that made her look exotic; her large, brown eyes that flashed with mischief; and her gleaming smile that lip rouge made even more sensual—all these corporeal emblems of identity enhanced her mystery, even as they intimated the deviousness of her character.

Her phantom image rose up to conspire with him once more.

"I am rarely surprised by anything or anyone," she was telling him in his dreams, exactly as she had told him a year ago, when they had first met. "But tonight I am absolutely astonished. I never imagined that devising a plan to murder a man that we do not know would be this easy."

"It will be easy, if you follow my directions," he had told her, while resisting her excessive display of enthusiasm. "Find a wealthy guy from your own class. Make him fall in love with you. Get him to marry you. Then leave the rest to me."

In his nightmare, he saw Lauren's ghostly face peering at him with excited eyes and laughing with an intimate glee that anchored its exhilaration to a new pleasure—the act of murder—that, to her jaded perspective, was as carnal as it was sensual and revivifying.

"Your plan amazes me," she was exclaiming, each time that her phantom face appeared to him in his nightmare. "It is just the thing that I need to avenge myself against a world that has treated me with rough indifference. The wonderful part of it is that I am going to choose the man who will die. I'll make a mockery of the codicil in my parents' will that requires me to reform my character and to marry a substantial man who belongs to my class. I'll marry such a man. Then, after you kill him, I'll inherit his fortune as well as the millions of dollars that my parents have left me, with all their stinking conditions. We'll be in this plan together—you even more than I. You are the one whose finger will press the trigger. For once, we'll deal with loaded dice and get away with it. We'll play God and win the game."

"Sure we will," he had told her, while offering her a sly grin that revealed his confidence and that kept them on a realistic path. "We are going to win everything that we want."

She laughed a ruthless laugh, while he observed her with furtive eyes and with a fake smile. Always at the end of this nightmare, her once-lovely face looked bedeviled, as if a spirit from hell had peeled away all the skin and all the beauty and left her with a skeleton's demeanor—a death's head that had been left to rot on a public gallows under the blazing sun.

Then the face turned into his face, and her body became his body—a hanging corpse reeking of decay and left on that same gallows that stood in a long-ago city square at the place in some predatory chapter of his life where three sinuous roads converged.

Always, in the middle of the night, the face of Ian Templeton flared into his nightmare. It was a face as sick as any tormented man's face that was crazed with grief and obsessed with his need to avenge the death of his daughter.

"You killed her!" he shouted, his voice both raspy and anguished. "You killed my Meredith! You brought her to a bad end! You were her death trap!"

Most of all, he thought about Meredith Templeton. That she loved him so completely left him, even now, both awed and regretful. Her capacity for loving awed him. His inability to recognize the honesty of her love filled him with sorrow.

He saw her night after night in his troubled sleep.

"Why can't you say it, Bryce?" she was asking him. "Why can't you tell me that you love me?"

In his nightmare, he tried to explain himself. He wanted her to understand why he had never said the words that she wanted to hear.

"I did not know how to say 'I love you.' I did not understand what I was feeling. But I understand now, and it is too late. I loved you then. I love you now. I'll go on loving you, even though I have lost you."

His words became a cry of anguish that woke him from his nightmare. Not even a quick shot of bourbon and the smoky tang of a cigarette could allay his grief. Nor could he escape from the unforgiving memories that rose like phantoms to torment him.

Even on the night before the murder, he thought about all these things. Then, at last, only minutes before a deep sleep overtook his anxious restlessness, he willed himself to turn away from his memories. He accepted the dark truth of himself. He was lost. He could not blame the Fates, who blindly spun out the decrees that determined the paths that he might take. The Fates were the jugglers of random chances. They offered him different kinds of scenarios. He could have chosen a path that would keep him on a proper course. But he did not do so. He disdained the choices that would lead him to a makeshift and impoverished life. He wanted wealth. He craved excitement. That was the life he desired, even if he had to kill to get it.

When he awoke six hours later, his resolve to murder Aaron Dowling wavered once more. The thought of his killing a man in cold blood weighed upon his conscience. Yet he saw no other way to save himself from the haphazard miseries of an uncertain future.

"Just do it," he told himself while he sat in his bed, propped against an array of soft white pillows and taking a drag every so often on his imported cigarette. "Don't *feel* any of it. Don't let your emotions trap you. Just kill the bastard."

Now he rose from his bed, showered and dressed quickly, and hurried into the sun-glanced streets where the day was nearly half over. He was intent upon following the schedule that he had always followed every Saturday. If the police were to trace his movements, they would find that he had treated the day with both casual and affirmative responses. As it was his habit, he drank Brazilian coffee and ate French rolls at Sardi's with an actor on his way to the top and with his savvy agent, who had joined them at his table. While he summoned a contrived enthusiasm, he conversed with them about popular New York plays and about a few Hollywood films. Lauren had introduced him to the two men during that first year when his relationship with her was at its happiest and most intense. He made a point of mentioning the time and the specific date to the two men who were sharing brunch with him. If the actor and his agent were questioned later, they would recall their casual meeting with him.

Right after that, he made an appearance at the exclusive men's salon where Ramon cut and styled his hair, as he had been doing every other Saturday for more than a year. He and Ramon spoke of the recent string of wins that the New York Jets had achieved. They shared reminiscences about hunting red stag, though not together, in Maine and in Colorado. Ramon gave him a tip about the prize stallion that was expected to win the Kentucky Derby. He left the salon with the assured manner that had become his trademark. Ramon, he knew, would keep in his meticulous appointment book a record of their meeting on this Saturday at precisely two o'clock.

At three o'clock, he drove Lauren's Bentley into the main garage of the dealership where she had bought it. Giovanni, the mechanic there, changed the oil, checked the tires, and filled the tank with gasoline. Everything went smoothly. He did his work with skill and efficiency. They exchanged friendly remarks about a recent boxing match at Madison Square Garden. A tall, dark Neapolitan in his late twenties, Giovanni joked about his imaginary escapades with the Italian film star Sophia Loren.

"You are reaching for the moon," he had told Giovanni. "Pay attention to the beautiful brunettes right here in the city."

"I've already slept with most of them," Giovanni said, without skipping a beat. "Now I need a thrill ride to the moon."

They laughed. They were buddies. Giovanni would remember the laughter. If the police questioned him, Giovanni would be certain to describe him as a good-humored gentleman who was always comfortable in his own skin.

At five o'clock, he headed back to his apartment. He shaved and showered again, dressed in his favorite tuxedo, and drove to the hotel on East Sixty-First Street, where Rhonda Darnell was staying. He arrived at her place at six o'clock.

Tonight, Rhonda looked more beautiful than he had ever seen her. With her red hair and green eyes, her turned-up nose and ruby lips, and with her fair, young skin, she looked especially radiant. She greeted him with a gleaming smile and with a breathlessness that told him she had been having a grand day.

"You will not believe it, Bryce," she said, as she allowed him to wrap her full-bodied figure in an ermine, floor-length coat that made her red, sequined gown appear even more dazzling. "Not merely one, but two Hollywood film executives will be attending my show tonight. One is a producer from MGM. The other is a director at Paramount. They want to sign me for romantic comedies and for musicals."

"You are flying high," he said. "You are headed for the big time in Hollywood."

She kissed him lightly as they entered the private elevator that would bring them to the main lobby and to his Bentley that was waiting outside the hotel.

"You are my lucky charm," she told him. "Every time that we come back to each other, something really good happens for my career."

"Of course, it does," he answered her, affecting a lightness of heart that was convincing, yet spurious. "I'm your lucky man."

"I would not have you any other way," she said, invoking her Irish sense of mischief as he guided her into the car. "I am a woman who has a special fondness for lucky men."

Like most celebrities, Rhonda was a narcissist. She was artificial. She was self-serving. Her glamour and her softness concealed an iron will and ruthless ambition. But, in spite of the contrivances that attended her persona, she was not a self-liar. She knew who she had once been, and she never lied about her origins. Like him, she had been a foundling. She had spent most of her childhood in an orphanage with its sadistic keepers and in foster homes with abusive guardians. No, she never lied about her shabby background—not to herself or to the public. Nor did she betray a friendship that had earned her hard-won loyalty or renege on a promise that she had made in the heat of erotic pleasure or with the impulsive enthusiasm that she brought to the relationships that she regarded as more than ordinary.

On this fatal night, when he was a few hours away from killing Aaron Dowling, he was pleased to be in Rhonda's company. She would provide him with a first-rate alibi, if the police were looking to pin a murder rap on him. Starting here and now, while he drove her to The Blue Note, where she would be singing, he was doing all the things that he needed to do, so that neither fair-weather friends nor wily foes, including the police, could prove that he was the thief who had robbed and murdered one of the heirs to the Dowling fortune.

On this holiday weekend, Rhonda was performing in three shows this evening. Each show lasted an hour and a half. Her first set began at seven o'clock. The second show started at nine-fifteen. The third show opened at midnight. Accompanied by a jazz combo, she sang bluesy interpretations of love ballads by the likes of Cole Porter, Harold Arlen, Stephen Sondheim, and Jerome Kern. Drawing upon a familiar habit, he remained in the audience for Rhonda's first show. At least sixty friends and acquaintances noticed his presence.

Rhonda was a gifted singer who discovered poignant subtexts in each ballad. The drama of her own life, widely publicized throughout the globe, spilled into the world of each of her songs. Yet the lost quality that she often conveyed through her singing was yoked to more than her life. The experience of being bruised by unexpected endings or of being cast adrift by the dark consequences of one's behavior also reflected the problematic biographies of those persons to whom she was singing. Her fans loved her. Even foreign visitors to New York admired her poise and the subtle nuances that deepened the emotional resonance of her singing. She was the real thing. For much of her show, he forgot about the murder that he was prepared to commit in only a few hours. But after she finished her first show, he became aware once more of the importance of hobnobbing with some of Rhonda's theater friends. For about ten minutes, he kept his place at the table where he had joined a group of actors and musicians who genuinely liked him, because he was as street-wise as they were and because he had a talent for making women like Rhonda happy.

Tonight, he went out of his way to be affable to these men and women who, like himself, had come from wayward and turbulent environments. He was a storehouse of anecdotes about football and soccer, about European cars, and about the American stock market. He listened to the trenchant words of tough-minded actors who recalled their most grievous disappointments. He enjoyed, particularly, the cynical comments of a few musicians about crooked politicians; about racism in the United States; and about rich, old men who devised wars that killed youths from the middle and lower classes. Afterwards, he spent a few minutes with Rhonda in her dressing room. She sipped

Champagne, and he drank a shot of bourbon. Then, he left her to be interviewed by journalists from the major newspapers and magazines and to have her seductive beauty captured by renowned photographers. At eight forty-five, he hurried across the street to the fashionable casino where high rollers and hucksters spent their free hours gambling. He played a few hands of poker. The croupier, a brooding and discontented fellow, recognized him and, as it was his habit, gave him a nod that indicated his presence there was familiar and acceptable. This croupier would vouch for him, if he needed a witness to verify that, on the night of the murder, he played poker with his usual sharp eyes and wise choices.

At nine-thirty, he returned to The Blue Note. Now, he joined a different group of Rhonda's friends and several friends of his own. Once more, Rhonda pleased her audience. Once again, he appeared to be self-assured and happy. Whether he was entering a discussion about horse racing in Saratoga Springs, New York, or about hunting in Patagonia or kayaking in the Adirondacks, he made certain that these friends would remember that he was both gregarious and good-natured.

After this second show, he made another visit to Rhonda in her dressing room. Once again, she sipped Champagne, and he swallowed a shot of bourbon. Artists and their latest paramours, stock brokers and their wives, and Rhonda's publicist and dressmaker were also drinking and imparting the witty repartee that, they knew, Rhonda always appreciated. Before he made an unobtrusive exit, Rhonda's Texas oilman arrived. Big-boned and muscular, Owen Garrett dominated the room. Yet there was about him none of the bullying authority of some of the wealthy men he had once served, as chauffeur or valet or bodyguard. He was deliberately low-key. He had come to New York without his wife. Ostensibly, business meetings with corporate leaders, with bankers, and with brokers had called him to the East Coast. But, apart from the wheeler dealing and the shrewd negotiations that would make him a richer man, Rhonda figured as a primary reason for his being here. After her third show, she would spend the night with Garrett in the palatial suite he had bought for her on the sixth floor of The Hotel Pierre.

If the police questioned her, Rhonda would convince them that he—Bryce Thompson, her occasional lover and convenient escort—had spent the night with her. She loathed policemen, having been roughly handled and even raped by them during her earlier days as a chanteuse in a dive that was a front for a narcotics ring. In her glamorous way and because of her harsh background, Rhonda had learned how to be a cool hustler, whether she was dealing with the police or with a Texas oilman.

At midnight, Rhonda returned to the sensual implications of The Blue Note and performed her third show. At a quarter past twelve, he slipped away after whispering to the couple next to him that he wanted to play another round of poker at the casino across the street. He, in fact, did play a hand or two and succeeded in winning. Then, informing some gambling friends that he was heading back to The Blue Note, he left the casino with the satisfied demeanor of a man who has just won twelve thousand dollars. Maintaining a natural pace, he made his way to the public garage where he had parked his Bentley earlier in the evening. A group of seven or eight persons had entered the garage at the same time that he did. Yet they gave him no special notice. Nor did the parking attendant, who was an aged and near-sighted man, look up from his cubicle to study him as he paid his fee and drove away.

At five minutes before two, he drove Lauren's Bentley to the private garage where she and Aaron shared a parking space. No one else was around, not even the security guard. Should the guard arrive in the interim, he might glance at the Bentley as a familiar vehicle that was parked in its appropriate space.

With a steady pace now, he walked into the elevator that carried him to the tenth floor. In his left hand, he was carrying the valise that contained the crowbar that would help him open the wall safe in Aaron's bathroom. Always, he held in the grip of his right hand the semi-automatic Colt Cobra .38 Special that was concealed in the right pocket of his black evening coat. When the elevator door opened on the tenth floor, he felt no trepidation as he moved across the capacious hall to Aaron Dowling's apartment. Because the hall was well lighted, he had no trouble fitting the key into the lock without making a sound and while opening the door with an equivalent stillness.

But, once he was inside the apartment, the stillness seemed eerie and disconcerted him. It was as if the apartment had turned into a living creature, with eyes that were watching him and with breath held taut. He felt his ghost passing near him. He became even more anxious after he moved with careful gait through the foyer and arrived inside the reception room. But there was no sign of Aaron here. Why should there be? According to information that Lauren had given him a week ago, Aaron would surely be sleeping at two o'clock, because he was scheduled to catch a flight to Palm Beach several hours later, at nine o'clock. He placed his valise on the carpeted floor directly beneath the Renoir that he planned to carry away with him after the murder. Now, as he brought his revolver from his coat pocket and held it before him, he quickened his pace. But his jitters would not leave him even when he recognized the objects that his earlier visit to the apartment had made familiar to his furtive glance. His careful scanning of the room showed his eyes the things that he expected to see: the light of the moon flowing from the French windows into the room and touching objects that the recessed lighting had already illumined; the amply upholstered sofas and chairs and the profusion of needlepoint pillows; the delicately-shaped statuary, vases, and lamps; and the canvases of Renoir, Monet, and Fragonard that hung on the cream-tinted walls.

The thought that he was only two minutes away from killing a human being left him short of breath. Nevertheless, he continued to move forward. Toughing his way through the experience that was unfolding, he made his way down the winding hall that was leading him to the master bedroom. Once again, he noticed to the right and left of this passage a montage of richly appointed rooms. He noticed, too, in an alcove of the hall about ten feet from the master bedroom, the mirror that hung above a small French Provençal table. As it had three days earlier, the recessed lighting in the hall partly illumined the world of the mirror, where there lurked the face of a thug whose brutalized features gave him the look of a villain. It was his own wretched face that he saw. It was a face that carried beneath its furrowed and wind-burned brow the chaos of fear and anger and hatred. The brown eyes glared back at him with murderous intent. This tall and muscular man that was wearing a black tuxedo and a black overcoat was pointing a pistol at him. He was that man. He was the savage in the mirror.

This image in the mirror, repulsive and accusing, stopped him in his tracks. He did not want to be that man. He did not want to be a killer.

He turned away from the mirror, intending to leave the apartment as quickly as he could. But, as he turned, he stumbled against the Provençal table beneath the mirror. With his well-honed agility, he retrieved himself in the midst of his fall and planted his feet on the threshold of the master bedroom. His hand still gripped his revolver and pointed it in the space ahead of him.

Suddenly, the lights of the bedroom were flashing on. In the distance, Aaron was jumping out of his bed and leaving behind him a naked blonde who was grabbing hold of a Beretta revolver from a bed table. The man was hurrying toward him. He was also naked, and he was wild-eyed. He was firing a Walther handgun.

He felt the first bullet rushing through his left arm. The second bullet pierced his right shoulder.

In the surprise and confusion of this attack, he froze on the threshold, even when the first bullets pushed his body back almost imperceptibly. He was still pointing his pistol in the space ahead of him. He could not will himself to press his finger against the trigger. He did not want to fire.

Yet Aaron was going to fire again.

"Don't do it, Aaron!" he heard himself shouting. "Don't make yourself a killer!"

But Aaron kept running toward him and kept firing his handgun. Then, just before another bullet ripped through his left lung and his chest, he saw that the man was not Aaron. The long angularity of his body and a slight scar around the left corner of his chin made him someone else.

The bullets punched their way into his lung and his chest. Blood was spilling out of him as he fell to the floor. The hall and the bedroom spun away from him and, seconds later, as if they were rushing through a vortex or funneling their way through a darkening tunnel, the hall and the room were hurling themselves back to him. The man, clad in a black robe now, was standing over him, and the woman, all in white, was standing right behind him. Each of them still clasped a revolver. Each of their faces looked startled and remorseful.

"Oh, Gavin, I think that you have killed him," the blonde woman was whispering.

"I didn't have any other choice," the man said. "He was pointing a gun at me."

His breath was coming fast now. The pain in his chest was fierce and unremitting. Blood was shooting up from his insides and spilling out of the corners of his mouth. He felt life rushing out of him.

"I wasn't going to," he heard himself trying to tell them. But, because he was slurring his words, the man and the woman could make no sense of them.

Then, in the last minutes of his consciousness, he remembered who these two persons were. He recalled hearing about a cousin of Aaron who resembled him. He recognized him now from the newspaper profiles and television coverage of his privileged and adventurous life. He also recognized the woman. She was Liam Dowling's widow.

So, these rich bastards had defeated him, after all.

The hall and the threshold of the bedroom threw themselves away from him again and disappeared. A dark cloud, like a shroud for the dead, was covering him. His life flashed before him. A montage of faces whirled around him. He saw the sadistic guard from the orphanage. He saw Mr. and Mrs. Baxter. He strained to see more clearly, as the faces sped away from him. He caught sight of Lauren and, even in his dying moments, understood that, no matter what was happening to him, she would run free of all blame. He saw himself as he had been—a con man, a huckster, a thief, and a hardhearted user of women. He saw Meredith Templeton, the one woman who really loved him and whom he had destroyed. He had loved her too late. He had always been too late. Even now, in these final moments, he had turned too late on a path to goodness.

The pain was swallowing him up. The black cloud, like the lid of a coffin, was closing down upon him. For the last time, he heard in silence the thought that his mind was speaking to him.

"It is ironic," his mind was telling him from far, far away, "and very sad that life is kicking me out of existence in the very hour that I refused to become a killer."

TO THE READER: GO TO THE NEXT PAGE FOR AN
ALTERNATE ENDING.

AN ALTERNATE NARRATIVE FOR THE READER
WHO BELIEVES IN HAPPIER ENDINGS

At five minutes before two, he drove Lauren's Bentley to the private garage where she and Aaron shared a parking space. No one else was around, not even the security guard. Should the guard arrive in the interim, he might glance at the Bentley as a familiar vehicle that was parked in its appropriate space.

With a steady pace now, he walked into the elevator that carried him to the tenth floor. In his left hand, he was carrying the valise that contained the crowbar that would help him open the wall safe in Aaron's bathroom. Always, he held in the grip of his right hand the semi-automatic Colt Cobra .38 Special that was concealed in the right pocket of his black evening coat. When the elevator door opened on the tenth floor, he felt no trepidation as he moved across the capacious hall to Aaron Dowling's apartment. Because the hall was well lighted, he had no trouble fitting the key into the lock without making a sound and while opening the door with an equivalent stillness.

But, once he was inside the apartment, the stillness seemed eerie and disconcerted him. It was as if the apartment had turned into a living creature, with eyes that were watching him and with breath held taut. He felt his ghost passing near him. He became even more anxious after he moved with careful gait through the foyer and arrived inside the reception room. But there was no sign of Aaron here. Why should there be? According to information that Lauren had given him a week ago, Aaron would surely be sleeping at two o'clock, because he was scheduled to catch a flight to Palm Beach several hours later, at nine o'clock. He placed his valise on the carpeted floor directly beneath the Renoir that he planned to carry away with him after the murder. Now, as he brought his revolver from his coat pocket and held it before him, he quickened his pace. But his jitters would not leave him even when he recognized the objects that his earlier visit to the apartment had made familiar to his furtive glance. His careful scanning of the room showed his eyes the things that he expected to see: the light of the moon flowing from the French windows into the room and touching objects that the recessed lighting had already illumined; the amply upholstered sofas and chairs and the profusion of needlepoint pillows; the delicately-shaped statuary, vases, and lamps; and the canvases of Renoir, Monet, and Fragonard that hung on the cream-tinted walls.

The thought that he was only two minutes away from killing a human being left him short of breath. Nevertheless, he continued to move forward. Toughing his way through the experience that was unfolding, he made his way down the winding hall that was leading him to the master bedroom. Once again, he noticed to the right and left of this passage a montage of richly appointed rooms. He noticed, too, in an alcove of the hall about ten feet from the master bedroom, the mirror that hung above a small French Provençal table. As it had three days earlier, the recessed lighting in the hall partly illumined the world of the mirror, where there lurked the face of a thug whose brutalized features gave him the look of a villain. It was his own wretched face that he saw. It was a face that carried beneath its furrowed and wind-burned brow the chaos of fear and anger and hatred.

The brown eyes glared back at him with murderous intent. This tall and muscular man that was wearing a black tuxedo and a black overcoat was pointing a pistol at him. He was that man. He was the savage in the mirror.

This image in the mirror, repulsive and accusing, stopped him in his tracks. He did not want to be that man. He did not want to be a killer.

He turned away from the mirror, intending to leave the apartment as quickly as he could. But, as he turned, he stumbled against the Provençal table beneath the mirror. With his well-honed agility, he retrieved himself in the midst of his fall and planted his feet on the threshold of the master bedroom. His hand still gripped his revolver and pointed it in the space ahead of him.

Suddenly, the lights of the bedroom were flashing on. In the distance, Aaron was jumping out of his bed and leaving behind him a naked blonde who was about to take hold of a Beretta revolver from a bed table. The man was also opening the drawer of the table flanking his side of the bed. He, too, was naked, and he was wild-eyed. His quick grasp was almost upon a Walther handgun.

He, Bryce Thompson, the lost man who had come there to kill him, reacted with swift fury. He fired a warning shot that blasted through the drawer of the bed table near this man that he had intended to kill. At the sound of the splintering wood and the sight of the intruder standing with his revolver pointed at his heart, his intended victim froze. So did the blonde.

In the same instant, he heard himself issuing a command both militant and threatening.

"Get away from the revolvers," he said. "Get back into bed, and you won't get hurt."

Something in his wild eyes, perhaps, and in the cautious, backward steps that were bringing him to the threshold of the room prodded their awareness that he was not going to kill them. Tense though they were, they followed his directive. They returned to the bed and covered their nakedness with the cobalt blue satin sheets that gleamed inside the radiance of the central lights. To do otherwise might have cost them their lives.

"I've made a mistake," he told them, as he reached the threshold of the room and as he repeated the words that echoed his brooding admission. "I've made a mistake."

Then, with the furtive speed that made his passage a blurring motion, he was gone.

He felt like a man who had rescued himself from the foul end to which his errant ways had chained him. He had not yet broken all of the chains. His would not be an overnight reformation. But he was making his way toward the probability of other self-rescues.

He hurried into the night, choosing to walk alongside newly washed, moonlit streets rather than to drive Lauren's Bentley. He headed northwest on East Fifty-Seventh Street toward First Avenue and, minutes later, turned left onto Second Avenue. Even at two in the morning, limousines and taxis were carrying passengers on those same glittering streets to upscale nightclubs and to after-theater parties at five-star restaurants. Young men and women in tuxes and gowns were emerging from the VIP exit of an impressive hotel. An equally young drunk and his four Navy buddies were weaving their way past him in rollicking fashion.

By the time he turned right onto East Forty-Ninth Street, he came face to face with two police officers who were carrying night sticks in their hands and revolvers in their holsters while they patrolled the area. With approving eyes that noticed his dapper tuxedo and his subdued manner, they nodded a friendly greeting. He returned the greeting, while simulating a casual mood that concealed his tightly harnessed tension.

When he reached Rockefeller Plaza, he was ready to rejoin the poker players at the casino. There, he would pick up one of the blondes who had sometimes spent the night with him. The prospect of spending this night with her eased his tension, though not completely. The thought that he had nearly killed a man still left him shaken. But he had not killed the man. That was a happier thought. That thought would sustain him through whatever hard times he might have to confront.

He was ready to walk out of Lauren's life now, once she came through with the money that she had promised him. She wouldn't make any trouble, nor did he intend to play rough with her. They were going their separate ways. At last, he was willing to turn away from her and from the murderous impulses that bonded with his own. He wondered how long it would take her and Aaron Dowling to become weary of one another.

With money in hand, he was going to try to make an acceptable life for himself. Maybe he'd train a young boxer here in New York or open a nightclub in Boston or Chicago. Maybe he'd buy into a baseball team on the West Coast or build a chain of restaurants in the southwest. These thoughts, nebulous and far-reaching though they were, also comforted him.

The night went on rising around him, offering the hum of its traffic, the gleaming presence of hotels, restaurants, and nightclubs, the lightheartedness of passersby, and the distant roar of a jet, sky-borne and elusive. He hurried forward, eager to greet the persons and places that often brought him temporary comfort. He was eager, as well, to begin a new cycle, with its extemporaneous promises, its unanticipated challenges, and its hard-won rewards. If things didn't work out exactly as he wanted, he'd hold on for as long as he could, trusting his nerve, his street savvy, and blind chance. For the first time in years, he felt truly alive. He felt grateful. On this trouble-haunted night, he had not killed anyone. Nor did he want to kill anyone. He had already killed his best self. There was no need for him to kill anyone else.

ABOUT THE AUTHOR

David Orsini is a Phi Beta Kappa graduate of Brown University, with degrees that include a Ph.D. in English Literature. David has taught literature, grammar, and composition at secondary schools and colleges in Rhode Island. He is a veteran of The United States Army. His novels include *The Woman Who Loved Too Well*; *The Ghost Lovers*; *The Weaver of Plots*; *Schemes, Disguises, & Traps*; *Vanishing by Degrees*; *The Reappearing*; *Prisoners of Desire*; *The Price of Happiness*; *The Enchantments*; and *What's Left Afterward*.

Visit https://quaternitybooks.com.

Also visit https://www.flipsnack.com/goldg/welcome-to-quaternity-books.html.